Fated to be mine

JODIE LARSON

Chapter 1

D<small>ID YOU KNOW THE AVERAGE</small> heartbeat in a normal human being is sixty to one hundred beats per minute? Did you know when your heart does not beat in a regular rhythm it's considered to be in arrhythmia? Did you know when you leave your heart across the Atlantic Ocean it stops beating altogether?

I do.

How do I know this? Because that's where my heart is, and it has not beat once since yesterday morning, back when everything was still perfect in my life.

The early morning rays of the sun peek in through my bedroom window after another restless night of tossing and turning. I should just give up on sleep altogether because I haven't had a good night's sleep since … well, let's just say it's been a couple of days. Days that will live vividly in my memory, wanting nothing more than to cherish and relive each one.

I can still feel the warmth of his arms wrapped around my body. Securing me and all my fears with their firm hold. Encasing me with feelings I've never felt in all of my twenty-six years on this earth. Andrew Parker, the name that's etched across the non-working organ in my chest, the man who changed my life and allowed me to feel as if someone out there cares for me. But like a dream, it's all just a lie, a fallacy, a passing snapshot into a life that is not mine. The unloved rarely find anything other than pain and isolation. And as I pull myself off my bedroom floor I've come to realize that any indication of a happy future is nothing more than a waking dream.

Wrapping the robe around my body, I slowly drag myself into my bathroom, feeling worn out and beaten, even if it's only my spirit. What I'm unprepared for is the reflection in the mirror staring back at me. A face so worn and sad it no longer looks like my own. The usual pasty white skin has been replaced with giant red blotches, indicating a night of crying myself to sleep. Add that to the dark smudges that ring around my eyes and the tangled mess that is my hair, hanging in knots and looking dull as ever. I could compete for best Halloween monster without even needing a costume.

I can see why Andrew would want nothing to do with me. My hands slam against the mirror, blocking the horrid view of what I have now become. Pain sweeps through my body as Andrew's memory continues to haunt me. It's too much to bear and I slowly sink onto the cold tile floor, letting the chill seep into me as I curl myself into a tight little ball.

Why did I tell him I loved him? Why was I stupid enough to think there would be a happy ending for me? More tears fall from my eyes, splashing onto the tiles. The coolness feels good on my heated face and I lie there for what seems an immeasurable amount of time, wallowing in my discomfort and sadness.

But I need to move. Lying here isn't doing me any good so I slowly pick myself up off the floor.

Staggering into the kitchen, I pull random things out of the cupboard, unsure of exactly what it is I'm searching for. The fog is still sitting heavy in my brain, the lead weight still pulling my heart down from where it's supposed to be. They say time heals all wounds. I guess I need to see if that's true or not because right now, time is not my friend. With each passing second my thoughts drift to Andrew; wondering what he's doing or if he misses me. Or worse, if there's someone else that has already taken my place.

No, I need to stop this line of thinking. I need to put London and everything that happened there behind me, force it into a little box to be kept in the back recesses of my memories. I need a distraction. With a new task at hand, I shuffle to the front door, grabbing the suitcase Chris had left there after he and Kara dropped me off last night. Just another humiliating scene to add to the many others my two friends have endured with me.

Dragging the heavy bag down the hall, my foot catches suddenly on the rug, causing my body to tumble to the ground. My knee hits with a hard thud against the wood floor, sending a new round of pain through my body.

"Just perfect," I mutter to myself, well aware I am alone and no one is around to help me. I pull myself off the floor and limp my way back to the bedroom, tossing the suitcase unceremoniously onto the bed. Flinging it open, I can't help but stare at the haphazardly packed clothing, forgetting I had packed in such a rush that nothing was folded and put neatly into place. No, I must not think about this. It's just clothing. Clothing that needs to be washed and put away in its proper place. And so I begin my chore, sorting out the clothes into piles so I can go wash them later.

Once my bedroom has been brought back to order, I make my way back to the kitchen, placing all the various items back into the cupboard and focus my attention on the coffee pot.

Caffeine. I am in definite need of caffeine.

Leaning my cheek against my folded arms on the counter, I watch the steady stream of life-giving brown liquid pour into the waiting carafe. As I watch the ribbons of liquid flow from the spout, I look at the color and realize it's the same color as Andrew's hair. That luxurious dark hair, all thick and expertly styled to look as if he's just had the fuck of his life. The thought of his sexy bedroom hair has my heart constricting again in my chest as I reach for an available mug, which just happens to be the perfect shade of sapphire blue. In my distracted thoughts, I barely register the scalding liquid falling onto my hand as it splashes over the side while I pour.

"Fuck me," I mutter, lunging for the sink to put an immediate stream of cold water on the reddening burn. This morning is not going well. I woke up with yet another migraine, courtesy of my never ending dream. Then the floor decided to reach up and grab my foot causing the growing purple mark on my knee. Now there's a large angry red blotch on my hand. Anything else want to happen this morning?

As if on cue, my phone rings in the living room. Funny, I don't remember turning it on last night when I came home. Kara must have done that for me, surely so she could call and check up on me today. Lucky me to have my own mother hen to rule my roost. I dampen a towel and wrap it around the burn to keep it cold and answer the call without looking to see who it is.

"Hello?"

"Tessa, you're back."

Perfect, it's Sharon. As if second-degree burns and swelling knees weren't bad enough, let's throw my stepmother into the mix. *Thank you, fate. You cruel, cruel bitch.*

"Hi, Sharon. Yes, I got back late last night. I would have called, but I didn't want to wake anyone."

I limp over to my couch and carefully lower myself to avoid hitting both my hand and knee on any unnecessary objects. My eyes close as my head falls back to rest on the cushion, waiting for whatever snide remark Sharon's about to unleash come my way.

"And we thank you for that. There is definitely no need to wake us for something as minor as you returning from wherever you were. Your father mentioned that he invited you to dinner tomorrow night?"

"Yes. He called me earlier and asked if I wanted to …."

"I am just calling to confirm you are still coming," Sharon says, cutting me off as if she isn't really interested in anything that I was saying, which she truly is not.

"Yes, I will be there," I say meekly.

The rustling of keys in the background and shifting of papers tells me she must be getting ready to head for her weekly spa treatments. Another way for her to waste my father's money and keep her social status in check. I pinch the bridge of my nose and sigh softly to myself.

"What time would you like me there?" I'm praying it's an early time because the sooner I can leave that house the better off I'll be.

"Miriam says she'll have dinner ready at six o'clock since your father has a rather large case to work on Monday morning."

"Okay, I'll be there just before six then."

She scoffs, causing my shoulders to rise slightly. "Not too much before. It's only dinner, not some fancy party with invited guests."

But I was invited I want to say, knowing that statement will only start another round of insults and arguments. Instead, it stays in my head, where all other thoughts go unspoken when dealing with her.

"Is there anything I can bring?"

A small laugh sounds and it makes me want to cry. "Miriam is taking care of everything. I trust her cooking skills so there's no need for your contribution." The beeping of her car door let me know the conversation is about to end. "Try not to be late Tessa. It's bad form and highly tacky."

I nod. "I won't be late."

The engine purrs softly to life and the click of her seatbelt sounds over the phone. "Good. I'm off for the day. I'm having a much-needed spa day with the mayor's wife. Remember, don't be late. Goodbye, Tessa."

"Goodbye, Shar-"

She hangs up before I even finish her name. Well, that took more energy than I wanted to use today. And she's going to lecture me on manners? Honestly, I'm not even sure why they bother with me. I am an adult after all and don't need checking up on. Why did I promise to have dinner with them? Once again, it all boils down to pity and obligation with my father, which I find completely ironic since he never cared about me until I was eighteen and a legal adult. And even then it was already too late. The damage was done and nothing could erase the years of pain that had been brought to my life. I slide down the couch further, wanting nothing more than to sleep the rest of the weekend away.

I stretch my arms above my head several hours later, feeling moderately refreshed and thankful to wake up still lying on the couch instead of the floor. But like everything else there's a sacrifice to be made. Instead of waking up with a bruised cheek or pounding head, I'm greeted with the not so pleasant cramping of my neck from being contorted awkwardly against the arm of the couch.

The sun is in its final descent, casting an orange hue along the buildings and trees outside my window. The howling of the wind causes a shiver to run down my spine as the newly fallen leaves dance down the street before being picked up and carried away to destinations unknown. *If only that could happen to me.* What I wouldn't give to be taken away from here, away from my life and all its problems. There was a possibility of that happening, at least I thought there was, but how mistaken I was in believing that good things happen to the damned.

His bright sapphire eyes still haunt me every time I close my eyes. The scent of his cologne invades my nose as I picture him standing near me, holding his hand out to me, telling me everything is going to be okay. That I really am his love, as he called me. Ugh, that stupid pet name. Damn sexy British men.

My phone beeps at my side, alerting me to an incoming message. Ice forms in my veins as I think about what the message could be and who its sender is. Realistically it would only be one of two people. I hesitantly pick up my phone and swipe my finger across the screen then sag back into the couch as I see Kara's name appear.

You better be alive. I'm coming over to check up on you.

Oh God, please no. I don't think I can entertain anyone right now, even if it is my best friend and boss.

Really, I'm okay. See, alive and well. No need to check up on me.

Within minutes, her response shows up, not shocking me in the least.

Too late. Couple blocks away. Be right there.

Damn. There goes my quiet night of self-loathing and private pity party. But then again maybe it won't be so bad. I mean it is Kara and she knows exactly how to stop my mind from working, which I would welcome with open arms right now. And Kara Thomas doesn't exactly take no for an answer.

Within five minutes, my door is being pounded on and I barely have time to stand before it flies open with Kara filling the frame, holding two bottles of wine out in front of her.

"Chickie! You and I are having a movie marathon tonight. And I knew one bottle would not be enough so I brought two." She walks right past me, putting her coat on a barstool and tossing a few DVDs from her bag onto the counter.

"Thanks, Kara, but you didn't need to come over. I'm okay, really." I pull the sash of my robe tighter around my body before taking down two wine glasses from the cupboard. Kara looks me up and down and starts laughing hysterically.

"Are you kidding me? You're still wearing a robe and your pajamas for crying out loud. And seriously, puppy dog slippers? What are you, five? I need to give you a makeover something fierce."

Kara brushes past me, grabbing the electric wine opener off the counter to uncork the first bottle. She fills the glasses with the already chilled white wine and hands me one, raising hers in the process to clink them together.

"Tonight we're not thinking about guys. It's a No Boys Allowed night."

I silently laugh and take a rather large sip of the wine, relaxing my shoulders a bit. Kara always gets the best wines and tonight her flavor of choice is a Riesling.

"Sounds good to me. So what movies did you bring?" I pick up the cases to give them a once over, making sure she won't be torturing me with scary movies.

"We are going to have a Sandra Bullock marathon tonight. We could use a little bit of comedy after this last week." She winks at me and ushers me back into my living room. Still holding onto the movies, I crawl to the player while Kara occupies the spot I just vacated on the couch, tucking her feet underneath her body. At least she dressed down slightly to come over here. Although even her yoga pants and off the shoulder sweatshirt still make her look runway-worthy.

"Which one first? The Proposal or Miss Congeniality?" I ask, waving the two movies in front of my face. Kara taps her fingernail against her wine glass as she brings it up to her lips.

"Such choices. Hmm."

I laugh as she smirks at me. "Give me a break. I know you want your Ryan Reynolds fix first." I open the case and put the DVD into the player before a pillow sails near my head, barely missing me.

"Shut up! It's you that has the unhealthy obsession with

him. How many of his movies do you own?" she asks, raising one perfectly plucked eyebrow at me. With the remote in my hand, I plop down on the couch next to her, turning the necessary devices on.

"That's not the point," I say with a chuckle. She laughs with me as I hit play. Five minutes of her being here and already my mood has lifted considerably. I love this woman to death. "Besides, you can't tell me you don't want to see Ryan Reynolds naked body."

"Hey, I never said that. I'm all for Ryan getting naked in every scene. In fact, that's what I'm going to do. Every scene he's in I'm going to pretend his beautiful ass is naked, even though he looks so hot in a suit."

"Kara, only you would do something like that."

"Don't judge. You'll be doing the same thing now that I put the idea in your head."

And she's right. I will. Because let's face it, the man has a smoking hot body. We watch for a little bit and my gaze falls on my feet.

"So you really don't like my puppy dog slippers?" I ask, knowing what the answer is.

The disgusted look on her face has me almost spitting my wine all over the coffee table in front of us. Luckily, I keep it in because I know that would be alcohol abuse, which is a grievous crime, punishable by weeks of ridicule.

"Tell me you're joking," she says dryly.

I shrug my shoulders. "So I have them. Big deal. It's not exactly like anyone is going to see me wearing them except you."

"You never know. Your dream pizza delivery guy could see you wearing those hideous things and be like, um, well, I was going to bang her. Then I saw her slippers and decided not to tap that after all."

I laugh and shove at her. "As if I'm going to go for the pizza delivery guy anyway. I need to find someone with a slightly more stable job and isn't sixteen and covered in acne."

She laughs and takes another sip of her wine. "Okay, very true." She pauses, seeming to consider her next statement carefully. "I still think Andrew is head over heels for you. There must have been a misunderstanding. There is absolutely no way he is going to turn down a hot piece of ass like you."

The spot above my heart begins to ache again as I try to rub the pain away. "Yeah, you've told me how hot I am in my current attire. Can't imagine him not wanting this. Besides, didn't you say this was a No Boys Allowed zone? No more talking about guys or London or events that happened over there."

Her face softens, placing a sympathetic hand on my knee. "You're right. Tonight is about funny women, wine, and pressing slow motion while Ryan gets naked. Then rewinding and doing it all over again."

I nod and clink my wine glass to hers. "I'll drink to that."

And then our scene comes on, and for the next twenty minutes we appreciate the fine male specimen on the TV in slow motion, still frame and reluctantly in regular motion to finish the movie.

Chapter 2

I T'S FINALLY HERE, SUNDAY NIGHT. I was hoping to maybe contract a sudden case of the flu, or maybe even the bubonic plague. Anything to get out of this dinner tonight with my father and Sharon. I can think of hundreds of things I'd rather do, including letting my heart bleed open and think about Andrew. But no, I'll play the part of the good daughter, imagining my father actually cares about me, and will engage in uncomfortable conversation for the next two hours.

I pass the sign welcoming me to Lilydale and instantly I want to turn around and go back downtown. My crappy car and less than designer clothes make me feel almost homeless just driving through the streets. Large mansion-like houses surround me, telling everyone just how well off they are. I am definitely out of my league here.

And yet, I pull into the circular drive of my father's house and park my car, thankful I arrived in one piece, and on time. My nerves get the best of me as I walk to the front door, constantly tucking and re-tucking strands of hair behind my ear.

As soon as I see the bright smiling face of the only friendly person in the house I instantly relax.

"Hello, Ms. Martin. How are you this evening?" Miriam says as she pulls me into a hug. I squeeze her back, thankful to see her. She's an older woman in her mid-sixties and reminds me of Betty White in her Golden Girls days. She has the same overly fluffed hair but in a shade of graying red instead of blond. She's a little round in the middle and slightly shorter than me. But her smiling face and cheery personality reminds me of my grandma and she treats me just like she used to.

"Miriam, I told you to call me Tess. You know I'm not like my dad and Sharon."

She reaches up to cup my cheek, her eyes glassing over a bit with emotions. Miriam has worked with my father for the past ten years. I was fortunate to really get to know her during the few months I lived here and thankful she was my saving grace from a life of depression and isolation.

"Of course, my dear. Come, come, in you go before you catch your death out there. You're not properly dressed for this weather, child." She takes my light jacket and hangs it up in the hall closet. Sitting on the bench, I slide my boots off, making sure to tuck them underneath so they don't get in the way. Also, so Sharon doesn't see them and starts to cast her judgment on my shoe choices.

"How has Colin been?" I ask. Colin Rafferty is Miriam's husband of the past forty-plus years. I've met him on a few occasions and he's just like her, a sweet little Irish man with a generous heart to match. He owns a small pub in downtown St. Paul and runs it most nights of the week.

"Oh, Colin is doing just fine. Been working day in and day

out now since they lost another bartender. Can't seem to keep young people around long enough anymore."

I shake my head and follow her down the hall, looping my arm around her waist and hugging her close to me. She squeezes my shoulder as we turn toward my father's study.

"That's a shame. Hopefully, you two still make time for each other. I know how crazy life can sometimes get." And really I only know this because of the past week. If you had asked me how crazy life can get a month ago, my answer would have been different.

"Why of course we do dear. We always see each other at night so don't worry your pretty little head about us." Never missing anything, Miriam's face falls slightly as she notices my appearance. "How about you? Is everything all right in your world?"

I fake my best smile for her, although I'm not sure she buys it. Heck, I don't even buy it. It's hard to fake happiness while in this house, along with the recent events of the past few days. "I'm good, Miriam. It's just been a little … stressful at work this last week. Lots of traveling and not enough sleep."

Miriam shakes her head, not buying what I'm selling. It doesn't stop her from enveloping me in an enormous hug, patting my back reassuringly, as only she could.

"You know if you need anything you can call me. And I baked your favorite dessert tonight, just for you."

My eyes light up. "Apple crisp?"

She nods. "With caramel topping. And I made an extra one for you to bring home."

I fling my arms around her again. "You're the best, Miriam."

She cups my cheek one last time and urges me into the study, where my father is waiting for me behind his massive desk. I knock on the door first to announce my presence. He looks up from his work and acknowledges me in the doorway.

"Tessa. It's good to see you. Please, come in." He motions for me to sit in one of the leather wingback chairs in front of the large mahogany desk. His greetings are always formal, but then again he is the Assistant Attorney General for the state. Formality is to be expected.

He takes off his glasses, setting them on top of the stacks of papers that litter his desk. He regards me for a moment and I can't help but fidget under his stare.

"Um, hi, Dad. How have you been?"

He leans back in his leather chair, making it creak slightly. Robert Martin looks like the influential lawyer he is behind his desk. You would never guess he has a twenty-six-year-old daughter just by looking at him. He's in his early fifties, having had me when he was young and just starting his law career, and is only now beginning to show signs of gray at his temples. He's tall, which is where I get my taller than average height from, and an athletic build, no doubt from the dedication he puts into the gym as his way to blow off steam. I can only imagine the stress he's under with his position. Actually no I can't since I'm just an administrative assistant. My life is pretty much the same thing every day. Well, at least it was.

"I've been doing well. Several larger cases will be keeping me plenty busy these next few months before I have to fly out to D.C. again."

I nod my head as he takes a sip of the amber liquid in his crystal tumbler. Brandy, no doubt. It's his drink of choice when he wants to avoid something. Probably me.

"So how was your business trip? Did you get everything accomplished that you needed to?" He asks with genuine interest, shocking me almost into silence. Wow, I wasn't expecting him to really ask me anything.

"Yes, we did. We met with the board of the Tree of Life Foundation, got all the contracts signed and we're working on strategy this week. I'm really excited because I love their mission statement and the work they do. I think it's a fitting cause for a person like me."

That last little jab was unintentional. Maybe I'll be lucky and he won't know what the Foundation does. At least I hope he won't. I'm not a mean person. Deep down, I do love my father, but it's hard not to hold on to some sort of resentment for the condition of my childhood and his direct part in it.

"Ah yes, I've heard of them. They do fantastic work and are most definitely a great cause. Aren't they based in London though?"

Shit. He has heard of them. If he was affected by my off the cuff comment, he sure doesn't show it. I blink rapidly and swallow hard. "Yes, they are. That's where we met the board last week. They gave us several tours of different centers to show us what they offer to the children."

"I see. You never mentioned you were going abroad. You should have told me. I'm still your father and would like to know when my daughter is leaving the country, even if she is a grown adult."

I bite my lip and look down at my lap. "I didn't want to make a big deal about it. I went as Kara's assistant so my role was pretty small. But I was grateful for the opportunity to see firsthand what the Foundation does and who we are going to represent."

Andrew's face quickly flashes into my head and I shake it off, not wanting to dwell on him while sitting in front of my dad. But then he stands, draining the liquid from the tumbler and setting it on the bar behind his desk.

"Of course, as her assistant. It was very nice of Ms. Thomas to take you with her."

And with that statement my mood plummets even further to the ground. That simple statement says so much more than what is on the surface. He was less than thrilled when I went to a two-year community college, only to graduate with my associates degree and a certificate for Administration Assistant. It's not exactly something he can brag about to his high and mighty friends, whose sons and daughters all followed in the family business, being doctors and lawyers and such. His absence from my life was a determining factor to not follow in his career path. That was not a life I wanted. If I should ever get the chance for a family, I wanted to be there and spend time with them, show them they are the most important thing in my life, not my career.

I follow him out of the room, making some idle small talk on our way to the living room. Sharon is perched on her stark white designer couch, casually flipping through the latest fashion magazine. My dad walks up behind her, placing his hands gently on her shoulders before dipping down and lightly kissing her cheek. Sharon beams brightly at him, leaning into the kiss yet never once stops turning the pages. I can never tell if she really loves my dad or if she's only interested in him for what he can give her. A scowl forms on her face when her eyes finally land on me, standing in the doorway to the great room. "Hello, Tessa. You look ... nice." Her nose crinkles as she glances over my appearance. Apparently jeans and a nice sweater aren't proper Sunday dinner attire, as she lounges in her Chanel suit, which I find as slightly overkill. It's the weekend and she doesn't work. Why on earth would she need to wear something like that? Oh yes, to rub it in my face how much of my dad's money she has and how little of it I have.

"Um, thanks, Sharon." My toe twists nervously against the cherry wood floors, thankful that I picked a pair of socks without a hole or worn out soles in them. I stand there for a few seconds in awkward silence before Miriam arrives to announce that dinner is ready.

Sharon gracefully rises from the couch and takes the offered arm from my dad as he leads her to the formal dining room. I silently follow, mindful not to bump into any tables or trip over the rugs lining the hallway. I don't need an embarrassing display right now. Dinner will be enough as it is.

My dad pulls out Sharon's chair for her, placing a kiss on the crown of her head as he lightly pushes it in. Memories appear of Andrew doing a similar gesture on numerous occasions over the last week, causing my heart to beat slightly faster. It's been two days since I've seen or heard from him and yes, I realize it's my own doing. A part of me was hoping he'd ignore my pleas for silence and contact me anyway. The last two messages I received from him were the day I left, begging me not to go and to talk to him. And I stupidly ignored them, too hurt and prideful to admit that I may have been wrong.

I brush the memory away, taking the seat to my dad's left. Tears will do me no good here. It doesn't stop me from rubbing the spot above my heart to ward off the impending hurt of watching Sharon and my dad hold hands before our plates are brought out to us.

Miriam is a miracle worker I swear. The food she brings is absolutely divine, serving it as if she was preparing for a major competition rather than just a regular Sunday dinner. And bless her heart she remembered that I don't eat very much and portioned me accordingly. Prime rib with roasted new potatoes and lemon green beans sit neatly on my plate. This is my dad's favorite meal and is definitely a step up from my normal dinner of soup or noodles.

My father pours us all a glass of Bordeaux, no doubt from his private collection, starting with Sharon and then serving me last. The delicious flavor blasts my senses as I take a sip, thankful to have the alcohol to numb my brain, if even just for a moment.

We start off in silence, each of us appreciating the excellent meal Miriam has prepared. I keep my head down, not wanting to make eye contact with either of them and bring any unwanted conversation. It's a short-lived dream as my dad is the first to break the silence.

"So, Tessa, were you able to see any sights while you were in London?"

I bite my lip, hoping to avoid anything regarding my trip. Sharon looks up and scowls slightly. Someone should tell her if she keeps doing that she'll develop wrinkles on her perfect face. Another comment that stays silent in my head.

"You were in London? I thought you said you had a business meeting to go to."

I take another sip of the wine for some courage. "I was

at a business meeting. We were negotiating with the Tree of Life Foundation, which is based in London. It's an incredible foundation and I'm really excited to start working with them. They help underprivileged children who have nowhere to go and give them a place to hang out and belong. They also run an orphanage and school and …"

Sharon cuts me off before I have the chance to finish. "Well, isn't that nice. So what exactly does that have to do with you?" She takes a bite of her prime rib, her perfectly pink lips sliding delicately over the silver fork, reminding me again how out of her class I am.

"My firm is doing the consulting work for them in the U.S. They want to expand their foundation stateside and we're helping them with the process of making that happen."

"I suppose it is a good cause. So why exactly did you have to tag along? You are, after all, only the secretary."

I retreat further into my chair, hoping it'll just swallow me up. My eyes drift over to my dad to see his reaction and I'm not surprised when there isn't one.

"Administrative Assistant. I accompanied Kara to help her set up the contracts, take notes for her when we met with the board, and various other things she needed help with while we were there."

I push the food around my plate, not really feeling hungry anymore. Not that I did in the first place. Just coming here is enough to lose my appetite. The best diet plan in the world.

Sharon rolls her eyes and takes a sip of her wine. "Again, if you ask me, it's a waste of company money to take you with. There's no reason why she couldn't do all those things by herself."

I drain the wine from my glass, praying the numbing effects will take over, or at least buy me time until I need to leave. Not that I want to be plastered when I have to battle the traffic to go home, but I'd like something to kill the pain of having to sit here and endure this inquisition.

I decide instead to focus on the question my father had asked me before Sharon dug her poisoned barbs into me. "I was able to do a little sightseeing. I rode the Tube; saw the Palace, Big Ben, and Westminster Abbey. I also took an enjoyable walk through Hyde Park with …" I stop before I divulge too much information. Unfortunately, it wasn't fast enough. Sharon catches it and raises one perfect brow.

"With whom? Don't tell me you met someone over there."

My eyes dart to the corner of the room, trying to focus on anything other than my stepmother. My dad has been silent this entire time, not once contributing to the conversation or stopping her line of questioning.

"I went for a walk with a gentleman I met on the flight over there, who coincidentally works for the Foundation, I later learned."

Now my dad gives his first sign of life, frowning at my last statement. "You allowed someone you met on a plane, a total stranger, to take you around London? How did you know he wasn't some lunatic who was going to take advantage of you somewhere? Plus, don't you think it is bad business to get romantically involved with someone who is employing you?"

My fingers twist in my lap as I contemplate my answer. "It wasn't anything like that. He's their head of operations and was willing to show me around. There's no relationship between us so you don't have to worry." I can barely choke out that last line as it gets caught in my throat, hoping he doesn't notice my discomfort.

Sharon doesn't fail though in putting me back in place. "Don't worry. You weren't there long enough to build a meaningful relationship with anyone. I mean, he's a COO and you're, well, you know." Her nose crinkles slightly as if she's laughing internally, which I'm sure she is.

I push the plate away from me, thoroughly finished with my meal and wanting desperately to go home and curl into a ball. Yes, I know better than anyone that a relationship between Andrew and I would never work. That insecurity alone was reason enough for me to run when faced with the harsh reality of our circumstances. He was Andrew and I was, well, me.

Finally, my dad gives Sharon a disapproving glare at her comment, the first sign showing he may actually care if my feelings get hurt. Sharon plays her role well by giving him a contrite look, feigning an apology I'm sure. I know I'll never hear it. His gaze returns to my barely touched plate with concerned eyes.

"Tessa, you cannot be finished eating. You've hardly touched anything on your plate, which wasn't much to start with."

"I'm just trying to save room for the apple crisp that Miriam made. I had a late lunch so I'm really not that hungry," I lie. He doesn't need to know I haven't had anything substantial to eat in a few days. My stomach hasn't exactly been into it. He seems to buy the lie because he doesn't push it further, just nods his head and resumes eating his own dinner.

So I sit as the dutiful daughter I am, listening as Sharon goes on and on about her spa day with the mayor's wife and her disgust at having her massage performed by someone else. Her regular masseuse was ill so now she's incredibly sore and isn't sure how she's going to function for the rest of the week. I refrain from rolling my eyes, only wishing those were my biggest problems in life.

Miriam comes back and clears our completed plates before returning with three dishes filled with warm apple crisp and a small scoop of vanilla ice cream. Salted caramel sauce is drizzled over the entire thing and I swear I'm drooling out of the corner of my mouth. The smell alone threatens to put me into a food coma and make me gain five pounds. But nothing compares to taking that very first bite. It is heaven disguised as a baked dessert. My dad actually half smiles at me as I sit and quietly enjoy this treat. It's nice to see some sort of positive emotion from him instead of indifference, which is what I get most of the time.

"So Tessa, we've decided to have Sharon's party this Friday night at seven p.m. Did Natasha get a hold of you yet?"

I shake my head and wipe the corner of my mouth with my linen napkin. "No, she hasn't yet." I almost forgot about my scheduled dress-up appointment.

"I'll make sure she calls you tomorrow to set up the appointment. Are you planning on bringing a date?"

Sharon scoffs loudly and I chew my bottom lip almost to the point of pain. "Yes, Tessa, is there someone special you plan on bringing?" She bats her eyelashes at me in an overly saccharine gesture. My spoon noisily falls to my plate, indicating that I'm done.

I need to leave. I can't be here anymore. My poor psyche is fragile as it is after this past week and Sharon is quickly pushing me over the edge.

"No, I don't have a date. I'll probably bring Kara with me, as usual. You both seem to like her."

My dad nods his head and pushes away his empty plate. "Yes, Ms. Thomas is a good choice. I'll make note of it. Remember, whatever you find at the boutique just put on my account. I'll take care of it for you." He gives me a genuine smile, which in turn causes Sharon to frown. She's not accustomed to sharing my dad's attention.

"And just so you know, I'll be wearing red."

Gotcha. Wear another color. Point taken.

"Thank you for doing this for me, Dad. I really appreciate it."

He gives me a curt nod. The corners of his lips turn up even more and warmth crosses over his face. "Of course, Tessa. It's nothing."

Except it's everything to me. Just having my dad acknowledge my existence is something to me. I'd never be reckless enough to ask him to love me. I know better than that. But inviting me to share his time with others, acknowledging me out in the open is good enough for me.

He stands and Sharon and I follow suit. She mutters something about needing to call a consultant for some fashion show so she excuses herself, but not before placing a large, passionate kiss on my father's lips. Gross. My dessert is threatening to reappear at that image now permanently carved into my brain.

"Thank you for the lovely meal, but I'm still jet-lagged from my trip and I want to catch up on some sleep before work tomorrow."

"Think nothing of it. I'll walk you to the door."

I follow him to the foyer in silence because I really don't know how to talk to him. I never know if he's really interested in anything about me or if he's just faking it for appearances. I'm sure it'd look bad in the public eye if the Assistant Attorney General didn't have a relationship with his daughter. Appearances are everything after all.

He grabs my jacket out of the closet while I sit on the bench and lace my boots up. Another frown appears on his face as he assists me in getting it over my arms.

"Don't you have a warmer jacket, Tessa? It's starting to get cold outside and I don't want to see you get sick."

"The zipper on my winter jacket from last year broke so this is all I have."

"When you go shopping please pick out a good winter coat as well. In fact, pick out a couple of different jackets if you need something different to wear to work other than your casual jacket."

I repeatedly blink at him. Whoa, where did that come from?

"Thank you. I'll see what they have and go from there. You know you don't have to do that."

His eyes soften and this time he fully smiles at me. "Do you need anything else? Any work clothes, shoes? You know what, when you go, please buy whatever you need and put it on my account. Don't worry about the cost or how many things you're getting."

I want to throw my arms around him to show how much that little gesture means to me. But I can't because it would be showing affection. Speech is lost to me and I shift from foot to foot.

"I don't know what to say. Thank you, Dad. That's very generous. I don't know how I could repay you." I choke back some tears that threaten to come forward, but they're quickly quashed as his indifference mask is put back on at my show of emotion.

"It's nothing. You are my daughter after all. It's what I should do for you."

Obligation. Right. How could I forget? He's not doing it because he loves me. He's doing it because he feels he should. It's when I take in my appearance that I realize he must be ashamed and embarrassed that I'm walking around the city, sharing his last name and looking the way I do. So I push the previous joy back into the recesses of my mind, locking them up and just nod my head.

"Well, I better get home. Thank you again for dinner. Please tell Miriam I said thank you as well." And speaking of the angel, she comes running down the hall, clutching a small dish of apple crisp for me to take home. She brushes my cheek with a swift kiss and waves goodbye to me. Thank heaven for Miriam.

My dad opens the front door and pats my shoulder as I walk toward my car. I never know if it's appropriate to give him a hug or a kiss goodbye, but the shoulder pat is at least some sort of connection. Sort of.

I turn back toward him at the top step and force a smile. "Goodnight, Dad. I'll see you Friday night."

"Drive safe, Tessa."

Then he turns and closes the door, leaving me in the glow of the front porch light. He doesn't look through the window next to the door to make sure I buckle my seatbelt or drive off with my headlights on. I'm effectively dismissed, having completed my task.

With my heart hanging heavy once again, I start my car and head back to my meager apartment, thankful to be away from that house. Merging back onto I94, I crank the radio when a Nickelback song comes on in an attempt to drown out the voice in my head. Just another successful dinner with my dad. Career is wrong, clothes are wrong. Basically, I am wrong. I focus on that thought as I pull up in front of my building and sigh. I'm just too exhausted to deal with any of it.

After putting the dessert in my fridge and securing my apartment, I get myself ready for another night of restless sleep. I check my phone one last time before setting the alarm and turning off my bedside light. Nothing. I guess this proves I was right. He doesn't want anything to do with me. So I close my eyes and pray tomorrow will be different and my heart won't hurt as much.

Chapter 3

THE START OF A BRAND new work week for me is a constant thorn in my side. Every Monday morning it's the same thing. It never changes and constantly finds me embarrassed about something that I did or didn't do over the weekend when people attempt to make polite conversation with me. I try to limit my responses to single word answers if possible. The less I engage in conversation, the better. Although Kara is trying her best to break me of this habit. It's a slow process.

I stare at my phone as I pass through the doors of my building. No new messages. Of course not. Why would he contact me? I mean, I ran off, broke the man's heart and begged him not to reach out to me. Well, the breaking of his heart thing is subject to debate. I still don't think he was quite as affected as I was, but then again I ran off without letting him explain anything. On the flip side, there could have been nothing to explain. This whole situation is making my head spin and I do not need this right away for my Monday.

Joining the crowd in front of the elevator, I watch as they all push into the available car, squeezing in like packed sardines. All they need is a little bit of oil to allow some sort of movement between them. I stop in my tracks. I know what will happen the moment I try to cram myself in there. I'll move to the back, unable to push the button to my floor. And no one else will be getting off there so I'll have to ride it all the way to the top before I can reach the buttons on the panel.

No. I need to break this endless cycle, stop my Bill Murray habit by changing just one little thing about my day. And this, not wanting to be embarrassed or squeezed to death by strangers looking down at me seems like a good start.

So instead, I wait until the door closes before pressing the up button to call the next elevator. Within minutes, the other descends, opening up and allowing a few people to exit. Only a few individuals are waiting now as we enter the car. I easily press the button for my floor without any awkward stares or unnecessary trips.

When I walk through the doors, I'm amazed that I'm not stumbling over my feet as usual. No, I'm on time, in fact. Amazing how one little change can make a world of difference to my routine. It's not a monumental life-changing event because all I did was wait for the next elevator. Nothing to get too hung up on.

I walk toward my cube with a newfound smile upon my lips, very unlike my typical Monday demeanor. I wave brightly at Kara as I pass her office and she literally stares at me as I walk by.

"Tess!" I hear her call out. I halt and turn back to her office, leaning against the door frame as she's still staring with her mouth wide open. "Holy shit, you're … not late." Her eyes dart from the clock to mine and then back again, in almost amused astonishment. And I can't help but laugh.

"Weird, huh? I guess waiting for the second elevator made that much of a difference."

I shrug my shoulders and move further into her office, occupying one of the available chairs in front of her desk. Kara's still staring at me, eyes bulging and mouth gaping open. I laugh because I don't know what else to do.

"Trying to rid the building of the fly situation?"

She shakes her head and tilts it slightly. "Huh?"

"You're staring at me with your mouth hanging open. Trying to catch flies?"

She laughs and leans back in her chair. "I guess you just caught me off guard. So, you waited for the second elevator. Didn't feel like riding up to the twentieth floor today or what?"

"No, I just wanted to keep my shoulders where they should be instead of scrunched together. I had a crazy image of sardines when I watched everyone pack into the first car. And you know how much I enjoy fish."

Kara picks her hands up and rests them on her stomach for a second. "And that one little change was enough to improve your day for the better. I see a new trend for you, Chickie. Maybe now you'll see that good things come to those who wait."

I roll my eyes at her. "It was an elevator ride, not a life lesson. Besides, I'm still me. I managed to put a small run in my nylons this morning. Luckily, it's high enough so it will be covered by my skirt."

She laughs and stands from her chair, rounding her desk

as I stand as well. Her arm slings over my shoulders and we exit toward my dull and lifeless cube.

"You know you're hilarious, right? One little change, one small decision can alter the entire course of your future. All you have to do is step back sometimes and look at the bigger picture. You can't tell me you didn't do that this morning by not jumping into the first elevator that arrived."

I swivel my chair and slowly lower myself onto it, tossing my purse in the bottom drawer. My brows furrow slightly as I think about her words. Did I really subconsciously do that this morning?

"Maybe, I guess. I don't know. Or my mind has been too preoccupied from … recent events."

She bypasses the last comment and I'm thankful for it. "That one decision saved probably a few minutes and some awkwardness on your morning, right?" She perches herself on the edge of my desk and my lower lip disappears between my teeth. Man, I hate it when she makes sense.

"Probably."

Kara's bright eyes find mine, locking me into place as she continues on. "Sometimes the answer is right in front of you and you just have to stand back to see it. And I'm not just talking about the elevator here, Tess. You have to know that if you just take a second to look at everything you can see what everyone else sees."

Confusion crosses my face as she lets out an exasperated sigh. She's frustrated with me and really, I am too. I understand what she's trying to say. Just stop and look around, take one second to see the world for what it truly is and not what I make it out to be. See it through different eyes, from a different point of view and a new perspective will appear; one that may make even more sense than what was originally thought. But my insecurities and self-doubt will never really let me see things.

But to appease her, I just nod my head and weakly smile back. "Yeah, okay Kara."

"I have a meeting at ten with the other executives this morning to give them the rundown of last week. Could you do me the hugest of huge favors? Could you get all of our materials together and get enough copies for everyone? I think I'll need seven copies total."

I nod my head and shake my mouse, bringing my computer to life. "Sure, no problem. I'll have them ready for you by then."

Kara hops off my desk and regards me quietly. "I have a feeling that today is going to be a good day for you, Tess."

My nose wrinkles as I think about her comment. "Because I chose to ride the second elevator this morning?"

She laughs, jabbing her index finger into my forehead. I wince slightly at the pain as she manages to hit my fresh bruise. That alone is contradictory to her statement.

"No, because you actually thought about something and it had a positive outcome. You assessed the situation and chose the correct path."

"It was an elevator ride," I say, slowly annunciating each word to her. "Let's not make a bigger deal of it than it really is. Now if you don't get out of my cube, I'll never have your materials ready for you before your meeting." I shove at her hip and she stumbles on her heels, laughing.

"Fine, don't believe me. You'll see. I think things will start looking up for you." Kara waves to me over her shoulder, a typical response when she wants to get the last word in and heads back to her office. Truly she needs to cut back on her coffee intake in the morning. It's going straight to her head, lacing it with ridiculous ideas. Turning my chair around to face my computer, I start clicking through the files, gathering all the information she needs for her meeting.

Time flies by and when I look down at the clock again I'm amazed it's already noon. I swear I just got here, but it's been one of those mornings, just a nonstop hustle and bustle type day, which always tends to make time speed up. Of that, I'm thankful because the closer it gets to five the closer it is for me to wallow on my couch and lick my wounds. Wounds that haven't even begun to scab over yet.

Needing to feed my body with something other than coffee, I call the local deli down the street. I order two salads and half a sandwich, one for me, and one for Kara since she still hasn't returned from her meeting. I'm sure after two hours of being stuck talking to the other executives she'll be chomping at the bit for something to eat. At least I know I would be.

As I hang up my desk phone, I have a sudden urge to check my cell phone for any news. Not that I'm expecting anything. I mean it's been pretty silent for the past three days so why would today be any different? Just because Kara says good things could happen to me today? She's way too optimistic and I'm, well, the opposite.

To my surprise, I do have a missed text message. I open the app, wondering who it's from. My breath catches in my throat. Holy shit, it's from Andrew. He's finally decided to reach out and ignore my request. Emotions war inside me, unsure if I should be happy or mad about this. I did ask for space, but I'm pretty sure three days and the Atlantic Ocean is taking it a bit far, even if I am the one who instigated it. You can't get much more space than that.

With shaking hands, I open the message. Instantly my hand flies to my mouth as I read his first words to me in days.

Tessa, it's been days since I've heard your soft voice. Please allow me to explain my actions from Friday. I'm not pleased by how we left things and I'm afraid there may have been a misunderstanding somewhere. I miss your face, your smile, your touch. I'm in agony. Please, love, let me explain. ~A~

My mind processes his words as I read them over and over again. He's apologizing to me when I was the one who ran away, left him dangling on a rope without explanation? Wait, I'm supposed to be upset with him and whoever this Evie person is who was garnering his attention that morning. Was it just a weekend thing between them? Had he used her too and now that she's gone he wants me?

It's too much. My chest hurts and my breath is coming in short spurts. Pretty sure this is the start of a panic attack. I bolt to the closest bathroom and stand in front of the sink, staring at my pale complexion in the mirror. Why? Why me? Why now?

Can I say that I don't feel the same about him? That I haven't missed his voice, his touch, his smile, his … everything? If I wanted to lie to myself, the answer would be no, but I can't do that. I can't deny my heart's feelings toward him when he puts his out there like that. To say I've missed him is a gross understatement. Andrew occupies too much of my mind when it's not focused on whatever task is at hand.

Standing just a bit taller, I smooth my hair back into position and calmly walk back to my desk. I stare at the phone, wondering how to handle his message. Should I ignore it? Should I reply? I rub the spot over my heart and decide to think about it on my way to pick up lunch. It's been three days. What's another half hour?

As I step out into the brisk autumn air, my phone beeps again in my purse. *No, just ignore it. Don't torture yourself.* How can I ignore him when he's reaching out? And do I really want to? Every time my eyes close I see his beautifully sculpted lips, remember how he kisses me with the finesse of a gentleman, treating me like the most precious thing on the planet. I remember his hands, his arms, his body pressed hard against mine, driving me wild with desire and yes, even that stupid four-letter word which shall go unsaid again.

Being a glutton for punishment, I stop and lean against the building, pulling my phone from my purse, anxious to see what the message says this time.

Tessa, please answer me. I know it's only been a few hours since my last message, but I'm desperate to hear your voice. I know you're at work and don't want to disturb you, but I must explain things. It's killing me to think that you believe I do not have any feelings for you. Talk to me. Please, Tessa, I miss you so much. ~A~

A few hours? I look at the timestamp of the first message and realize he had sent it to me while I was making copies this morning for Kara. And now he's reaching out, trying to draw me back in. Do I want to be drawn in again? The hole in my heart says it wants to be filled with the emotions that only Andrew can bring.

But I shove my phone back into my purse. Maybe after lunch it'll be something I can deal with. With purposeful strides, I walk the short distance to the deli, avoiding any eye contact along the way for fear of something setting me off. I feel too vulnerable to the outside world at the moment.

As if the universe enjoys screwing with me, my purse strap falls off my shoulder while I wait in line, dumping the entire contents onto the floor. Loose change and various personal items spread like water along the tile floor. The ground can swallow me up any time now. Instantly, I drop to my knees, still mindful of the massive bruise from this weekend, and begin the tedious task of gathering every nickel and dime scattered about.

The guy ahead of me bends down and starts to help me, picking up pens and receipts and a few loose coins as well. He dumps them into my opened purse on the floor and I follow suit, thankful for the help. That's when I look up and see his bright dazzling smile at me. My mouth opens to thank him, but the words never come out. A set of warm, brown eyes regards me, halting all thoughts of performing any necessary human functions. Those eyes are powerful yet friendly and crinkle slightly in the corners when he smiles.

He helps me stand and my eyes travel the full length of him. He must be some sort of businessman, dressed in a navy pinstripe suit, complete with matching navy tie. He's young, maybe slightly older than me. His blond hair has a small wave to it like it's just slightly overgrown from how it's normally cut. All in all, he's definitely someone worth giving a second look to.

"Thank you so much. I can't believe I just did that," I say.

I shift nervously from foot to foot thinking Kara is completely full of bullshit now, saying that good things will happen to me today. Crawling across a tile floor on my hands and knees, gathering change and various other items isn't what I would call a good start.

"It's not a problem. We've all been there." His voice is soft and kind, just like his eyes, as he speaks to me. But his voice is not the one in my head, the one my heart hurts for. Then again no one has *his* voice, the one that lights my soul on fire the instant I hear it.

"Well, thank you again." I tuck a strand of hair behind my ear, my telltale nervous gesture. His eyes narrow in thought as we move up the line.

"You look familiar to me. Do you work close by?" My eyes are drawn to his long fingers scratching at his chin while his eyes stay focused on my face.

I nod my head. "Yes, I work in the building a few blocks away, at Mattson and Associates."

His smile broadens and he snaps his fingers. "That's where I've seen you. I work in the same building on the fifteenth floor. I believe you've been in the elevator a couple of times when I've been in there."

Oh no. Please don't say he's seen me riding the elevator well past my floor. A flush creeps across my cheeks, causing him to smile even more.

He really is kind of cute when he smiles.

"I'm sure that's a good possibility."

The line shifts again and somehow he manages to move forward while still facing me. If I were to attempt that I'd be sprawled on my ass in two seconds flat. He holds his hand out to me, his eyes still hovering over my features.

"Michael Fontaine."

"Tessa Martin."

He gives me another grin and the lady behind the counter calls for the next person in line, repeating it louder this time. I can't help the giggle that escapes as I point over his shoulder.

"I think she's calling for you."

Michael turns around and only then notices he's next in line. Shaking his head, he approaches the counter and gets his order. Briefly, I appreciate him from behind, especially his broad shoulders and the way he stands so confident in himself as if nothing could ever bother him. I wish for that type of confidence.

I step to the counter and give the lady my name and she quickly returns with the order. Michael's still standing beside me, making me slightly nervous as I move to grab my wallet from my purse.

"Here, allow me to get that for you." He gives her some money, smiling politely.

"Thank you. You really didn't have to do that for me."

He shakes his head and I turn to follow him through the front door. "It's nothing. I just didn't want you to risk dumping your purse out again." He gives me a wink and I instantly blush. He's quite the smooth talker. Definitely a businessman, if it wasn't already apparent by his attire.

We start walking toward our building, making small talk and casually getting to know each other. I learn that he's not a businessman, but worse, a lawyer at Lyman Burns & Goldman. I'll hold off my judgment for now. Perhaps not all lawyers are workaholics like my father.

Michael tells me that he grew up in Eden Prairie, went to college at Northwestern and got his law degree from Harvard. So on top of being an adorable lawyer, he's smart as well. Now I feel insignificant at being just a lowly assistant with nothing more than an AA degree. Perhaps the pizza delivery guy is more in my league after all.

"What about you? What do you do at Mattson? Let me guess, senior executive?"

I shake my head and look down at my feet. "No, I'm just an administrative assistant to Kara Thomas."

Michael quickly stands in front of me, causing me to stop and look up at him. Our building is less than half a block away and I can't figure out why we're just standing here.

"Hey, don't be ashamed of your job. I'd be lost without my assistant. I honestly think she works harder than I do."

Well, this is something new. Someone who doesn't look down at my position but actually thinks it's something worthwhile and significant. Okay, he's not the first person and if I was honest with myself, there are really only four people who make me feel like my job is important. Everyone else doesn't share that view. I flash him a weak smile and we resume walking toward the building, allowing him to usher me into the lobby as he holds the door open for me.

As we wait for the elevator to arrive, Michael asks me about my family, my least favorite subject to talk about, and I quietly tell him who my dad is.

"No way. Your dad is Assistant Attorney General Robert Martin? I've followed his career around the state for the past few years. He's a shoo-in for Attorney General in the next election. He's tried and won some of the biggest cases in the state."

Great. Another fan of my father. Not that I can blame him. My dad is kind of a celebrity in his own right. His face gets flashed across the news channels almost weekly due to the cases he works on. Part of me is proud of him. The other part of me is still the little girl he left crying in the driveway, just wanting her daddy to come back to her.

"Yep, that's him. I don't know much about my dad really. We just recently reconnected a few years ago due to my parents' divorce when I was little."

Michael's eyes soften more at the small tidbit of information I just shelled out. I don't like too many people knowing my personal matter and I'm not sure why I divulged it in the first place. I guess I feel comfortable talking with him, like a long lost friend or something. Is it possible to have that kind of connection with someone? *You fell in love with Andrew in less than a week. Pretty sure you can find a friend in less than that* the snarky bitch in my head says.

When we enter the empty elevator, I'm immediately assaulted with the intense smell of his cologne. I would catch whiffs of it when we walked outside, but I wasn't entirely sure it came from him. But now, standing here next to him, clutching the takeout bag for dear life, I know it's coming from him. It smells good, but it doesn't drive me wild. Not like Andrew's, how it would wrap around me and make every nerve ending tingle and spark to life. Between his cologne and his natural scent, my body would go haywire. A much different reaction than what I'm currently experiencing with Michael. He doesn't make my skin jump or my heart beat faster with just a look or a simple touch of his hand. There's just nothing. And that's okay. I'm not looking for anything more than a friend right now.

40

Chapter 4

WHEN THE DOORS OPEN ON my floor, I gracefully step out, thankful to be back on home ground. He holds the door open, leaning against it with his shoulder. I extend my hand to Michael, who shakes it with a smile on his face.

"It was a pleasure meeting you, Michael. I'm sure we'll run into each other again sometime."

"It was nice meeting you too, Tessa. And you can guarantee that we'll see each other around."

Michael winks at me one last time then steps back, allowing the doors to swallow him up and bring him to his floor. Well, that was definitely an eventful lunch hour.

Walking down the hallway to my desk, I glance over quickly to see if Kara is back. A sigh of relief flows through me as I quietly enter her office, taking note that she's feverishly typing away on her computer and her phone is pressed against her ear. I always love watching her brain work a mile a minute. It just amazes me but also shows how she got to where she is now.

I place the salad and sandwich on her desk, just off to the side of the papers she's studying. Kara glances up and mouths a "thank you" to me. Funny that she hasn't said a word to the person on the other line. Kara is not one to halt a conversation if I enter the room. She carries on as if I'm not there, a real professional. But I find it strange when her eyes follow me out, still not acknowledging the person on the other line until I'm fully out of her office.

After putting my things away, I sit back at my desk and open my meager lunch. I know this is way more food than I'll ever eat but hey, I'm ambitious today. Now that I've stopped moving, my mind focuses on Andrew's text messages again while I stab away at my salad. It's all so confusing. I drop the fork and cradle my head in my hands, propping my elbows on top of my desk. I feel a headache coming on.

Andrew says he misses me, yet he couldn't stop talking to another woman while I was still in his bed. Well, not literally in his bed but you know what I mean. My stomach growls and I take a few more bites of my lunch, discarding half of the contents into the garbage. My stomach is too upset to eat right now.

After an hour of diving head first into my afternoon assignments, a faint knock pulls me out of my thoughts. I turn and find Chris perching himself on the corner of my desk.

"Tessa, hey, how are you?"

What is it about the corner of my desk that invites everyone to sit there? Not that there's any other option in my tiny space. It's not exactly like I have an extra chair or anything like that.

"I'm good, thanks. How's everything coming with the Tree

of Life Foundation?" My hands fall into my lap, clasping them tightly together so I don't continually run them through my hair or twist my fingers together. Just the mention of the Foundation brings Andrew back to my thoughts, causing my heart to accelerate, as well as my breathing. It's amazing that he can still affect me this way even after three days apart.

"That's what I wanted to talk to you about. If you could join me in Kara's office for a moment, I'd appreciate it."

His tone has switched to all business, the light and friendly voice he usually uses with me now gone. Did I screw something up? Maybe the other executives caught wind of my tryst with Andrew and they're unhappy about it, wanting me to resign my position with the company for fear of backlash. I swallow harshly and nod, following him into Kara's office.

Kara glances up from her desk, still eating the lunch I brought her. The soft click of the door closing next to me causes another wave of nerves to flow through my bloodstream. A closed door is never a good sign. What if this is about the phone call I walked in on earlier? Maybe Kara didn't say anything because it directly affected me. Oh crap, I'm going to be fired. In a nervous twitch, my leg begins bouncing in place. Kara regards me with curious eyes and her hands folded neatly in front of her.

"Tessa, relax. It's not bad, I promise."

It's only then I realize both her and Chris are beaming brightly at me. My eyes dart from one to the other, giving them each a perplexed look.

"Um, okay. Am I in trouble? Did I screw something up in one of the contracts?" There's a slight tremble in my voice as I quietly speak to them. Chris's eyes soften, realizing how paranoid I am right now and places a friendly hand on my shoulder, instantly relaxing me.

"No, the contracts were excellent. Everything about them was fantastic. The other executives were really amazed at how fast you were able to draw them up and put everything we needed in there."

They were talking about me this morning? Me? A lowly secretary? Okay, admin assistant but I'm not going to correct myself. I reserve that only for my dad and Sharon in regards to my profession. Chris clears his throat and steeples his fingers beneath his chin on his propped up elbows.

"So during our meeting this morning we were informed that because of our growing clientele, and now with this giant project, we will need to add another junior account executive."

My stomach flutters with the wings of thousands of butterflies. An out of body experience starts to take over as I concentrate on what he's saying. Could he really be talking about what I think he is? I glance over at Kara and she's beaming.

"Yep, so I put in my recommendation to promote internally and you were the first person that came to mind. In these past four years, you have more than proven you can handle the stress and know the ins and outs of the game. You've drawn up every contract for me, attended almost every single meeting, and know how to close the deal. You were the obvious choice for the position in my mind. And apparently the rest of the executives agreed with me."

Shock. That's what I'm in. My fingers feel cold and numb. My hands can't stop shaking. Is she actually saying this to me? Did I choke on my food at my desk and now am having one of those 'what if' moments? I clear my throat and tuck a strand of hair behind my ear.

"Really? You think I'm ready for that? But I don't have a marketing degree or any sort of business degree."

Chris shakes his head. "You have something better. You have experience. A degree means nothing if you've never actually worked in the field. You've put in your time, learned the tricks of the trade and excelled at everything you do. So on behalf of myself and the other executives, I am offering you, Tessa Martin, the position of junior account executive. What do you say?"

I blink back at him a few times, allowing my brain to catch up. I can't believe it. I never thought my hard work would ever be noticed. Not that I was doing it to bring attention to myself. It's my job and I just wanted to make sure I did it well.

Kara tilts her head slightly and waves a hand in front of my face as I stare at a spot over her shoulder.

"Tessa? Hello? What do you say?"

Coming back into myself, I can't help the ear-splitting grin. "Yes. I say yes."

Chris pats me on the shoulder and shakes my hand while Kara jumps out of her chair and rounds her desk to engulf me in a giant hug.

"Congratulations, Chickie! I knew you'd move up the corporate ladder soon." She gives me one more death squeeze before releasing me to Chris, who hugs me as well.

"We're all very proud of the work you do and are very excited to see you move into this position. We know you will exceed our every expectation."

A lone tear trickles down my cheek and I quickly wipe it away. The amount of love and support that my two dear friends are giving me is overwhelming. I've never had confidence in my abilities or myself for that matter. But these two have never faltered in their opinion of me, never once treating me as if I was a lesser person. Instead, I was their equal.

It's just all too much.

"I don't know what to say. Just, wow. I never thought this would happen to me. Thank you so much for this opportunity. I'll do my best not to let you down."

Kara waves her hand in front of her face, dismissing my comment. "As if you could let us down. We know you all too well, remember? But now we have something to celebrate tonight. Dinner at Capital Grille?"

I nod my head and smile again. "Sounds good to me."

Kara leans up, stealing a kiss from Chris before they have to go back to hiding their relationship. "Okay, you need to go now. I have to talk to Tessa for a bit without an abundance of testosterone in the air."

Chris leans over, looking as if he's going to whisper something in her ear. Instead, he reaches around and pinches Kara's ass, causing her to yelp in a mixture of surprise and pain.

"Watch it, little girl, or you may get worse than that later tonight." His lips curl up into a wickedly teasing smile. Kara matches his smile and I prepare myself in case World War III decides to appear.

"Promises, promises. Seriously, get out. Highly important things need to be discussed without you."

"Girl talk?" he says, cocking his head to the side.

"Go!" she half whispers, half yells. He laughs and takes her mouth again, leaving her a mess as he walks back to his office. Kara regains her composure and rounds the desk, sliding back into her high leather chair.

"I didn't get the chance to thank you for lunch earlier. It was exactly what I needed." She picks up another forkful and shoves it in her mouth.

I shrug, playing it off as nothing. "Once I saw you were still stuck in that meeting I figured you'd be ready for lunch when you got out. Besides," I pause, thinking about whether or not I want to tell her about my lunch escapade. "I didn't even buy it for you."

Kara raises her head, tilting it to the side. "No? Who did then?"

"Well, there's a story behind that. You'll laugh about it I'm sure."

I go into the whole embarrassing story, not leaving any part out. She sits there, almost stoic and listens as I talk about Michael and the coincidence that he works in this building. The smile on her face slips slightly.

"Tell me more about this Michael guy."

I shrug my shoulders. "He's nice, good looking, and kind. I guess I never really gave any thought to it. He's just a stranger, well, acquaintance now I suppose."

There's a tapping noise echoing through the quiet office and I realize it's coming from Kara. She only taps her pen when she's deep in thought, but I can't figure out what it is about my story that has her mind in overdrive.

"Have you heard from Andrew today?" she asks.

And there's the reason for her curiosity of Michael. My face is indifferent as I nod my head, unsure of how I feel about hearing from him today. Part of me is elated. The other part of me is scared and upset.

"He sent me a few text messages. There's really nothing more to say to him, especially since I won't be working on the account anymore. So we have no chance or need to ever see each other again."

Kara leans over the desk and holds me in a stare. "But you want to."

Images of Andrew assault my mind as I picture his beautiful face and body, smiling and laughing as we walk the streets of London. My most favorite memory of that trip. Well, one of them.

"I do, but I don't."

"Do you love him?"

I sigh. "What does it matter? What's done is done. I'm here, he's over there. A relationship between the two of us is impossible, regardless of what I may or may not be currently feeling for him."

"That's bullshit and you know it. I can see it written all over your face. You try your best to hide it, but you fail miserably every time. You are head over heels in love with that man and nothing should ever stand in your way. If you've found love, then you need to grab hold of it with two hands and don't let anyone or anything take it away from you."

Kara should know. Her love for Chris is one she has to hide, but it doesn't stop them from being together. I don't want a relationship like that. I don't want to hide in the shadows and steal time to be with him. I want a relationship that's out in the open, where we can go anywhere and do anything anytime we wanted. But if Andrew is there and I am here it's impossible.

"Look, no offense, but I'm still not quite ready to dive into what if situations where Andrew is involved." I stand and turn toward the door. A look of sadness crosses Kara's face as she nods her head dejectedly.

"Oh, by the way, my dad is throwing a birthday party for Sharon on Friday night at the Millennium. Will you come with me as my guest? You know I hate going to these things alone." She checks her calendar and then nods her head.

"I've got Friday free and clear so it shouldn't be a problem. Formal affair again I'm assuming?" Kara knows from the last party she went to that my dad goes all out for Sharon because it's what she expects.

I nod my head and sigh. "Yeah, he's making Natasha set up an appointment at some boutique to get me clothes, you know, so I don't embarrass him further."

Kara shakes her head. "Your dad frustrates me sometimes."

I stand in the doorway and sadly laugh. "Try being his daughter." I wave to her as I walk back to my desk.

My head is swimming at everything that's happened over the course of the day so far. A new position, an embarrassing meeting with a random stranger, and then Andrew finally making contact with me. The last little bit has me reaching for my phone, anxious to see if he's messaged back, even though I have yet to reply to his last two messages.

Tessa, please. I miss you and I need to speak with you. Just give me five minutes of your time. ~A~

This is exhausting, fighting my feelings for him. I want to reach through my phone and hold him, kiss him, feel his body touching mine. This last message seems sad, tortured even. And I love him too much to hurt him further. But Andrew must understand it just wouldn't work. There are too many things stacked against us, the largest being our jobs. Still, I find myself texting him back, unable to resist his pull any longer.

Andrew, it's not going to work. We're from two different worlds. You don't need to explain anything to me. Really. We had fun and I'll cherish those memories forever. ~T~

A part of me wants to slap myself for not going to him while the other part is striving for self-preservation. I can't live in my dreams, knowing they'll never come true. But there has to be a purpose to all of this. Why would he be pursuing me, knowing it's an impossible dream?

Within minutes, my phone beeps in response.

Apparently I do need to explain. I believe there has been a misunderstanding and it must be rectified. There is something between us Tessa and you know it. Please don't shut me out yet. ~A~

There is something between us. I cannot deny that, even though I try. My mind cannot let go of our time spent together because it truly was the happiest time of my life. The way Andrew would touch me, hold me, make love to me … all of it. No one has ever looked at me with such adoration before. No one has made me their world in that short a time. It still seems impossible all this transpired over the course of a week. Such an insignificant amount of time. A blink of an eye in the grand scheme of life. But that one week changed my life and I know it's largely in part to the man whose heart I'm breaking.

Andrew, there's nothing to explain. This is hard enough as it is. It's just not going to work. You'll find someone else and move on, someone who lives in London and can see you every day and give you more than I ever could. I just want you to be happy. ~T~

I won't survive without you and no one will ever take your place. You are the one who makes me happy. I am not done with you. I told you, I am yours and you are mine. ~A~

I read the text over and over again, slowly letting the words seep back into my shattered heart. I remember him saying those words to me before. Words which hold so much hope for a future that still hangs right in front of my eyes. Could we actually work? Is it possible?

Kara emails me, asking me to move all her files into her drive so she can access them before I move into my new position. A position I'm still walking in the clouds about. But those same clouds carry me to Andrew and my heart hurts again. Deep down I know I don't want to move on from Andrew because I do still love him with every fiber of my being. But can we go back? Can we make this work between us? Too many questions float in the air as I buckle down, focusing on the task at hand instead of the tall, dark-haired British man who has me rethinking everything I thought was true.

Chapter 5

HAVE YOU EVER BEEN so rushed that you've forgotten things in the most obvious places? Spent hours searching for something that was actually right in your hands? Or have you ever been trapped in your car door because you're too distracted by your thoughts? Then realize you shut the door when your coat wasn't fully out and now you can't reach the lock to open the door?

So here I stand with my coat stuck in the locked car door, unable to access the handle because my ass is pressed tightly against said door. And heaven forbid my car should be new enough to have a fancy key fob where I could just press a button to unlock the door and free myself. Not that it would help right now anyway with my keys out of reach on the ground. No, instead I get to sit here looking like a fool, waiting patiently for someone else to enter the nearly empty parking garage and be my hero. Is this how my day is going to go? If this is any indication, I'm calling in sick now.

And just as I'm fumbling for my phone, on the verge of

tears, I hear the soft laugh of a man approaching me. Oh no. Please don't let it be some crazed lunatic who wants to lock me in his basement, keeping me in a hole and telling me put lotion on my skin or I'll get the hose again.

The soft footsteps grow closer and a gentle hand is placed on my shoulder. "Need some help there?" His smooth voice falls over me and I instantly sag backward.

"Oh, Michael, thank God you're here. Could you help me? I've managed to trap my jacket in the door and I can't reach the lock."

"Of course. Where are your keys?"

I point to the ground about a foot away and he starts laughing again.

"Don't laugh! I'm embarrassed enough as it is. They accidentally fell to the ground when I realized I was stuck."

He bends down smoothly and retrieves the missing keys. I attempt to move to the side but with my position right in front of the handle it's going to be difficult to find the lock.

Michael smiles, leaning close to me. "Just hold still. I'm going to try and find the lock this way." His arms snake around my waist, his hands feeling for the door, which in turn also moves against my back and body. He presses further into me and I close my eyes at his closeness. He smells good, fresh and clean shaven, like linen that's been hanging out in the sun to dry or what I would imagine rain smells like if it had a scent. And he's close, so close. Close enough that if I just lean over a few inches our lips would be pressed together.

I hear the key slip into the lock, his hand turning the mechanism, involuntarily pressing it against my ass. A tingle runs up my spine at the contact. It's been five days since anyone has made that kind of contact with me. Well, okay, not *that* kind of contact but it's been five days since a man has been anywhere close to me, just as Michael is now.

The door handle is lifted up and I'm freed from my prison, thankful that no one observed my distress, outside of Michael.

"There you go, little damsel in distress," he laughs.

I don't step away as I look into his deep brown eyes, feeling my mouth go dry by just looking at him. He leans closer and I brace myself for a kiss, feeling the heavy lids of my eyes start to close until the jingling of my keys in front of my face breaks me of my trance. Oh God, could I make any more of a fool of myself in front of this man?

"Thank you. This wasn't exactly how I pictured running into you again."

I lock my car, this time making sure my jacket is free and clear of the door. When I turn to face Michael, his lips have curled up into an arresting smile.

"So you've thought about running into me again is what you're saying."

Why can't I control the words escaping my mouth? Did my filter permanently take a vacation or just decide to stop working altogether when faced with drop dead gorgeous males? If there were ever a time for one of the plagues of Egypt to happen, now would be as good a time as any. I'd take a swarm of locusts over standing here making a complete ass of myself any day of the week.

"I … um … well … that is …"

Great. And now, apparently, I can't speak either. If he doesn't take off running, I'd be surprised. And Chris wants to give me a promotion? Hell, I can't even speak coherently in mildly stressful situations. *I need a drink and I don't care if it's not even eight in the morning yet.*

He's leaning into me, barely a breath between us. My breathing picks up slightly at his nearness and I watch his eyes travel over my features before locking onto my lips. Mine do the same and without realizing it, I lick my dry lips. Michael clears his throat, breaking his stare and shakes his head before offering me his arm to escort me out of the garage.

He wasn't going to kiss you. Get a hold of yourself. Seriously, that drink?

"Well, now that you're free from your car I better make sure you get safely to work. I wouldn't want you getting stuck anywhere else."

I laugh nervously as we cross the street, letting him hold open the door for me as we enter the lobby of our building. His hand rests gently on my lower back as he ushers me into the elevator, guiding me close to him as people begin to file in with us. But he keeps me to his front near the panel of buttons. He must remember my elevator rides all too well since I never actually told him about my prior predicaments.

We don't talk on the ride up, which is good because the only way I'd be able to hear him is if he whispered directly into my ear. And I don't think my body would be up for that right now. It'd be too intimate and confusing to my already swimming head.

As I approach my floor, Michael squeezes my side slightly, drawing my attention to him. He smiles down at me and looks nervous for some reason.

"Tessa, would you like to meet me for coffee tomorrow morning?" His eyes sparkle in the fluorescent lights of the elevator as the cheesy music swirls around us. I pause, giving it a moment of serious thought. Michael is a good guy and we have this easy rapport between us, making it seem as if I could talk to him about anything without feeling embarrassed about it. And I can always use another friend.

"Sure, coffee sounds good. You let me know where and when."

"How about seven o'clock at the Caribou Coffee place on the corner?" He still looks nervous, a slight blush crawling across his cheeks. It's kind of cute in a way.

I smile. "Sounds perfect. I'll see you then." Michael lightly grabs my hand, squeezing it before I walk through the open doors to my office. I turn back to look at him as the doors close and he gifts me with his perfectly white smile.

As I turn the corner, making note that this is now two days in a row I have arrived on time to work, I hear Kara call out to me as I pass her office. I backtrack slightly, peeking my head through the open doorway. She smiles and holds a finger up to me.

"One second." She presses the receiver of the phone into the palm of her hand. "Hey, are you available for lunch today?" I nod. "Perfect. Does noon work for you?" she asks in a hushed voice.

"Noon is good for me."

"Awesome. I'm in meetings again all morning so I'll come get you when I'm done." She uncovers the phone and resumes her conversation, never breaking stride. Someday I hope to be a tenth of the businesswoman she is.

I've just unpacked my things at my desk when Kara bounds into my cube, grabbing her perch on the corner of my desk.

"Change of plans. You're coming with me to my meetings this morning. I am in desperate need of your far-more-superior-than-mine note taking skills. And besides, you're technically still my assistant so I'm utilizing my boss-like power over you."

It's hard to take someone seriously when they say things like that and swing their legs back and forth like a six-year-old. I swivel in my chair, placing my hands on the armrests and laugh.

"Seriously, you need to cut back on your coffee intake in the mornings."

She shoves my shoulder and laughs. "No, you need to drink more. It's not right to only have one cup of coffee a day. It's sacrilege and makes people all crazy-like."

"Says the woman who's swinging her legs at my desk and talking like she's on fire."

Kara laughs and waves her hand in a dismissing manner. "Pfft. Whatever."

"Well, tomorrow I'll definitely be getting my recommended caffeine intake. Michael saved me this morning when I got stuck in my car door. Then he invited me to coffee tomorrow morning."

The smile falls from her face instantly. Why is she not happy about this? She's always been one to tell me to get out there, break out, find someone and date. Well, I really don't have plans to date Michael, but there's nothing wrong with two people enjoying a cup of coffee together, right?

"So you're going on a date tomorrow morning?"

"It's not a date. It's just coffee with a friend before work."

She's forcing a smile at me, feigning happiness. She may

be good at a lot of things, but I still know how to read her. And right now she's not happy about this little development.

"No, I mean, yeah, that's awesome. Super! I guess I'm just surprised you're meeting up with Michael again."

My brow furrows at her statement. "Why is it surprising? I mean he's cute and friendly. We get along well; at least I think we do. So far, all I've managed to do is make an ass of myself in front of him. Besides, aren't you always the one who says I need to put myself out there more?"

There's a pause while she thinks of her answer. A stray lock of blond hair falls onto her forehead and she brushes it aside. "No, it's not that. Yes, I'm happy you're putting yourself out there. I'm glad. I've only been asking you to do it for the past four years. It's just ... what about Andrew?"

Why does it always come back to this? I shake my head and sigh. "What about him? Kara, it's over, never going to work. He has someone else who apparently wants him and who lives in London. He doesn't want me, at least not in the way that I want him."

Kara just stares at me, narrowing her eyes slightly. "Are you sure about that?"

Am I sure about anything? Hell no. My mind is a jumbled mess and any moment it'll scatter the contents across the floor. That stupid text message comes back to haunt me. Andrew says he misses me. Why would he miss me if he didn't want me? He also told me I am his and he is mine. But honestly what does that mean anyway? I rub my temples, trying to ward off an impending headache.

"No, I'm not sure about anything. The only thing I'm sure of is I'm hurting inside and it's excruciating sometimes. I still cry myself to sleep at night because I can't get him out of my mind. But I need to move on, stop living in the dream that Andrew and I will ride off happily into the sunset."

Kara stands and grips my shoulders. "Tessa, I love you. You know I do. But please, for once in your life, listen to me. You're following your brain in this situation and normally it wouldn't let you down. Just don't silence your heart, because it also knows what's best for you.

"Do you know how long I fought my feelings for Chris? Years. And it sucks I wasted all that time fighting them because he is the best thing that's ever happened to me. Yes, we fight. Yes, I've gone weeks without speaking to him outside of work because of something stupid we've said to each other. But at the end of it all, we belong together. He's the only man who has ever made me feel so alive and so helpless at the same time."

Right now, I know that feeling all too well. I'm helpless to stop my attraction to Andrew, I know this. But my brain is telling me logic should prevail and logically, given the information at hand, it just wouldn't work out between us.

"Tell me what to do Kara? I feel lost and alone and I don't want to go back to the girl I was before I met Andrew. But I hurt. Every day I hurt because Andrew isn't here. And this morning when Michael helped me, it was the first time in a few days that the pain was manageable, even if it was only for a second."

"All I'm saying is to keep an open mind. I'm glad you made a friend in Michael. But don't forget what could still be out there waiting for you. And you can start by actually talking to the poor man."

Kara hands me my notepad and favorite pen as we walk

back to her office. "I'll try, but I may need a few more days. It still hurts."

She nods her head and grabs her laptop. "Then it'll take a few days. As long as you try. That's all I'm asking." We start walking toward the conference room until she suddenly stops in her tracks, remembering something from before. "Wait, did you say you got stuck in your car door this morning?"

I laugh and drag her back down the hallway. "Don't ask. It was embarrassing to live through the first time around."

"Oh, now I need to hear the story. You can't dangle that carrot in front of me and not expect me to bite."

We laugh as we enter the room. Chris is already sitting at the table in front of the TV we use for video conferencing.

"Christopher," Kara purrs, sliding into the seat next to him. He rolls his eyes and places his hand beneath the table onto her leg. I'm not sure what he does, nor do I want to know, but whatever it is made her almost jump entirely out of her seat with a squeal of delight. I take my seat next to Kara and open my notebook.

"Okay ladies, are we all set?" Chris asks, opening his own notebook and clicking a few buttons on his computer, bringing the TV to life. Kara never told me what the meeting was for, so just to be on the safe side I find a clean sheet of paper but still feel unprepared.

The murmuring of voices on the TV suddenly get louder and I freeze. My breath catches in my throat and I try to swallow. I know those voices. Slowly, I turn my head to Kara, who gives me a sideways, unapologetic glance. Sly little witch. She mouths "you're welcome" to me and I feel my cheeks reddening by the second.

I try to keep my eyes cast down, for I know what I'll see if I look at the screen. But I can't very well sit on a conference call and not make eye contact with everyone. Biting the bullet, I raise my head slowly, finding three very familiar faces in front of me. Two of them are smiling brightly, but the third, the one sitting directly in front of me, is the one that makes me stop breathing again. He looks horrible. Well, not entirely awful. He's still gorgeous to me, but he looks ragged and worn out. Dark circles rim his tired blue eyes and his generally well-styled hair is more of a mess than usual. Those beautiful full lips that I've felt on almost every inch of my body are turned down at the corners, causing the ache in my chest to expand to an almost painful level.

There's a delay in the video feed but as I take him in, fully take in his beauty after not seeing him for five days, I know the moment he sees me. Andrew takes a sharp breath, almost inaudible to everyone except me. But that's because I can always hear him just like I always see him. Our eyes lock, hazel to blue, as the others begin talking around us. Their voices fade into the background, becoming nothing but a hushed murmur. Still aware of everything around me, I kick Kara under the table and she discreetly elbows me in the side. She's going to pay for this one.

"Thank you for meeting us this way. Video conferencing is always more efficient than teleconferencing. At least I think so." Chris laughs. "Of course, you remember Kara and Tessa."

"Yes, of course. Lovely to see you both again," Charles says with a broad smile.

I nod my head, but only because I'm too distracted by Andrew to do anything else. A joke is told and everyone around us laughs. Everyone but Andrew and I. He just keeps looking at me, his eyes raking over my face nonstop. I watch as his chest expands, taking in a deep breath, as if sitting there is painful for him. *Well, you and me both, buddy.* My heart hurts just looking at him, knowing he's there and seemingly suffering like me. Although I must say, I'm slightly more put together, at least on the outside.

Breaking our staring contest, I focus on the paper in front of me, taking down notes as the other four people involved begin talking about strategies, timelines, and accomplishments. But as I write feverishly on the paper, I can feel Andrew's eyes follow every small movement I make. Every time I tuck a strand of hair behind my ear, I hear a faint groan. My eyes flicker to his and sure enough they're still locked on me.

"Andrew should arrive the week after next to oversee the building site, making sure that it's still a good fit. He'll bring the designs for you to give to your contacts to begin the bidding process," Priscilla says.

My head snaps up so fast it felt like it was going to fall off. Did she just say Andrew was coming here? As in Minnesota? In two weeks? The butterflies begin fluttering in my stomach again at the prospect of seeing him in the flesh, being close enough to touch him again and fuel the flames that have dimmed in my blood. My body yearns for him to touch me again, not fully realizing it until this very moment, when reality and fantasy could potentially crash together.

"Yes, I'm very excited to meet up with you and Tessa so we can go over the plans together." Andrew's lips turn up in the corners for the first time as his tongue caresses my name. God I love the way he says my name, letting it roll off his tongue as if he's said it thousands of times. But there's also a note of pain in his voice. A pain I have caused by my lack of communication and the Dear John letter I left for him before leaving without an explanation. Apparently, he doesn't know my new situation yet and once again it's up to me to break the bad news to him.

"Actually, you'll just be meeting with Kara. I've been given a promotion and will no longer be working on this project."

My heart goes into full arrest as the beautiful smile that graced his face falls, pulling his entire demeanor with it. Can he really be that upset that I'm no longer working with him?

Charles and Priscilla both congratulate me as I force a smile on my face. "Thank you. I'm very grateful for the pro-motion and am saddened to not be working on this project anymore. I really do love the work your Foundation does."

"Well, we will definitely miss your presence but at the same time are glad that you're able to move forward in your career with other projects," Priscilla says.

The meeting continues, banter flowing freely between the five of them, well, really the four of them. My eyes find An-drew's occasionally and he's almost stoic now, looking forward or down, his gaze only skirting over me when he thinks I'm not looking. I take down the notes of everything that will be needed prior to Andrew's arrival. Sadness sweeps over me as I realize this will be the last thing I do before I leave this project and never have to work next to Andrew again.

Chris's booming voice brings me out of my melancholy as we say our goodbyes. Risking a glance, I lock eyes with Andrew and he smiles at me. And not the forced smile he was giving before. A genuine smile. My favorite smile. The one reserved only for me. Andrew mouths something to me, but I can't quite make it out. My brows furrow and confusion clouds my face as I shake my head. And then the call ends. The screen goes blank and yet Andrew is still sitting there in my mind's eye, smiling at me. I turn to Kara and glower at her.

"Okay, explain to me why I needed to be here for that? I know it wasn't for my superior note taking skills, as you so kindly put it." The loud thumping of my pen against the paper causes a laugh to bubble up from Kara's throat.

"I figured you needed a little push. Don't hate me because I'm right."

I lean across her body to catch Chris's gaze. He, too, gives me the same not-so-apologizing grin as Kara. Great, they're both plotting against me. I do not stand a chance at this point.

"You need to do something with her. Her matchmaker skills need to be tamped down a touch."

He shakes his head and laughs. "You think I can control her? I've been trying for years. You know how stubborn she is. Once she has her mind set on something it's hard to convince her otherwise." I groan loudly and put my head on my folded arms on top of the table. The muffled sound of their laughter is not welcome as I lay here and wallow.

He looked so broken, so sad. The light that is usually in his eyes wasn't there. They seemed almost dull and lifeless; missing the spark that had drawn me in the first time I saw them. Am I really the cause of his pain, just as he's the cause of mine? No, I caused this pain all on my own, first with my stupidity of falling in love with him and second with voicing that same stupidity to him.

Somehow I gather my strength and pull away from the table, standing to my full height. Kara and Chris are whispering to each other, giving loving caresses before having to go back to the public eye of the office.

"Well, if you two are quite done meddling in my life I think I'll head back to my desk and get to work on this new task." I glance down at my watch and note the time. "Are we still doing lunch at noon?" I ask, turning in the doorway.

Kara nods and wraps her arms around Chris's waist. "Yep, I think Thai sounds good," she says in answer to my question but never once taking her eyes off of Chris. "How about you, hot stuff? Care to partake in some pleasant female companion-ship during the noon hour?" It's almost obscene the way she's batting her eyes and running her tongue over her teeth at him. Just short of stripping down to her garters and bra, although I wouldn't put it past her. I know she's done it before.

Chris leans down and kisses the tip of her nose before grabbing her ass and squeezing hard. "I will pass on lunch with you two. However, I am expecting dessert later." Kara cups his face, gently pressing her lips to his.

"Fine. Have it your way."

"I always do."

"Come on, Tessa. I think the special today is Cream of Some Young Guy. And you know I'm all over that." She casually tosses her arm over my shoulder as Chris stands there, mouth gaping as we laugh down the hallway.

I glance over at her and roll my eyes. "You are so going to get it later for that comment."

Kara wipes a tear from the corner of her eye. "I know, but it'll be worth it."

I leave her at her office and slide into my chair. Andrew's distraught face still haunts my mind as I try to make sense of this new situation. Kara's previous words also float in my head from before. Should I listen to my head or my heart?

The text message alert draws me from my thoughts and I know who it is before I even open it.

It was wonderful to see you, Tessa. You looked just as lovely as I picture you every day in my mind. Can we talk, please? ~A~

How can I deny him now that I've seen him? We do need to talk, that much is true, especially if we'll be seeing each other in two weeks. I won't be able to avoid him then because he'll come find me if he doesn't see me in the office. That I know for a fact. But the ache in my chest tightens at the thought of cutting him out of my life completely. Kara's right. We do need to talk.

You looked sad Andrew and I'm sorry I'm the cause of your pain. But just so you know, I'm hurting too and it's not something I can turn off overnight. I'm not saying that I don't want to talk, but I'm just asking for some time to think. ~T~

There, I've said it. It's not a brush off, but it's not a promise that anything will happen. There has to be a level of caution with us. Things started fast the first time around. If anything happens now, it needs to go slow.

We're both hurting unnecessarily and I apologize for that. It pains me to know you're hurting. But my feelings for you haven't changed Tessa. They're just as strong as ever. ~A~

I just need some time to sort a few things out. Please give me that, Andrew. ~T~

Okay, love. Just please promise to think of me, of us, while you're sorting things out. I miss you deeply. ~A~

He's not going to make this easy is he? Time. Time is what I need. Time to sort out my feelings for him and see if they're strong enough to survive my dark thoughts. But I miss him too and it brings me some comfort to hear that he feels the same.

Hauling up the numerous garment bags from my shopping appointment that Natasha set up for me, I groan as I shut the door to my apartment with my foot. Honestly, I didn't think I had bought this many items. Okay, *I* didn't buy them but it seemed like far fewer things when I just kept handing them to the young lady helping me out.

I promptly hang them in my closet to avoid any wrinkles and stare. The closet is almost full now, at least three-quarters. Business suits, dresses, and several new jackets now occupy the once nearly empty space. And, of course, it was required that I get shoes to match each outfit, which are now lined on the floor underneath the clothes.

Lastly, I put away the formal gown for Friday night's party. I stare at it as it sits awkwardly next to my older clothes. In my mind, I keep singing *one of these things is not like the others; one of these things just isn't the same.* Pathetic? Probably. Nerdy? Most definitely. God, I can't even be normal in my own head. My hand runs over the satin and beads, still unbelieving that it's really mine. It was perfect the minute I put it on. Trudy, the lady helping me, said not to bother looking at anything else because this was the one.

I crawl onto my bed and sit cross-legged, just staring into the closet full of clothes. Reaching for my phone, I dial my father's number and listen to the ringing on the other end. Maybe he's not home? And if he's not, please don't let Sharon answer. On the third ring, someone finally picks up.

"Tessa?" He seems surprised that I'm calling, which I sort of am too. It's not as if we have that natural father/daughter relationship where I call every night and tell him about my day or he calls wondering what I'm doing for the night.

"Hi, Dad. Um, is this a bad time?" This suddenly seems like an awful idea as I pluck the little fuzz balls off my slipper socks, my replacement for the puppy dog slippers that I threw away Sunday morning after Kara's chiding remarks.

He clears his throat and the clicking of his study door can be heard over the line. "No, it's fine. Is everything okay?"

Why would he think that something's wrong? Oh, probably because I never call him. "Yes, everything is fine. I had my appointment with Trudy and I just wanted to thank you for the clothes."

His voice softens and warms. "You're welcome, Tessa. Did you find everything you needed? Please tell me that you picked up a new winter jacket at the very least." I think he's smiling over the phone. You can almost hear it in his voice. The thought causes me to smile in return.

"Yes, I did. And I took your advice and picked up two, one for work, and one for everyday wear. Oh, that reminds me. I wanted to let you know I got a promotion at work."

There's a small pause as I hear the creak of his leather chair. "Promotion you say? What is your new job title?"

"Junior account executive." The title still is shocking to me and I can't believe it's mine. It sounds so foreign, so unlike me. But there's pride in my voice as I say it because it's a title that I earned on my own through hard work and dedication.

"That is a substantial promotion. Congratulations, Tessa. I'm very proud of you."

Whoa. Silence falls between us as I let his words sink in. He's proud of me. Now that is a phrase I never imagined hearing from him and directed toward me.

"Um, thanks, Dad. I'm very excited about it. Chris wants me to start Monday so I'll be tying up my loose ends this week as Kara's assistant. Also, I hope you don't mind, but I picked up some new clothes for work today, you know, because of the promotion."

I nervously chew on my lip, still hoping he was serious about wanting me to buy more things. Not that money or clothes can buy my love. Perhaps this is the only way he knows how to show affection, through material things. If only he knew I didn't care about all that. I just wanted my dad.

"Did you get enough? What did you end up finding?"

I run through the list, excitedly describing my shopping experience with him, only to realize that I actually did have fun today. He seems genuinely pleased with my selections, even saying that I should have bought more. I tell him it's not necessary and that I'll be okay now for a while.

"Well, if you ever need more just call Trudy and let her know. She's been instructed to help you with anything you need."

"Thanks, Dad."

Just then, Sharon's shrill voice comes across the line as she calls out to him. He clears his throat and suddenly there's static on the line, along with muffled voices. My guess is he placed the phone on his shoulder to talk to her. The voices start to rise and then the door to his study slams with a loud bang.

"Sorry, Tessa, but I have to go. Again, I'm very happy about your promotion at work and really am proud of you for doing this all on your own. You're still coming on Friday?"

And just like that he's back to his serious persona. This is the dad I know, not the kind and concerned one I had just been talking to for the last few minutes.

"Yes, Kara and I will both be there. Thank you again for everything today. It means a lot to me."

"You're welcome. It's a good investment for your future."

A good investment for my future? I throw myself back onto my pillows and rub my forehead with my free hand.

"Okay, well, I'll see you Friday night. Goodnight, Dad."

There's a pause before he speaks again. "Goodnight, Tessa."

He's always so formal with me. It drives me absolutely insane, at least when I let it. Typically I try not to let him get to me, but today has been all over the place so it completely fits in with everything else. Between seeing Andrew, making a coffee non-date, my utter humiliation in the parking garage and finally some sort of affection from my father, it's just too much. I fall asleep, still fully clothed on top of my sheets and not caring one bit about it.

Chapter 6

I T'S STILL DARK OUTSIDE AS I pull myself off the floor once again, my usual morning habit. This whole early rising thing had best not be an everyday thing. If it is, I'll have to learn how to go to bed earlier at night. On the plus side, I am going to a coffee shop so that should aid in my quest to not be a zombie for the day.

Coffee.

Michael.

It still feels strange that I'm doing this, considering the few times Michael and I have seen each other I've managed to make a complete fool of myself. First there was the whole purse thing in the deli and then the incident yesterday where my car decided to eat my jacket. So he knows I'm nothing more than a clumsy fool. But what do I really know about him? He's obviously smart (just look at his alma maters and the fact that he's a lawyer), well dressed and has a charming personality. Plus he has a penchant for saving damsels in distress. Or just me. All I can hope for today is just to be normal and not be completely lame by cracking stupid jokes or spilling coffee all over myself. And on that note, I put the white sweater back in my closet, opting for something maybe in a darker color. Just in case.

The nice thing about arriving this early to the parking garage is you get your pick of prime parking spots. Most normal people aren't at work yet and the ones who are, they're the workaholics that practically live in their office. And since Caribou is just down the block I don't have to deal with finding a parking spot there as well. I exit my car and take extra caution to make sure my new coat doesn't get caught in the door. I don't need to be rescued again today. At least not yet.

The bell chimes above the door as I enter and instantly I'm assaulted with the intense smell of roasted coffee. Such a delightful smell, ranking high on my list of favorite scents. I've seen people keep coffee beans in a jar on their desk, using it as a pencil holder, letting the aroma float around them subtly all day long. That may not be a bad idea for when I move into my new office.

My office.

That still sounds so weird to me.

A table opens up toward the back so I quickly grab it. It's busy for this early in the morning, but then again it is a coffee shop. I think early mornings and coffee just go hand in hand.

I smooth my hands down the dark purple sweater dress I finally decided on this morning while I nervously wait for Michael to show up. There's no reason for me to be nervous, though. We're just two people meeting for coffee.

The bell chimes again and my head turns to the sound. That's when I see him standing there in his neatly pressed light gray suit, paired with a yellow tie that beautifully compliments his expressive brown eyes. Those same eyes look around the shop until they finally land on mine, allowing a smile to form on his face. My palms begin to sweat and my black knee high boots nervously tap against the leg of the table.

He strides to my table, ignoring several glances from women as he passes by. Not that I blame them for looking. He is a rather striking man.

"Good morning," I say a little too brightly.

"Good morning. You look beautiful." He occupies the chair across from me, folding his hands in front of him while silently staring at me.

"Thank you. You look beautiful as well. Handsome," I quickly correct myself. "I mean, you look handsome as well." *Come on brain, catch up with me here.*

He swipes his hand down his tie before unbuttoning his suit coat. My fingers twist in my lap and I resist the urge to touch my hair.

"I'll take beautiful, as long as it's coming from you." I flush at his compliment and look up at him through my lashes. He really isn't bad on the eyes. And he's sweet "Did I keep you long?"

"Oh, um, no. I just got here a few minutes ago. I wasn't really expecting you for another ten minutes or so."

"To be honest, I was here a few minutes earlier. I saw you sitting there through the window and I just couldn't help but look at you."

Did you hear the loud thud? That was my subconscious falling over in complete and utter shock and awe. How did he know just the perfect thing to say at that moment? Here I was nervous about meeting him, arriving early and looking like a fool only to find out he had seen me and was staring at me, unable to go inside. My eyes travel over him again and it's like I'm actually seeing him for the first time. His full lips that are turned up with his shy smile, his slightly crooked nose which must have been broken at some point in his younger years. And those dark brown eyes of melted chocolate with flecks of gold sprinkled around the edges, catching the light from above us.

My eyes travel further and take note of the athletic build underneath his perfect suit. My fingertips tingle with a sudden curiosity about what lies underneath. I bite my lip, needing to drive those wayward thoughts from my mind. People don't think of their friends like that. And Michael is a friend. A hot and gorgeous friend, but still a friend. My eyes pause briefly on his lips before meeting his eyes again.

"You did? Really?" I somehow manage to squeak out; yet I can't help the smile that crosses my face. It is definitely a boost to my self-esteem considering the hundreds, no, thousands of women who are far more beautiful than me.

He looks down and clears his throat quietly. "I hope you don't find that creepy."

"No, not at all. Actually, I find it rather sweet," I say, placing my hand on the top of his. "You were really just looking at me?"

His eyes meet mine again and I'm rewarded with that beautiful smile. "Of course. You are easily the most beautiful woman in here."

I look around and realize the crowd has dwindled, leaving only about a dozen people sitting around tables and talking to each other or reading their books.

I laugh. "That's not saying much since there's hardly anyone here."

He laughs with me and I watch as his cheeks pink up slightly. He looks positively adorable when he's embarrassed. It's nice to know I'm not the only one who gets embarrassed easily.

"You know what I mean. If this place were filled to capacity, I would still find you the most beautiful woman here."

"Even if a bus full of Victoria's Secret supermodels came traipsing in, all scantily clad in their angel wings and whatnot?" Now it's my turn to blush.

"Why, are they here?" Michael says, frantically looking around and then wiping his hand across his forehead in mock relief, making me laugh. "Well, thank God they're not here. I don't think I could handle them being so jealous of your good looks."

He gives my hand a squeeze, causing warmth to spread through my chest. He really is a nice guy. I wonder why we've never met before.

"Would you like some coffee?" I nod my head and start to stand up from my chair, but he motions for me to remain in my seat as he stands from his. "No, you sit. I'll get it. What would you like?"

It's been a while since I've had coffee that wasn't made in my tiny kitchen, but I do remember the only thing on this menu that I enjoyed.

"A small Northern Lite Caramel High Rise, no whip."

"Any muffins? Oatmeal? Breakfast sandwich?"

I shake my head and giggle. His hand rests on the back of his chair and leans forward slightly. "Just the coffee will be good enough for me."

Michael turns towards the counter with a smile plastered across his face and eyes bouncing with amusement. I watch as he waits in line, one hand shoved in his pocket as he reads the menu hanging above the barista. A few girls walk through the door, giggling loudly and looking him up and down as they stand behind him. He doesn't even acknowledge their presence, which makes me smile. I lean my cheek into my propped up hand and admire him. The view from behind is almost as good as the front.

Almost.

Okay, so I like him, attracted to him even. How could anyone not be? There's just an ease between us that's effortless and I feel myself relaxing more and more with him. It's not awkward or pushing, just comfortable. Safe.

Michael returns with a tray holding both our coffees and a bowl of oatmeal.

"Where were you just then? Daydreaming?"

Damn, I got caught. I flush and spin the coffee cup in my hand, unable to meet his eyes. He laughs, probably knowing exactly what I was doing but nice enough not to bring it to attention. His fingers loosen the button of his coat as he sinks back into his chair, pulling it marginally closer to me this time. My poor senses are on overdrive with the combined smells of his cologne, our coffees and the maple in his oatmeal. Each smells delicious in their own right, but making me slightly dizzy when joined together.

He takes a bite of his oatmeal and wipes the corners of his mouth with a napkin. "Tell me, anything new with you? We didn't exactly have the opportunity to talk much yesterday."

I laugh, recalling the reason why and take a sip of my coffee. "I suppose not since you were busy playing the part of my rescuer." He smiles and it warms me more than the coffee I'm drinking right now. "Actually, I got a promotion Monday afternoon."

I'm still giddy about the whole thing and I feel ridiculous about it. People get promotions every day and I'm sure none of them act like I am right now.

"Congratulations. That's definitely something new then. What's your new position?"

"Junior account executive. They needed to add another spot with all the clients we've acquired and some of the larger accounts will be taking up more time than anticipated. I'm kind of nervous about it because I really don't think I have the experience or the degree to do this sort of thing."

His warm smile eases my fears slightly. "If they didn't have confidence in your abilities they wouldn't have picked you. You should trust their judgment on this. How long have you worked there?"

"Four years, but only as an assistant." I try to look down again, but he brings his head down with mine, drawing my gaze back up.

"But you must have paid attention to everything your boss was doing. Who was it that recommended you?"

"It was Kara, my boss. She always had me drawing up the contracts for each account, sit in every meeting with her clients and watch as she closed each deal."

He nods. "See. Then they definitely picked the right person for the job. A degree is just a piece of paper saying you spent a lot of money on an education that doesn't quite prepare you for the working world. Trust me. The best way to gain experience is by actually doing it."

That's what Chris told me too. And now with Michael telling me the same thing I'm feeling much better about it. Just hearing that someone else believes in me means more than he could ever possibly know.

"I don't know. I'm still pretty nervous about it and I'm afraid I'll never live up to their expectations."

He leans forward and gives me a reassuring smile. "I have confidence in you. You'll be great, I just know it."

I tilt my head to the side. "How do you know? We barely know each other."

Michael takes a sip of his coffee and smirks. "Call it a hunch. I don't see someone like you letting things get the best of you at work. You seem like the type who does everything by the letter. A problem-solver of sorts."

"You're pretty good at reading people," I remark.

"It's what I get paid to do."

The tension I was previously feeling regarding my promotion lifts even more now that someone else has confidence in my abilities. We spend the next half hour laughing and exchanging work horror stories. I'm wiping away tears and gripping my stomach from laughing so hard. When I look at Michael, who's doubled over with laughter, I notice the small dimples that appear when he smiles. And I like the way his eyes crinkle in the corners, making him look distinguished and carefree at the same time. The knot in my stomach loosens a little, letting me relax a bit more.

"Well, if we're not careful we're both going to be late for work, even though I would much rather sit here laughing with you than spend my day in court."

We stand together and Michael grabs our empty cups from the table, tossing them and his oatmeal bowl in the trash. I struggle to get my new jacket on, but he comes up behind me and holds it open for me so I can easily slip my arms into the sleeves. He's quite the gentleman. Does he have any flaws?

Slinging my purse over my shoulder, I walk up next to him and wait while he buttons his suit coat. He flashes me a quick smile, then picks up my hand and gently kisses the back of it. His lips are warm from the coffee although I'm sure they'd be warm without it too.

"Ready?" he asks.

I nod. "As I'll ever be."

Michael threads my arm into his as he escorts me out the door and down the sidewalk to our building. The cool, crisp October air hits us as we walk the short distance to our building. I can feel Michael's body heat through my jacket, warming up my goose bumped skin instantly. Idly, I wonder if it's more than just his heat that's warming me up. Whatever it is I don't want to dwell on it too much. We're friends. Friends who walk down the street arm in arm and have coffee dates before work. Regular friend stuff, right?

We continue our journey of discovery with each other on the elevator ride up, laughing and comparing stories once again. It's then I realize that he hasn't let go of me since we left the coffee shop. I'm not entirely sure what to make of it or how I should act. But I push the strange new feelings aside, not wanting to make them more than what they really are or could be. I've done that once. I won't do it again.

The doors open and Michael reluctantly lets me go. He walks me into the lobby area of my office and places his hands in his coat pockets. It's quiet for a moment because we're still trying to get to know each other and don't know how we should say goodbye. So I decide to give him an awkward wave and smile, which he returns, making us both laugh.

"I'm glad you invited me out for coffee. It was fun."

He smiles and pushes the call button for the elevator. "Same time again tomorrow?"

I nod. "Sure. I'd like that. Have fun in court today."

Michael groans and pretends to hang himself with his tie, his tongue hanging out the side of his mouth playfully. I clasp my hand over my mouth to stifle the giggle. He waves to me and I wave back before the doors close.

I slowly turn and begin walking toward my desk when a stern sounding voice yells at me as I turn the corner.

"Tessa Marie, you wait right there!"

Kara is practically sprinting behind me, her long blond ponytail swinging behind her. I glance at my watch and note that I'm on time, early even. What could she possibly be yelling at me about?

I turn and face her, thinking maybe this has something to do with seeing Michael by the elevator with me. I can feel the redness creep up my neck as I cock an eyebrow at her, hoping to throw her off balance.

"Really? Is the middle name necessary?"

Kara grabs my hand and practically drags me into her office, shutting the door behind her.

"It is absolutely necessary. Was that Michael I saw with you by the elevator?"

I nod. "Yes, that was him."

Kara surprises me by letting out a whistle and waving a

hand in front of her face.

"Wow, he's kind of hot. Not Chris hot or Andrew hot, but he's a damn close third."

I roll my eyes and start to stand from the chair I was thrown into.

"Okay," I say, dragging the word out slowly. "I don't want to sit here and discuss my crazy life right now so I'm going to go to my desk and get some work done."

Kara laughs and holds me back by my arm. "Come·on, say it with me. Your *love* life. You know that thing you actually have now? I feel like a proud momma. Two guys fighting over you. Ah, every girl's fantasy."

She cannot be serious. I slap her arm and she rubs the spot, pretending to be hurt.

"First of all, no one is fighting over me. They don't even know about each other and they don't need to. Nothing is going on with either of them. Last time I checked I was still single. And second, I'm not looking for anything right now. Look what happened the last time I decided to word vomit all over a guy."

Kara rolls her eyes and throws an arm over my shoulder, walking me back to my desk.

"You didn't word vomit all over him so knock that shit off. Just be happy. That's all I want for you right now." She flashes a grin, showing me her less than honorable intentions behind it.

My eyes narrow in suspicion at her. "What are you planning you conniving little vixen?"

She bats her long eyelashes at me, putting on her most innocent looking face, which is comical enough as it is.

"Me? Conniving? Why Tessa I'm hurt. Shocked, even, that

you would think I have something up my sleeve. Just for that I'm going back to my office to wallow in self-pity."

"I know you. You have something planned. Spill it, Thomas, now."

Kara sticks her tongue out at me and waves over her shoulder as she heads back to her office. Frustrating woman. She's lucky I love her.

My morning flies by as I drown myself in work, getting things prepared for next week. Kara has been in and out of my cube, digging for details on my morning, which I refuse to give to fuel the fire. She's up to no good. I just know it.

Around noon, a delivery guy appears around the corner carrying a vase filled with beautiful red roses and a clipboard.

"Miss Tessa Martin?"

I turn in my chair and nod. "Yes, I'm Tessa."

He hands me the clipboard, points to where I need to sign and then gives me the vase.

"Have a good day, Miss." He nods and retreats back the way he came.

I set the vase on my desk and lean in to absorb the delicate fragrance the flowers are giving off. Classic red. They're pretty. Not my favorite, but still very beautiful. I hear Kara's office door open and I count to three, waiting for her to find her perch on the corner of my desk.

"Lucky bitch! Who are they from?"

"I don't know yet. I haven't checked the card."

I pluck the small cardboard square from the plastic stake and carefully read the very masculine writing.

Congratulations
Tessa on your job
promotion. I know
you'll do great.

Michael

I hand Kara the card and lean in to get another fix of the heavenly fragrance again.

"Wow. Coffee and flowers all in one day? The boy is definitely putting on the charm. You are one lucky girl."

"It's not what you're thinking. I was telling him how nervous I am about my promotion and he probably sent these to help ease my mind. That's all."

There's a weak smile on her face as she hands back the card. "It's still very sweet of him."

"What's wrong?" I ask.

She shakes her head. "Nothing's wrong. I'm happy for you. Really. So are you seeing him again?"

"Tomorrow morning. We're doing the coffee thing again."

She nods and pushes herself up from my desk. A strange feeling still lingers in the air, like she's holding something back from me, although I really don't know what it could be.

"Kara, we're not going out. We're not even dating. We're two friends who are having coffee together." I don't know why I feel the need to justify the situation with her, but she's giving off this strange vibe and it's making me uneasy.

"Hmm."

She places her hand on my shoulder, nods once, and walks silently back to her office, closing the door behind her.

What was that all about? Maybe she's having an off day with Chris? Or perhaps she put a scuff in her brand new Prada pumps. It's hard to say with her. I just hope whatever it is gets worked out soon. I miss my perky friend.

I hate dinner. Why can't it just make itself? Better yet, why can't I just go without food because the hassle of doing this seemingly simple task is incredibly daunting right now? My head still aches from trying to figure out Kara's strange mood this morning. Then there's Andrew. It always comes back to him as I try to deal with my still lingering emotions where he's concerned.

Which leads me to my current predicament, tapping my foot as I stare at the cupboard, unable to decide if I want the gourmet meal of Mac and Cheese or Cinnamon Toast Crunch?

A text alert sounds from my phone and I open it quickly. My breath catches when Andrew's name appears. I glance at the clock and do a quick time conversion, realizing that it's close to two in the morning in London right now.

Dearest Tessa. I love your bright smile. The one that lights up any room you are in, that shows off your dimples and the laugh lines around your perfect lips. A smile that allows others to see what I already know, which is just how beautiful you really are. ~A~

I read his message over and over again, taking his words straight into my aching heart. He loves my smile. And just as he described it, that same smile appears out of nowhere, smiling down onto my phone in hopes that he could see it where he is. My eyes close when an image of him flashes in my mind, whispering those beautiful words into my ear as his finger gently strokes my cheek, sparking a trail of fire in its path. It is the sweetest, most endearing message anyone has ever sent me.

I need to respond back. How could I not?

Thank you, Andrew. You should be sleeping right now. It's so late over there. But I just wanted to let you know your text has brought that smile to my face. It was beautiful. ~T~

Abandoning my quest for food, I walk over to the couch and lower myself onto the arm. The red flowers sitting on my counter catch the corner of my eye, reminding me of my morning with Michael. My mind bounces between thoughts of Michael and then Andrew, noting the difference between the two. Not that I needed reminding. They are nothing alike.

Another message from Andrew brings my attention back to my phone.

I was up thinking of our time together and wanted to let you know that you were in my thoughts. But I shall sleep well now, knowing I have brought that beautiful smile to your face. Goodnight my sweet Tessa. ~A~

I place my phone on the coffee table, my spirit feeling lighter after Andrew's messages. The hole in my heart slowly fills as his words replay over and over in my head. Once again, he stealthily found his way into my heart and I'm not sure I'm ready to let him leave just yet.

Chapter 7

THIS WEEK HAS BEEN NOTHING but a rollercoaster of emotions for me. First there was my job. Then there was meeting Michael and the events which have followed since. Both are exciting and weird but in oddly good ways. Coffee this morning was just the same as yesterday, nothing but laughter and story-telling as we slowly get to know one another. He's quickly growing on me and I'm slowly learning that he has a funny personality. And he's an excellent listener, which is a rare trait for a guy. Well, at least in another guy. I know of one more.

Then there's Andrew, who always seems to occupy my mind in some way. Seeing him was hard, only because he looked so sad and defeated. And I helped in that. Could things have been different if I would have allowed him to explain what happened Friday morning? Did anything happen? The more I replay it over and over in my mind, the more I think I'm crazy and that I imagined things that weren't there. All because I was scared, scared of leaving, scared of my feelings for him, scared of a possible future when nothing was ever possible before.

I glance down at the clock on my computer, noting that it's time to leave already. Where has the day gone? I shut everything down, grab my things and start making my way to the elevator, noting that I'm almost the last person to leave the office. A very rare occurrence for me.

A familiar face greets me as the elevator doors open and I smile brightly at him.

"Hey you. I thought you'd be gone by now," I say, moving back to where he's standing in the corner. Michael turns to face me, his bright eyes shining under the fluorescent lights.

"Actually, this is early for me since my court case was settled. It frees up my next three nights."

"Well, that's good news. I always love pleasant surprises like that. Would you really have had to work the next three nights on it? I mean, that's the entire weekend."

He nods as we exit the elevator and holds the door open for me before we walk outside.

"Yes, I really would have but now I'm free."

"Honestly, working on a case sounds like more fun than what I'll be doing tomorrow night."

He turns a quizzical eye to me. "Why? What could possibly be worse than sitting down all night surrounded by case studies and notes?"

We pause next to my car and I lean up against it. "My stepmother's birthday party. My dad is throwing this huge event, a gala almost because she's turning forty. And I'm invited, along with a plus one. But I'm taking Kara like I always do, because I don't know anyone else. So it'll be the two of us, sitting around, not talking to anyone because we won't know the people attending since they're all friends with my dad. Plus I have to get dressed up in a formal dress, which is not what I'm used to for a Friday night. My Fridays are reserved for my Kindle and sweatpants."

"It could still be fun."

I shake my head. "No, it can't. I don't know what to talk to lawyers about, or the mayor or his wife, for that matter. I'm dreading it."

He taps his lip for a second in quiet thought. "You should bring your own hot lawyer with you. That way he can help guide you through the conversations and make things a little less painful."

I laugh. "Oh, is that what I should do? Do you happen to know of any hot lawyers who are available tomorrow night?"

He grins widely. "As a matter of fact I do. His Friday night just opened up and he has nothing planned yet."

I laugh and clasp my hands in front of me in a begging form. "Would you, please? You would be saving my life and sanity if you could."

"If it's a matter of life or death, how could I refuse?"

We laugh and I feel a weight lift off my shoulders. Michael would have more fun at the party than Kara. It's more his scene and he will more than likely know the people attending anyway. Plus it could be good for his career. Helping him with that would be the least I could do.

"Thank you, Michael. I really appreciate it."

"Think nothing of it. What time should I pick you up?"

"The party starts at seven, so around six-thirty?"

Michael nods and shoves a hand into his pocket to dig out his phone.

"Six-thirty it is then. I suppose I better get your address so I know where to pick you up."

He hands me his phone and I enter all my contact information into it while he does the same to mine. We hand back the phones and say our goodbyes with a smile.

"It's formal so I hope you have a tux handy," I say as he starts to walk away.

"It just so happens that I keep one around for such emergencies." Michael gives me a wink and walks down the aisle to his car. I slide into my driver's seat and crank up the radio when my favorite Pitbull song comes on, making my rush hour commute feel like a five-minute drive.

After getting into my lounge clothes, I flop onto the couch, ready to break the news to Kara regarding my changed plans for tomorrow night.

"Hello?" she pants out.

"Please tell me you're exercising and not doing something else."

She laughs and I can hear the motor of her treadmill in the background as her feet slap against the track.

"Now who has the dirty mind? You're a funny, funny girl, you know that? So what's up?"

"It's about tomorrow night. I hope you don't mind, but Michael offered to take me instead. Are you okay with that?"

The background noise stops abruptly on her end, causing me to chew nervously on my lower lip. Kara's breathing slows minutely, although she's still gulping in huge breaths of air.

"Michael's taking you?"

Maybe this wasn't such a good idea if Kara is shocked enough to interrupt her workout. I can only imagine where her mind is going or what scenarios are swirling around.

"He is. Do you mind?"

I begin pacing my living room, anxious about what she's going to say. She stays silent for a moment then lets out a puff of air.

"Yeah, that's cool with me. No biggie. Besides, he's a lawyer right? He can hob knob with all the other stuffed shirts there."

Her laugh is off, not her usual upbeat tone at all. Perhaps she's just winded from her run. It couldn't possibly be from anything else, could it?

"That's what I thought too after he suggested it. Thanks, Kara. You know you're the best right?"

The treadmill starts again but softer this time. She must be walking now, probably needing to start slow before she goes back into her full run.

"Yeah I know. I tell myself that every morning when I wake up. But you owe me lunch tomorrow then."

I nod my head and laugh. "You bet. I'll let you get back to your workout. I'll see you tomorrow."

"Sounds good Chickie. Night."

The call disconnects and I stretch my body across my couch. I must be crazy if I want to drag Michael into the debacle that awaits him regarding tomorrow night. My only hope is that Sharon ignores us for the night so we won't have to deal with her.

My stomach growls loudly and I walk to the kitchen, opening up a can of soup to tide me over. I stare at the bowl and glance over my shoulder to the cabinet above the fridge. All this thought about Kara's strange mood and having Michael accompany me to the party tomorrow has my head hurting more than usual. I think I need a drink instead.

Two hours later finds me sitting on my couch, watching my favorite Thursday night indulgence. My phone beeps next to me and I can't help the smile that appears with Andrew's name.

My sweet darling Tessa. I love how beautiful you look when your hair blows across your face and the sun shines down on the silky strands, creating a halo effect. I could run my fingers through them all day while looking into your heavenly eyes. An angel sent from above. ~A~

Tears prick the corners of my eyes. His words hit me hard, pulling at the fragile strings of my heart. How can he manage to take my breath away from a different continent? The message is so beautiful that I can't stop the few tears that escape. I bring the phone to my chest, convinced that by doing so Andrew will crawl through it and hug me like I want him to.

I miss him. I miss him so much it hurts. He must feel something for me. No one says things like that without having some sort of feelings behind it. And he'll be here in another week, so I know I still have time to figure this out.

I pull the phone back and type my response.

I can't even put into words how beautiful that was. Thank you. Sweet dreams Andrew. ~T~

His reply is instantaneous.

My dreams are always sweet because they are of you. Goodnight my sweet Tessa. ~A~

Grabbing my blanket, I lay down on the pillows of my

couch, not wanting to leave my spot as I cling to my phone. With a lingering smile, I imagine a warm breeze blowing through my hair and sapphire eyes looking over me.

Chapter 8

THIS FEELS ABSOLUTELY WEIRD. I feel out of place, lost in time or stuck in some parallel universe. The reflection staring back at me is not my own. No, this reflection is of a perfectly coiffed female, hair shiny and curled, with flawless makeup and jewelry to perfectly offset her elegant ball gown. No, this is not me. And yet, the smile on my face and dancing hazel eyes tells me that it is.

The diamond and pearl pendant hanging from my neck sparkles in the overhead lights of my bathroom. A gift from my father on my twenty-first birthday, no doubt a way for him to make up for the birthdays he missed when I was growing up. On second thought, probably not. If he truly cared about those birthdays he would have made an effort back then. Instead, I went without presents those years, getting nothing more than a piece of toast or whatever else I could find around the house. And where was my mother? Locked away in her room, stuck in her own personal hell of depression and hatred for my existence.

The strapless navy blue satin gown feels so different than the sweatpants I'm accustomed to wearing on my typical Friday nights. Trudy was right, though. It is the perfect dress for me. Silver ivy-like embellishments crawl across the skirt, wrapping around the cinched waist before crossing in front of my bodice. And as an added bonus, it's unnecessary for me to wear a strapless bra due to the cinching of the bust. At least I won't embarrass myself by trying to discretely adjust and readjust a stupid bra all night.

I slip on the silver strappy heels, picked out again by Trudy, that have a buckle at the ankle. I feel like Cinderella for once in my life instead of like one of the ugly stepsisters. It's not often I play dress up like this and I've never put this much effort into it before. Usually, I'd borrow a dress from Kara or find one at a secondhand thrift shop that still looked decent to wear in public. But this gown makes me feel special, beautiful even. An illusion of elegance, even if it's all just pretend.

Right on time, there's a knock on my door. I smile, swiping my finger under my bottom lip to get rid of a lipstick smudge before making my way to the front. All I can hope for tonight is that I don't fall flat on my face in these heels. It's going to take some effort to remember to pick up the front of the dress so I don't trip on that either. I'm not exactly what you would call ladylike if you haven't noticed. Feminine, yes. Sophisticated, no.

When I open the door, I'm greeted to a very regal looking Michael, who is boasting a rather large smile. His eyes take me in as he twirls me around, holding my hand above my head to take in the full package.

"My God Tessa, you are stunning. No, that's not the right word. Breathtaking. Or stunningly breathtaking. Even better."

I flush at his compliment and push against his chest. I'm not surprised by the hardness I find beneath the shirt. A man looking the way he does knows how to take care of his body. And my guess is he puts as much detail into everything else in his life too. I like him in his suits, but he's gorgeous in his tux. Very classy and elegant and way out of my league. At least I can appreciate him as a friend without it getting weird.

"You're crazy but thank you. You look very stunningly breathtaking yourself."

"Hey, I only speak the truth." Michael's beautiful brown eyes shine, showing me how excited he is to be here with me.

"I can't thank you enough for offering to take me tonight. I just hope it'll be worth your while and not too boring."

He gives me a dimpled smile. "Boring? With you? Never. We're going to cut a rug and rub elbows with the snobs of high society. It's going to be fun. Besides, we wouldn't want to disappoint the Assistant Attorney General by not showing up."

I cringe internally when he brings up my father's official title. I could care less about titles or material things. To me, he's just Robert Martin, my sometimes father when it's convenient for him. Maybe someday that will change, but for now it is what it is.

Grabbing my clutch from the counter, I turn and link my arm through Michael's as we exit, pausing to allow me to lock up my apartment.

When we reach the sidewalk, I stop mid-stride. Not because of the chill in the evening air or the blowing of a soft breeze. It's due to the large stretch limo that's parked next to the curb. I turn my head to face Michael, who's grinning from ear to ear.

"You rented a limo for tonight?" I whisper, my voice unsteady.

"I did. I figured we may as well arrive in style if we're going to play with the big boys."

"This is too much, Michael."

He shakes his head and holds his arm out, gesturing me to move closer to the vehicle. "It's nothing. Besides, what are friends for?"

The driver holds the door open for us and Michael slides in next to me on the bench seat. My leg bounces up and down nervously, but he places a hand on my knee, halting the movement.

"Don't worry. Everything will be fine."

I turn my head and chew on my bottom lip. "I hope so."

I remind myself that taking Michael is a good thing. He can meet new people in his field, talk with others and relate to their stories better than I ever could. It's Sharon that scares me. Will she try to pull her same usual crap or make a bigger deal than necessary of the fact that I'm arriving with a date instead of Kara? My stomach twists again as we head towards downtown and the ticking clock of the evening ahead.

Hitting the button to the fourteenth floor, Michael and I stand at the back of the elevator, surrounded by several other couples dressed similarly to us. Obviously guests of my father. I highly doubt many people walk around downtown Minneapolis dressed like this or wander into hotels in the hopes of crashing a high-class event. But then again, what do I know. I sit on my couch like a lump most nights of the week.

The ballroom of the Millennium is by far one of the best venues downtown Minneapolis has to offer for an event such as this. It's a beautifully decorated hall with floor to ceiling windows in a dome shape. The twinkling lights of the surrounding buildings shine in through the windows as a beautiful backdrop. There's a dance area set up on one side of the room, where a small stringed quintet is playing. Behind them, there appears to be a set up for a larger band to play later in the evening.

Multiple small banquet tables occupy the back of the ballroom, each holding several stands of hors d'oeuvres. Tall standing tables and a few shorter ones, all draped in white linens and bright pink flowers in crystal vases decorate the remaining space. Small decorative trees laced with white lights are set up around the perimeter, giving the whole room an incredibly romantic feel.

I sneak a glance at Michael, who gives me a wink as we look over our surroundings.

"Your dad sure knows how to throw a party."

I roll my eyes and he laughs. "Yes, nothing but the best for step mommy dearest," I reply dryly.

We make our way through the room and decide to find a spot close to the windows. Michael holds a chair out for me and I graciously sit down. It's only been a half hour since we left my apartment and my feet are already starting to hurt. And we haven't even started dancing yet. This is the reason why I don't wear heels very often.

When Michael takes a seat next to me, I glance down at his cuff links and notice the ivy-like pattern swirling around the white gold. It's so similar to the embellishments on my gown that it's almost uncanny. There's no way Michael would have known what I was wearing.

"Hey, your cuff links match my dress."

He glances down and smiles. "So they do. I guess I made a good choice then. Wouldn't want to clash against such a beautiful gown."

We both laugh until the sound of someone quietly clearing their throat behind us draws our attention.

"Tessa. I'm glad to see you made it," my dad says, eyeing up Michael. I move to stand and Michael follows my lead. We may as well get this part of the night over with.

"Dad, this is a friend of mine, Michael Fontaine. Michael, this is my dad, Robert Martin." The two men shake hands and Michael flashes him a smile.

"It's a pleasure to meet you, sir."

My dad looks him up and down again and I swear I see the makings of a smile appear on his face. My eyes bounce between the two of them, confused as to what's not being said.

"Fontaine you say? Do you happen to work for Lyman Burns & Goldman?"

And just like that, the smile fully appears on his face, obviously thrilled that I brought a lawyer instead of Kara. He must know who Michael is, which doesn't surprise me. My dad knows almost every single attorney in the state.

Michael's smile never falters as he nods his head. "Why yes, I do. I'm actually a little embarrassed to admit this, but I've followed your career for quite some time. You've handled some major cases across the state and I use them often as reference points for some of my own trials."

Again, my dad smiles, a very strange thing to see, at least

for me it is. He claps Michael on the shoulder. "Thank you. It just so happens that I'm friends with Adam Burns. He's told me about a few of your cases. In fact, he and I were just talking about you yesterday during lunch. Congratulations on settling the Stockman case early. It must have been a relief to have that one finished, and in your favor no less."

At this point, I've already tuned them out as they talk shop. I look around the room at all the people donning fancy party attire, mingling with society's finest, drinking from fluted champagne glasses and feeling generally superior to the ordinary man. Not that I can verify the last part. Just a hunch.

My dad's laugh pulls me back to their conversation. "Yes, it's very fortunate that you and my daughter work in the same building." He turns his attention to me and smiles. "You look lovely tonight Tessa."

And now a compliment from him? Did I step into the Twilight Zone when we exited the elevator? But I'm not one to squander a compliment from him.

"Thank you, Dad."

He makes a move as if he may come over to hug me, but I see the blond bitch in red slinking up behind him. Sharon slithers her way around his body and loudly kisses him in front of us. Michael leans down to whisper in my ear.

"Who's that?"

I turn my head to face him, our lips just inches apart. "That's my stepmother, Sharon."

He gives me a sympathetic look and takes hold of my hand. He must have seen my body stiffen at her arrival, feeling a sense of unease crawl into my chest. Sharon is hanging all over my dad in a possessive way, trying to exert her power over me I'm sure. It's when she takes a good look at Michael that she starts putting on her best show.

"Tessa, you almost appear to fit in with high society tonight. But we all know it's just for show."

I step back and hang my head slightly. I know how out of place I feel being here and I certainly don't need to be reminded of it by her. In a surprising move, my dad extricates himself from her hold, throwing down her arms in a non-gentle manner before stepping to the side.

"Tessa, Michael. If you'll excuse me, please." He glares at Sharon and turns to walk over to a group of men talking around one of the taller tables across the room. Sharon sneers at my dad's back and then turns her attention back to us. After looking Michael up and down in apparent appreciation, she molds her collagen filled red lips into a seductive smile.

"Sharon Martin." She holds out her hand, which is covered with diamonds and rubies. "And you are?"

Michael takes her hand, shaking it with as little contact as possible. "Michael Fontaine, a friend of Tessa's, and her date tonight."

He pulls me closer to his side, attempting to shield me from Sharon's blows. The loud cackle of her laugh startles me as the fake smile she had on before falls from her face.

"Date? Please. No one ever dates Tessa. She's more of a charity case. Always playing up the sympathy card to everyone she meets. Surely that must be why you're here. Either that or you lost a bet."

The anger and tension in Michael's body are palpable as he stands there stoically, listening to the venom being spit by this snake. But he doesn't falter, doesn't show that she's getting to him, which is her ultimate goal. Instead, he surprises me by sweetly smiling at her.

"If anything, I have won the lottery by being her date as she is hands down, without a doubt, the most gorgeous, electrifying woman in this room. Not one other woman holds a candle to her sheer beauty."

Sharon steps back slightly as if he's slapped her. To really solidify his words, Michael kisses me softly, eliciting a quiet moan from the back of my throat. When he pulls back, I'm dumbstruck. The kiss took me by surprise, stealing my breath slightly. I know it was all for show, but a small part of me is smiling when it sees the disgust on Sharon's face.

Michael turns his attention back to Sharon, who looks like she's about to have snakes sprouting from her head. "If you'll excuse us, I need to go monopolize my time with this ravishing beauty."

Michael guides us to the back of the room, getting as far away from Sharon as we can. The cool windows feel good against my heated skin as I lean briefly against them. A wave of nausea and dizziness hits me, and I pray I don't pass out in front of everyone present. Sharon must be drunk already. She has never acted like that in front of people before. That's usually a persona she saves for behind closed doors at her house, where she can control the situation and leave me a shrunken pile of nothing. Michael stands before me and holds his hand out to me. I take it and squeeze it with whatever strength is left in my body. He gives a slight tug and I fall into his arms, letting him comfort me.

"I can't believe your dad puts up with someone like her. Is she always that mean to you?"

I nod my head, unwilling to pick it up off his shoulder to look him in the eye. "Yes. She hates my existence, especially when my dad buys me things or pays any kind of attention to me. Even though it's not as often as I would like, he's been better about reaching out to me lately. She never wanted kids and would be more than thrilled to have me disappear entirely from my dad's life."

Sharon's latest stunt has my nerves fried, but I refuse to give her power over me. Not tonight. I really don't want to give her the satisfaction of knowing I let her words get to me, even though she knows they did. Michael pulls back and gently tips my chin toward him.

"Nothing she said is true. You are not a charity case, and I certainly did not lose a bet to be here with you. What I said was the absolute truth. You are the most beautiful, most stunning, most amazing woman in this room. Hell, in this city for that matter. I am lucky enough that you let me come here as your date."

I nod my head and force a smile. "Thank you, Michael. I'm really glad you're here with me."

"Sorry about the kiss. I just needed to shut her up and the best way I thought of was having her see how beautiful you really are. And nothing makes a woman look more beautiful than when she's being kissed. You're not mad, are you?"

I shake my head and smile. "No, I'm not mad. The look on her face was pretty priceless. I didn't think it was possible to stupefy her, but I guess you did."

He chuckles and flashes me a dimpled smile and I know everything will be okay from here on out. I know that Michael will watch out for me and keep Sharon at bay as much as possible. He makes me feel safe, and it's a new feeling for me. Well, slightly new. There's only been one other man to make me feel safe, but he isn't here. And, as always, my thoughts drift to him, making me miss him even more.

We decide to grab a plate of food and retake our seats at the table. A passing waiter offers us flutes of champagne, and I eagerly take one of the bubbling glasses from the tray. Alcohol is most definitely needed for the night. Anything to take the edge off that still lingers after the run-in with Sharon. Throughout our meal, Michael makes me laugh, telling me silly jokes or stories about his clients. It aids in taking my mind off of everything and I relax just a little bit more.

Soon we hear the hum of a microphone and see my dad occupying the stage at the front. We turn together and listen to my dad make a toast to Sharon, who slightly stumbles onto the stage and blows over-exaggerated kisses to the crowd. Everyone raises their glasses in unison, wishing the drunken tramp a happy birthday. Not wanting to draw any more negative attention, my dad offers Sharon his hand, leading her to the dance floor for the first dance of the night. The band begins playing a soft melody as the crowd watches them glide across the dance floor. Well, my dad is gliding and Sharon is limply hanging there. I wonder if she knows how ridiculous she looks or how embarrassing it must be for my dad.

A few couples join them on the dance floor at the next song selection and Michael stands, offering his hand to me.

"May I have the pleasure of this dance?"

I smile and nod, biting my bottom lip as he helps me stand from my chair. As soon as our feet hit the floor, he twirls me slightly before pulling me close to his body. We entwine our hands and hold them to our sides with our elbows bent close to our bodies. My free arm lays on his shoulder, allowing my fingers to rest across the muscular planes of his upper back. A Billie Holiday song floats through the hall, one I actually know, and we sway in rhythm with the music. Michael guides us around the floor with grace and ease.

"You're an excellent dancer," I remark.

His cheeks pink up and a nervous laugh escapes. "That's ten years of dance lessons with Madame Tousignant. My mom made me do it when I was growing up because my sister refused to go by herself."

I press my lips together and try my best not to laugh. "Ten years? Why didn't you quit as you got older?"

He shakes his head and lets out a quiet laugh. "Because, at that point, I started to enjoy it. She was teaching me all these advanced dances, you know, the kind you see on Dancing With the Stars? I can do almost all of them. Well, maybe not anymore. I am older and a little rusty."

"Damn. And I was hoping you could show me a few things."

He wags his eyebrows and twirls me out in front of him before pulling me back into the safety of his body.

"I've still got a few moves left in me."

We laugh and dance to a few more songs before my dad approaches, sporting a broad grin. I've never seen him smile this much in my life. Maybe he's drunk too.

"Michael, there are a few people out on the veranda that I'd like you to meet. Tessa, would you mind if I borrow him for a while?"

"Sure, that's okay with me."

Michael smiles and walks away with my dad while I head back to our table, thankful to get off my feet for a moment. Whoever said shoes were meant for fashion and not for comfort should be shot. I grab another flute of champagne from a passing waiter and partake in my favorite pastime. I don't know one single person here, outside of my dad, Sharon and Michael. These are all of my dad's friends and associates and I'm sure several people from their country club. I'm pretty sure I recognized the mayor and his wife, but I can't be positive. I've only seen them in pictures and never actually met them in real life. There are at least two hundred people in attendance, making it easy for me to be the wallflower that I like to be.

My phone beeps in my clutch as the champagne bubbles tickle my nose. I roll my eyes, guessing that it's Kara wanting the gossip on what's going on or how my date is going so far. But nothing prepared me for seeing Andrew's name on my screen, making my eyes go wide as saucers.

My darling, beautiful Tessa. I love the way you look with your hair swept back behind your shoulders in soft, delicate curls. I can see you in a blue strapless gown with intricate silver designs, and diamond earrings gracing your delicate lobes. Nothing compares to your smile which outshines the soft glow of the candles that surround you.
~A~

I freeze and nervously start looking around me. Either he has a very active imagination or ... or. I don't even get the chance to finish that thought as I feel him come up behind me, running his hands down my arms, leaning so close to me it sends a chill across my skin. My body erupts in goose bumps and desire takes the place of surprise.

Oh. My. God. He's here. He's really here.

"I also imagine your soft pink lips, slightly parted as a small gasp escapes them. The same sound you make when you're sleeping next to me or making love with me," he whispers in that soft, sexy British accent of his. My breathing accelerates and I shift in my chair. My head turns slightly, needing to see those bright blue eyes that I've longed for. The air has been completely drained from my lungs as I stare into Andrew's gorgeous face. A face that has haunted my waking dreams, causing my heart so much pain and yet so much longing. Those full lips that I want to kiss caress my cheek as his fingertip ignites a trail of fire down my neck.

"It's so good to see you, Tessa. I've been counting the days until we would be reunited again. I've done nothing but dream of you every second of every day since we departed last." Andrew's warm breath tickles the area behind my ear, allowing his lips to explore the area. I feel dizzy with pleasure, my eyes closing as my breath comes in short bursts. I feel as if we're making a scene, or at least we could be. However, when I look around, I realize that no one is looking at us. Not one person is aware of the reunion taking place, of the man who melts my soul and completes my very existence.

I turn in my chair, needing to fully see him as he takes the seat that Michael occupied not less than an hour ago.

"What are you doing here?" I whisper hoarsely. Andrew knows exactly how he affects me, how to turn me into a raging pile of hormones without actually having to touch me or do anything. His blue eyes shine in the soft glow of the candlelight, making my heart leap inside my chest.

"I came here for you. It couldn't wait one more week. I

needed to see you right away."

He came for me. He wanted to see me, no, *needed* to see me. How do I respond to that? Do I say how big of a fool I was for leaving like I did? Or that I needed to see him too? My hungry eyes take him in, admiring his freshly shaven face, his beautiful masculine features, and that sexy dark hair I love running my fingers through. And he's wearing a tux. Holy shit. If I thought he was hot in tailored suits, he's to die for in a tux.

I swallow past the lump in my throat, needing to regain some control of my body.

"Why?"

Need and desire mix together as I nervously canvas the room again, hoping that Sharon isn't watching. My hand rubs the area above my heart, trying to ward off the pain. Andrew ignores my question and grabs the hand at my chest, bringing it up to his lips before pressing it against his own beating heart.

"You don't have to hurt there anymore, love. I promise you will never have to hurt there again as long as I'm here." He leans forward, pressing our foreheads together, leaving my hand to cover his heart. "I've missed you so much, Tessa. I'm so sorry, more than you will ever know."

We close the distance to each other, pressing our mouths together in a whisper soft kiss. My lip trembles slightly as a flood of memories assaults my mind; each memory bringing back all the joy and pleasure those lips have brought me. My body takes over and I wrap my free hand around his neck. Pulling him closer to me, we seal our mouths together, succumbing to the kiss I've longed for since I last felt it. A kiss that is so perfect and natural. It's a kiss I could see myself giving and receiving for the rest of my life.

"Do you feel that, Tessa?" Andrew whispers against my lips. "My heart beats only for you. My heart longs for only you. It's not complete without you in my life."

I pull back slightly, leaving my hand still resting on his chest. "I can't do this here, not now. There are too many people around and Michael …" My eyes look everywhere but his. I stand from my chair, letting my hand fall from his body as I turn away from him. Andrew is instantly behind me, close enough for me to feel him even though he's not touching me.

"Your date is currently occupied outside on the veranda with your father and several other gentlemen. It appears he's left you alone so someone else can snatch you away."

I turn and try to move away from him. He lightly grabs my elbow, anchoring my body against his. The hard muscles beneath his tux flex and tighten as he wraps an arm around my waist. I try not to picture those same muscles as they flex and tighten while he's above me, worshipping my body while giving me immense pleasure.

I shake my head. "Andrew, please, not here. I can't do this tonight." My voice is weak and small. The fight behind the words is not there, indicating that I'm really not willing to let him go. Deep down, I want this. I want him.

He ducks down and brings my gaze to meet his. Confused hazels meet pleading blues as he softly cups my cheek in his hand.

"One dance. Please, grant me one dance for tonight then I promise to leave. But only for this evening. I told you that I came here for you, to beg your forgiveness and to clear up whatever misunderstandings we have between us. I belong to you Tessa, body and soul, and I won't stop until you see it too."

My willpower is fading quickly. With a final glance around, I place my hand in his, letting him lead me to the dance floor. "One dance, Andrew. That's it."

My hand tingles at the skin-to-skin contact, his thumb lazily grazing over my own repeatedly. I can't believe I'm doing this, here, right now, in front of all these people. Although it's not uncommon to dance with people you didn't arrive with. No one really even knows who I am so why would they care that I'm not dancing with Michael? But as Andrew's arm wraps around my waist and brings our joined hands to his chest, I can't stop myself from looping my own arm around his shoulders. I press up against him, close enough so our chests and stomachs are touching. This feels more intimate than the dance Michael and I shared earlier. Yet this also feels like home, like the universe is aligned in perfect formation.

The song switches and the familiar strains of "It Had to Be You" fill the air. *Fate, you really are trying to kill me, aren't you?* We sway together as we dance gracefully in a circle. We're barely moving yet it feels like we're floating at the same time. Andrew's hand flexes at the small of my back and gently rubs up and down my spine.

He leans his head down to rest against my cheek, whispering his thoughts into my ear. "Words cannot describe how beautiful you look tonight, love. It took everything I had to stay away and watch you from afar. Seeing you with your date, watching you laugh with him and dance closely, knowing that it should be me out there instead of him, about drove me mad. I have never been a jealous man, but seeing you with him made me feel something I have never felt before."

His words swirl in my head, my brain running a million

miles a minute at this bit of information. How long has he been here? What if he saw my run-in with Sharon, or worse yet, heard what she had said to me? But then I realize he was watching me, staring at me, jealous of my time with Michael. Even though he has nothing to be jealous of, he doesn't know that yet.

He really did come here to see me. The pain in my heart lessens as I let that wash over me.

I pull my head back slightly, needing to look into the blue eyes that I love, praying to find some answers to questions I'm not ready to verbalize tonight. What I see surprises me, although I'm not sure why. I see regret, sadness, and hope. Could he have possibly known I had secretly wanted him to follow me, to rescue me from myself and my crazy insecurities? To drag me away to places unknown, hidden from the world where we could reconnect and rediscover each other? Then I remember the pain I felt one week ago, the feeling of betrayal and believing he didn't want me and didn't return my affections. A lone tear slips down my cheek as my gaze falls onto the floor. Andrew releases my hand, gently sweeping away the tear with his thumb. A soft sob escapes me as he cups my cheek and pulls me closer to him.

"Please, don't cry. It breaks my heart to watch you cry and it shatters me whole to know that I am the reason behind those tears."

Another tear slips down my cheek, but he quickly brushes it away. We've stopped dancing, even though the music is still playing. Andrew's wet thumb brushes over my quivering bottom lip, allowing the wetness to seep into my mouth, letting me taste my salty tears. Tears of joy, tears of sorrow, tears of confusion, all running together and releasing from my body. And I'm trying really hard to guard my heart and not let it rule my body, but I'm finding it more and more difficult the longer I'm around Andrew.

"Andrew," I whisper.

He closes the distance between us, gently stroking his lips against mine. It's soft and familiar, making me sigh softly as we continue to move against each other's lips. He doesn't push me to open for him. It feels like he's restraining himself, letting me guide him as to what I want to happen. The spark that I love runs through our connection, lighting up the room even if it's only in my mind. Andrew places several soft pecks against my lips before pulling away, guiding my head down to rest upon his shoulder as he holds me tight with both arms around me.

Tonight has been more emotional than I anticipated it to be. First, Sharon shows her colors outside of the house. Then Andrew, the keeper of my heart and the one who makes my life shine brightly with promises of hope and love shows up, professing his need to be with me and to win me back.

The music stops and we slowly pull away from each other, making me miss the contact instantly. He grabs my hand and presses his lips against my skin, sending a new round of shockwaves through my system.

"Thank you for the dance, Tessa. I promised I would leave after our dance and I plan on fulfilling that promise. But before I go, I need to know I'll be able to see you tomorrow. Can we meet somewhere to talk? There's so much that I need to say."

Andrew's eyes bounce back and forth across my face, searching, pleading, begging me to hear him out. I exhale a breath and nod my head.

"How about we meet up for lunch? Let's say around one o'clock?"

He smiles, cupping my face gently in his hands. "One o'clock it is. Until then, my sweet Tessa."

His lips slant over mine, allowing me to bask in his taste once again. A taste I have missed for the past week and one that my body craves more than anything in the world. How do you forget the person who gave you your first real kiss, even if he never knew it?

Andrew keeps his promise and leaves me standing on the dance floor with my body longing for his, instantly missing him. My eyes open and watch his retreating form head for the bank of elevators, praying silently that he'll turn around for a final glance. As if he could read my thoughts, Andrew turns his head and mouths something to me before disappearing around the corner.

I need to improve my lip reading skills if he's going to continue doing that.

With a swipe of my finger, I wipe away any black smudges of mascara that may have appeared after my emotional dance with Andrew. My body still quakes, still feels his touch over my skin and his warm breath against my neck. I'm not sure how I can continue on with the rest of my night after Andrew's presence here. So I go seek Michael out, hoping that I can convince him to leave.

Michael stands in a circle with several other men, my father included, all laughing loudly while holding their crystal tumblers filled with an amber liquid. His head turns as I approach, a smile gracing his face. He makes room for me to join them and I flash nervous grins to everyone in the circle.

"And who is this lovely young lady, Michael?" asks one of the men standing directly across from us.

"This is Tessa, who I am lucky enough to be escorting here tonight." There's pride in his voice as the men around us all nod their head in agreement.

"Yes, gentlemen, this is my daughter. Michael is a very lucky man indeed."

Is that another compliment from my dad? This night has to rank high on my weird scale. I brightly smile at him, appreciating the sentiment, strange as it may feel.

"How long was I gone? I guess we got a little carried away, talking politics and whatnot. Hopefully, you're not too mad at me."

"No, I'm not mad. But I was beginning to wonder if you had abandoned me."

He taps the end of my nose and smiles. "Never."

The light feeling that I held before is gone, leaving me nothing but a pile of nerves and twisting emotions. Michael must see it in my eyes because he reaches out to the surrounding men, shaking each of their hands.

"Well gentlemen, it's getting late and I must take this gorgeous treasure back home. I wouldn't want her father getting upset with me for having her out so late." They all erupt in laughter and my dad claps him on the shoulder.

"It was very nice meeting you, Michael. I hope to see more of you soon."

They shake hands and then, in a shocking move, my dad leans down and kisses the top of my head.

"Goodnight, Tessa. I'm so glad you came. You really do look lovely tonight. And please, don't be afraid to bring Michael around. Maybe the three of us could do lunch sometime?"

I repeatedly blink, trying my best not to look shell-shocked. "Um, sure, Dad. That would be wonderful. What about you, Michael?"

"Lunch with the two of you would be perfect. We'll try to set something up soon. Robert, again, thank you for the wonderful party. I'll see to it that Tessa gets home safe."

They shake hands a final time and Michael ushers us back through the doors to retrieve our things that we left at the table. With his hand at the small of my back, we leave the ballroom and head down toward the lobby, eager to get home. Well, at least I am.

He opens my apartment door for me as I hobble inside, dying to free my feet from the constraints of the devil shoes I'm wearing. Trudy and I need to talk about fashion and comfort. There must be a balance between the two.

"Thank you so much for everything tonight, Michael. I really had a lot of fun. And you being there with me made it bearable."

"It was my pleasure, Tessa. I had fun as well. Met a lot of new contacts and got some pretty great advice from your dad. He's a pretty cool guy and knows his stuff."

I lean up against the counter and sigh. "Yeah, one thing he knows really well is work. It's all he does. I'm glad you were able to meet some people and possibly help your career along."

Michael steps forward and gives me a giant hug. I return the favor and silently thank whoever placed him in my life.

"Coffee on Monday?"

I smile. "You bet. We should just plan to do it every morning. I seem to function better when I've had caffeine that doesn't come from my house."

He laughs and mock knocks my chin. "Have a good weekend, Tess."

"You too."

Michael slowly backs out into the hallway and I wave at him before closing the door and securing it. With a heavy sigh, I slump back against the door, thankful for the night to be over. My head is pounding and it's not even from the several glasses of champagne I consumed. No, the pounding is due to the confusing nature of the night.

My dad was outwardly showing me affection, which is strange in its own right. Michael saved me after Sharon showed her true colors in public. And then there's Andrew, appearing out of the blue, telling me that he needs me, came for me, and still wants me to be his.

I find myself opening the cabinet above the refrigerator and pulling out a bottle of vodka, needing the burning shot to calm my nerves so I can sleep. After the second one, the pleasant numbness starts to set in and the jumbled thoughts in my head dissipate slightly.

My phone beeps in my clutch, drawing my attention to it again.

Thank you for the dance tonight, love. You have no idea how happy I was to hold you in my arms again, even if it was just for a short amount of time. Please let me know when you have returned home safe. I look forward to seeing you tomorrow. ~A~

One more shot for good measure should do it. I swallow the liquid, feeling the burn hit my stomach as I limp back to my bedroom, eager to rid myself of the oppressive clothes.

I crawl into bed and turn off the light on the table beside me while staring at the phone in my hands. I should reply to him. I don't want him to worry about whether or not I've returned home. I've put that man through enough worry for one lifetime already.

I have arrived home safe and sound. It really was nice to see you tonight. Looking forward to tomorrow. Goodnight, Andrew. ~T~

Placing the phone on the table, my mind wanders through the hazy fog of my thoughts. Images of Andrew appear behind my lids, garnering my attention. His hand reaches out to mine, pulling me close and promises to give me the forever I've always wanted. Now I just need to know if it's all a dream or not.

Chapter 9

THE WAITRESS HURRIES PAST MY table again, giving another glance at my half empty glass of Diet Coke. My gaze wanders around nervously, even though I have nothing to be nervous about. The noise is a good distraction, though; plates clanging together, the loud murmuring of conversations, and the occasional wail of an unhappy toddler. All of it aids in my distraction as my leg bounces up and down underneath the table.

He's not going to show. Another glance at my watch shows only one minute has passed since the last time I checked it and is still showing that it's not quite one o'clock yet. But I wanted to be early. I wanted to be the one to see Andrew walk through the door, watch as he searches the room until his eyes land upon mine. That's when the magic happens. Those dreamy blue eyes soften as he smiles; the worry lines across his face ease and fade, making him even more impossibly handsome than he already is. I would watch as he swaggers over to me, pulling me from my chair. Then he'd bend me backward to claim my mouth, his tongue stroking deep and long, hard and soft, possessing, owning, branding me as his, leaving me a breathless mess.

Did I mention I'm daydreaming? Because there is no way that scenario is happening. Life is not a chick flick. Life is messy and filled with many complications. And you can't get more complicated than fighting your own thoughts, making you believe the one person you want doesn't want you back.

I glance over the menu again, unsure if my stomach could handle any food right now. The smell of coffee and grease is thick in the air but is suddenly overpowered by an all too familiar smell; one that I can pick out blindfolded and know exactly who it belongs to. My head turns and my breath catches in my throat. There he is, lowering himself into the empty seat next to me, still not wanting to sit away from me. The sentiment is endearing and highly romantic.

Andrew moves his chair so close to mine they're almost touching. The only thing getting in the way is the corner of the table. His long slender fingers reach out, desperately seeking the comfort of my own. The tips of our fingers play with each other; the slight contact sends warmth through the connection straight into my chest. It's a simple touch, one typically done by two teenagers trying to sneak around, needing to feel each other but not wanting to make it obvious. Andrew's larger hand fully engulfs my own and I sigh, not realizing how much I needed the contact.

A light tug sends me forward, the perfect position for Andrew to lean into a kiss. Only he doesn't. Instead, his big beautiful eyes close as he softly inhales, taking in the moment. I follow suit, allowing the smell of his cologne to swirl into my nose, calming my nerves and stopping the bouncing leg beneath the table. There's something about his smell that calms me like nothing before. No amounts of lavender or chamomile will ever soothe my senses like Andrew.

His eyes open and I see multiple emotions flash across his face.

Hope … longing … need … desire.

I'm afraid to put a name on the last one because if it's not true, if he doesn't feel that way about me then I'll make a fool of myself again. I don't want to do that anymore.

The distance closes between our lips, moving slowly over one another, soft and wet, gentle and sure. It brings my body to life, sending an electrical arc to race through my nervous system.

"Hi," Andrew whispers against my lips, reaching up to cup my cheek in his hand. My shoulders relax with the gentle strokes of his thumb, relieving the tension right out of my body.

"Hi," I whisper back.

From the outside, this looks like an intimate lover's reunion, unlike the one from last night. There's a familiarity that our bodies recognize because they're drawn together. Fated if you will. He is the matching half of my soul. At least I thought he was, or maybe he still could be. My neuroses could very well be clouding my judgment.

But the closer he stays to me, the more I feel myself falling back into the familiar emotions we draw from each other. The previous sounds I needed to aid in my distraction before have now faded to nothing. It's as if the two of us are seated in our own little bubble, content on just staring into each other's eyes. Without thought, my hand reaches up and strokes the side of his face, feeling the day old stubble underneath. How I loved feeling those whiskers against my fingers and other places along the expanse of my body. Andrew must have remembered because he's usually so clean shaven at this point in the day.

"You have no idea how much I have missed your touch. I've craved it daily, longed for it nightly, begged for it every conscious moment. After what happened last week … the way we parted from each other … I wasn't sure when I'd be able to feel it again."

My hand falls from his face like a lead weight. Feelings of confusion, betrayal, love, and hurt swirl before my eyes. He winces slightly as if I have struck him. My head fills with the questions I long to have the answers for, wondering what it is about me that makes him not want to return my sentiment.

"If I said I didn't feel the same way I would be lying." My voice is scratchy and raw, trying to fight back the emotions I don't want to show. At least not yet.

"Then please, talk to me, Tessa. What did I do that was so wrong last Friday? Why did you run off and leave me behind without a second glance?"

I look into his tormented eyes, eyes which frequently bring me solace. I lean back and take several deep breaths, thankful that the noises around us are still drowned out by the closeness of Andrew.

"I just felt inadequate. You were preoccupied all morning with several messages and phone calls. I wasn't sure if you were trying to get rid of me quickly so you could go back to whatever or whoever it was that needed you."

"Inadequate? Did I make you feel that way? If I did I greatly apologize. There is nothing inadequate about you. You are everything to me, everything that I need and could ever hope to have. I've been going over this in my head, taking it apart and piecing it back together. The only thing I can determine is you saw the message from Evie."

Just the mention of her name causes a chill to run down my spine. "Yes, I saw it," I say. "I saw that she desperately needed you and that she was coming over within the hour. So I thought it would be easier if I left before you had the awkward meeting between your fling and your girlfriend. I was saving us both the heartache that scene would most definitely cause."

"That's what I thought you'd say," he sighs. Andrew leans back in his chair, putting more distance between us. I mimic his pose, wrapping my arms protectively around my body. He closes his eyes for a moment, exhaling a large breath and then slowly begins his story.

"Do you remember me taking a phone call the morning before while we were still in your hotel room?" I nod. "That phone call was from my mate, John. There was an incident with his younger sister, Sarah, and he wanted some advice on the situation. Sarah is sixteen and like any other sixteen-year-old, she thinks she knows what's best for her. She's been seeing this boy recently and had been coming home later and later after curfew. I gave him some advice based on my dealings with some of the teenagers at the center. John said that he'd try it out, see what happens and maybe she'll come around.

"Sometime during the night, Sarah had snuck out with the boyfriend. She had mentioned going to a concert with him that next evening, but it was out of town and her parents forbade it. Evie and Clive are very strict with her because she's their only daughter and the baby to boot."

That name echoes loudly through my head. "Evie?"

Andrew nods his head. "Yes, Sarah's mother. The same Evie you saw in that text message the next morning. She went to Sarah's room to check on her, make sure everything was okay after an argument the night before. When she opened the door, Sarah was gone. Evie messaged me initially asking if I would check the centers to see if Sarah had shown up there. I told her that I wasn't going in until noon so I'd make some calls to put the word out in case she showed up before I got out there.

"At some point John must have called the MPS, wanting to know if there had been any calls overnight regarding two teenagers. Apparently, there was a stolen vehicle call about a kilometer from their house, the description of the suspects matching Sarah and her boyfriend. John told Evie, who then messaged me right away, saying she needed to speak to me urgently."

"The message I saw," I gasp.

"Yes, love, that message. She needed to let me know about the new development regarding Sarah and her urgency to figure out what happened. So when I came out of the bathroom to discover that you weren't there, I saw the message. I wasn't sure what had happened to you, if you were all right or why you had taken off without me. Evie was the furthest thing from my mind, even though she's like a mother to me."

"So you chased after me instead of going to look for your best friend's sixteen-year-old sister?" My face heats up, realizing how stupid I was, misconstruing that message into my own twisted insecurities. Evie wasn't a girlfriend or sometimes lover. Evie was his best friend's mom, who was going through her own personal crisis. And what did I do? Add to the stress of the situation by just walking away without so much as an explanation or reason. I feel so stupid.

"Yes, I chased after you. John had the MPS looking for Sarah so they were covered that way. But I needed to find you because, at that point, you were missing to me. I had so many plans and ideas I wanted to share with you, things that I needed to say, but you were gone, disappeared like an apparition in the night."

I swallow hard, my throat threatening to close up. "Did you find her?"

Andrew sighs and reaches out for my hand. "On my way home from the hotel, I happened to take the long way, needing to get my thoughts straight after reading your note and finding you had already left. I glanced out my window, barely seeing anything until a shock of red hair grabbed my attention. That's when I saw Sarah with her sleazy boyfriend, pushing himself on her against the back of the stolen vehicle down a side street not heavily traveled. I quickly turned my car around, dialed John and headed for them. Luckily I got there in time before anything could happen to her. She had some bruising around her eye, several cuts along her arms and face and her shirt was torn off her shoulders. I held the boyfriend down, waiting for John to arrive with the MPS. Sarah was shaking so hard, but I couldn't do anything to comfort her while I held the sleaze away from her.

"Finally John arrived, along with the MPS. They cuffed him instantly and sent the medics to check on Sarah, who was shaking violently in John's arms. Thankfully that was the only thing that happened, but I shudder to think of a different outcome had I not taken that route home."

"A route you wouldn't have taken if I had been there."

His lip curls slightly in the corner and nods his head. "That's true. If you had still been with me, I would not have been driving that way. I would have been preoccupied with you."

"Driving me to the airport no doubt," I say.

"I was going to ignore your note and drive there anyway, but I had this feeling that I should heed your words and just go home. That's when I found her."

Andrew's story slowly sinks into my brain. This poor girl, his best friend's sister, was beaten on a side street. And who knows how far her boyfriend would have gone had Andrew not arrived when he did. The scenarios that flood my mind take me to a dark, familiar place, somewhere I'd rather not go.

That morning I left accusing him in my mind of cheating on me, convinced we were nothing more than a fling. I feel so stupid right now. This is a misunderstanding to trump them all. But what would have happened if I would have stayed? Would Sarah have been found in time? Would she have made the same choices leading to her being in that car?

Andrew dips his head, drawing my gaze back up to his. "Tell me what you're thinking? I know you get locked in your head, creating stories and scenes which aren't real. I know you feel insecure about us, but I can't begin fixing this until you talk to me. I need to know what you're thinking and feeling."

I sigh and play with his fingers again. "I'm playing the 'what if' game in my head. What if I wasn't that stupid insecure girl? What would have happened to Sarah if I would have just trusted you to think of me as more than just a fling?"

Andrew's hand squeezes tighter around my fingers. "You were never a fling. Why didn't you believe me when I told you this before?" His voice gets quiet, apparently displeased I still thought that way after he had reassured me over and over that we weren't.

"My insecurities tend to get in the way more often than not, creating roadblocks which aren't there and making things into more than what they seem. And I'm trying not to be that way with you, but it was so fast, so sudden, so …"

"Perfect," he says, completing my sentence for me.

"Yeah, perfect. There just had to be something wrong with us. Nothing in my life has ever been easy or … perfect. So I got scared and went into flight mode. I couldn't fight because I knew who I would be picking the war against … me."

With a gentle sweep, Andrew's knuckles graze my cheek, brushing away a tear that somehow had leaked from my eye. His features soften as he continues stroking his hand up and down my face. I feel guilty for my behavior from before, letting my pride and fears rule my heart, knowing deep down there was never any hope of leaving this man. If all of this is true, why didn't he say something when I blurted out those stupid words?

"Andrew?" I ask with a trembling voice.

"You're thinking again, I can see it in your eyes. Talk to me, Tessa. Ask me anything you want and I will answer it. You must know by now there isn't anything I wouldn't do for you."

Maybe he didn't hear me that night. And if so, would it be worth bringing up now? How can I ask him if he heard my words and not be hurt if he didn't return the sentiment? And deep down do I honestly believe that he doesn't? Andrew flew across an ocean for me, a week before he knew he was going to see me. What does that say about him? Is that the action of a man who just likes a girl?

"It's just … I don't know how to …"

"Do you still love me?" Andrew blurts out.

I freeze, unsure of what to do. Oh God, he did hear me. My head pulls back, allowing his hand to drop from my cheek. A hurt look crosses his face at my reaction, making my own flinch from causing him more unnecessary pain.

"Andrew, I …"

"Please tell me you haven't stopped. Tell me I'm not too late, that you haven't already moved on with another man."

A million things swirl in my brain, all jumbling together, creating a vortex of emotions and scenarios, none of which can be easily picked out. "Andrew, it's more complicated than a simple yes or no answer. That night … I didn't mean to … there were so many emotions in me … I just …"

I'm stammering like an idiot, unable to form a coherent sentence if my life depended on it. And right now it almost seems like it does.

"Tell me you love me. Tell me there's still a chance of that love between us. We can find our way back to each other and heal the pain we've both caused by our lack of communication and misunderstandings. That night, that glorious, magical night, was the best night of my life. I couldn't forget it if I tried and won't forget it for as long as I live. I want to create many more nights exactly like it. I want your mornings, your afternoons, and your nights. I want them all. So I need to know that the woman who is the center of my whole world and is sitting right here beside me after I never thought she would, still loves me."

The weight of his words hangs heavy in my head and chest,

pulling my heart down yet lifting it up at the same time. Was that a declaration of love? Because it sure felt like it was. Words become lost within the still swirling vortex as a fresh tear escapes from my closed lids, still trying to process what Andrew is telling me.

"I know this, Andrew. I know that I have incredibly strong feelings for you; ones I'm not used to or fully understand what they are. It could be love, but we spent less than a week together. It's impossible to love someone after that short amount of time, right? It could have just been the heat of the moment when I said those words. I'm not saying this to hurt you. I just think we were moving too fast before and I don't want to get thrown off the merry-go-round at full speed only to hit a brick wall in the end. We still don't know each other very well and I realize it's partly my fault.

"But our situation hasn't really changed either. There's still the problem of you living in London and me living here. The odds are stacked against us and I can't just throw caution to the wind like my heart is begging me to. My brain keeps focusing on the obstacles we need to overcome first, one of them being an ocean."

Andrew's warm hand runs down my arm, leaving a trail of goose bumps in its wake before lacing his fingers with my own. "The odds are whatever we make them out to be, love. You may not believe me right now, but you will. Somehow I'll just have to prove to you that we are worth the fight so you can stop flying away from me."

I lean forward, curious to see what he has planned. "What do you suggest then, to keep me from flying?"

The smile on his face rips a new tear in my heart. "You

say we don't know each other well. Or at least you don't seem to think so. I, however, beg to differ. I know you. I know your heart. And I will show you we are meant to be. As I've said before, fate has brought us together."

Oh yes, fate. You have no idea how much I dislike that meddling little witch right now. If I weren't so insecure, this would be easier.

"But I must know, are you seeing the other gent, the one you attended the party with last night?"

I clear my scratchy throat before speaking. "No, Michael is just a friend, nothing more. He offered to take me to the party last night so I wouldn't have to go with Kara and torture myself. Besides, he's a lawyer and was doing a little networking to better his career, so I was happy to help him do that."

Andrew leans forward again. "Just to be clear, you are not seeing him then?"

I shake my head. "No, I am not seeing him. We're friends. Nothing more."

He blows out a shaky breath before relaxing back into the chair again. "Good. I was nervous last night when I saw the two of you together. The way you were laughing and touching him had me believing I was too late.

"But I also saw that he doesn't look at you the same way I do, so part of me knew there was nothing between you."

My brows furrow together. "And how does he look at me?"

Andrew leans forward again, putting us close but not yet touching. "He looks at you with warmth in his eyes but no fire. He would protect you and guard you but that's it. He wouldn't push the boundaries any further than that. There's no heat between you two, no unbridled passion that ignites the air and sends fireworks into the sky to light up the dark."

"And what does that look like," I ask nervously.

"That's the look you and I share, one that will never be duplicated or replaced by anyone else. What you and I have is priceless, unique, and solely ours."

"You saw all that about Michael and I from a distance? How could you be so sure?"

Andrew presses his forehead against mine; his soft whisper touches my lips. "Because when you looked at me for the first time that night, I knew there was no one else for you but me. Your eyes gave you away."

My eyes search his in our intimate pose. "They did?"

He nods. "They called to me, begged me to kiss you again, even though you tried your best to fight it. Your eyes are the portal to your soul, something I'm well acquainted with. I want to ask you something without you overthinking it."

I swallow hard. "I can't promise you that I won't, but okay."

He pulls back and blinks several times while staring into my eyes. "I want to date you, formally, this time around. I want to get to know your life here, see how you live and prove to you how easy our relationship would fit into your life."

My brows draw together slightly. "But you're only here for a short amount of time. How is this going to work exactly?"

Andrew smiles that delicious smile of his and I can't help but smile back. "It appears my time here is open-ended until I am satisfied with all plans being made. So it seems we have nothing but time. I have faith in us that everything will go according to the fate's plans."

"So confident," I say, looking down briefly. "We need to take it slow this time. I don't want to rush into anything too soon. We need to find our way, make time for each other and learn to trust again after the damage we've caused."

I'm not sure if I'm trying to convince him or me of this more. But this is something we need to do. He needs to trust that I won't fly away and I need to believe that he'll stay.

"There's no damage to repair, but I will do anything for you, love. We'll start over and just take our time if that's what you need."

We reach up simultaneously and press our lips together to seal our agreement. The warm familiarity of his lips moving seductively across mine bring back happy memories and I allow them to flow, thankful that I'm in a better place with Andrew now. Those memories don't hurt like they did before. Instead, they bring on joyful emotions, along with the feeling of invincibility and forever. But that last one I shake off because if there's to be a chance for us, forever cannot be uttered yet.

We disengage our lips with both of us sporting equally stupid grins. And just for nostalgic reasons, my stomach decides to enter the conversation, growling so loudly that several patrons next to us turn to stare. My cheeks enflame and I cover my face while suppressing a laugh. Andrew, however, is not as nice and loudly laughs at my stomach's outburst.

"Apparently I need to feed you."

The suppressed laugh breaks free and my hands drop to the table. "I swear it only does this when you're around."

"I could say something right now, but I'm going to withhold the comment. Instead, I'll just kindly ask you to pick out your cheeseburger before your stomach starts eating the table."

The next hour breezes by quickly. Andrew fills me in on the past week regarding the Foundation, telling me that a few of the children had been asking about me, which touched me deeply to know they remembered and were thinking of me. I just wonder if it was the little kids I read the story to or the teenage boys I played basketball with. I tell him about my promotion and my nervousness about starting a new position. Andrew gives me encouraging words and helps boost my confidence in a way only he can.

It feels good to just sit here and talk like we used to when we were first discovering each other. We laugh and talk and laugh some more until we get scathing glares from the waitress, who probably wants us to leave so she can clean up the table for some paying customers.

Being the perfect gentleman, Andrew walks me to my car with our joined hands swinging between us. The same electrical current runs through me and I smile a genuine smile, thankful to have that wonderful feeling back.

When we reach my car, Andrew closes the distance between us and presses me against the door. A rather intimate scene, but one I won't deny from happening. My body craves him like an addict craves its next hit. The way he ignites my blood makes me almost dizzy yet it's not enough to make me stop wanting him. His hands move along my backside, following the curves before settling on my hips. I pull him closer to me, loving the feel of his body pressed up against mine.

I'm not sure slow is in our vocabulary.

This is going to be harder than I thought.

"Which hotel are you staying at?" I ask, trying in vain to keep my underlying desire hidden from him. A lascivious gleam shines in Andrew's bright blues as he gives me a smirk.

"Why? Are you planning on breaking the rules already by

visiting me at night?"

He's teasing me. I shove his shoulder and laugh, causing his own laughter to mix with mine. But then he presses against me again, making me stop everything I'm doing. A longing desire fills me instead, a need which can only be satiated by him. He's tempting me and it's not fair. His body is forbidden fruit at the moment, something to look at but not touch.

But the serpent is there, tempting me at every turn and the knowledge of knowing how juicy the fruit is, has my mouth salivating already.

"The Radisson downtown," Andrew says, seeing the new dilemma in my eyes.

I nod and am amazed my head can even do that. But the pull I have toward him can only be ignored for so long. My chin lifts, seeking him out. Andrew reads my silent plea and dips his head down to brush our lips together. When his arms wrap around me, I can't stop the shaking of my body. Our lips press lightly together before parting, allowing our tongues to gently dance with each other. Never pushing or taking, just casually getting to know one another again. The heat of his breath mixes with my own as my fingers dive into his hair, a place they've yearned to touch since he walked into the diner.

"This is going to kill me, leaving you right now." His voice dips low as he whispers against my lips. "I've missed you too much to want this to stop."

Our eyes lock together with our lips just a whisper apart. "I've missed you too, Andrew. I know this will be difficult, but if we're going to give this a real try it needs to happen. We need to take it slow. Almost like we need to forget what happened in London."

Andrew shakes his head. "Not forget. It's impossible, even if our brains want it to be that way. The best we can hope for is temporary amnesia. Because the power between us, the gravitational pull we have is too strong for it to be completely forgotten."

I lean back, biting my lip as I nod in agreement. "Temporary amnesia. I like that." And really I do. It's a perfect way to describe what needs to happen.

"Until next time sweet Tessa." Andrew lightly kisses the back of my hand before opening my car door. Smart man, staying away from my lips because I think we both know if we had one more kiss like that, our resolve would be obsolete. "I'll call you soon to set up our first official date."

"I can't wait."

"You're going to see how good we can be together. I promise."

Andrew shuts my door, closing me in on my thoughts. I live in my head way too much where nothing good happens when left alone to think. As his form gets smaller and smaller in my rearview mirror, my heart grows larger and larger. He came here for me, wants to date me, and is willing to go at my pace, even though we already know how good we are for each other. Perhaps there is hope for us after all.

Chapter 10

"I DIDN'T THINK IT WOULD be this hard," I grumble, leaning over my desk with my head in my hands. Kara laughs at me and shakes her head.

"Welcome to my world, Chickie. You were an easy choice for my assistant. But now, well you definitely have your work cut out for you."

Out of sheer frustration and her amusement of my dilemma, I toss the Post-It pad at her head. It narrowly misses her, causing her to cackle even louder.

"You are absolutely no help, you know that? Did you find my replacement yet?"

Kara shakes her head on a sigh. "No, but I have half a mind to hire some random hot guy just to get a reaction out of Chris. He's been acting weird all week and it's starting to piss me off. Do you know what's going on with him?"

Trying to keep my best poker face on, I shake my head while avoiding eye contact with her because I know I'll break if I do. The fact is I do know what's going on with him. And if all goes according to plan she will love it. I just need to keep her in my office for a little bit longer while everything gets set up.

"Nope, not a clue. I haven't really noticed anything different about him. Then again, I'm not sleeping with him either and I've been slightly busy around here doing my own thing. I've barely had time to do anything other than getting myself organized, setting up my new accounts and fighting the urge to eat every piece of chocolate in the city."

Kara's brows furrow together as she points a slender finger at me. "You know you're a shit liar, right?"

Unable to suppress it any longer I smile and laugh. "Yeah, I know."

Sitting on her new perch on my desk, she swings her feet, letting her heels dangle off the ends of her toes. "What's he planning? Come on, help a sister out."

For once in my life it's my turn to exact some sort of revenge against my loving best friend and boss, er, coworker. For all the torment and situations she's put me through, only to gloat at my expense when things work out in her favor, this was my time to shine. And what Chris is doing is the utmost romantic thing I have actually ever witnessed. My heart constricts as I wonder if anything like that will ever happen to me.

But to torture her more, I shake my head and pinch her leg hard.

"Ow! What in the hell was that for?" she cries, rubbing the abused spot.

"That, my dear friend, was for last Friday. You can't tell me it's sheer coincidence that I call you Thursday night to say Michael is bringing me to the party and then magically Andrew shows up to crash it. Especially since he wasn't supposed to arrive until next week. Huh, I wonder who tipped him off."

Her hands rise in defeat but still sporting her amused grin. "Okay fine, it was me. I knew you needed a push and that seemed like the best opportunity to get you two together." I pinch her leg again and she punches me in the arm, causing us both to laugh. "Knock it off! You're going to give me a bruise! Then I'm going to have to explain it to Chris, who will more than likely get ideas of his own and he does not need help in that department."

Wiping a tear away, I recline back in my chair, clutching my stomach. "Oh my God, I do not need that visual." With a heavy sigh, I lean forward again and resume my prior position. I place my head in hands and look over the applications, feeling the beginnings of a headache at my temples. "But seriously, a little help here would be appreciated. I need to make this decision."

"You need to relax a little," Kara says wryly. "How are things with Andrew going?"

My head slips out of my hands, landing with a thud on the hardwood desk. I have decided that Operation Take Things Slow is the hardest thing I have ever done with Andrew. Every part of my body craves him when he's around and it's killing me to hold back my true feelings for him. Every day this week he's shown me something new about him, letting me dive a little deeper into his soul. A soul that is already mine, according to him.

We've been keeping it to lunches every day and then the occasional office visit during breaks in our schedule. We laugh and talk and laugh some more. It's like he's becoming a permanent figure in my life, which is exactly his plan. He told me that our relationship would seamlessly fit into my life and I can see now how possible it could be.

But a woman has needs and taking sex completely out of the equation has aided in my growing frustration of this little experiment. It's virtually impossible to sit next to Andrew for any extended period of time and not want to rip his clothes off. It's just not possible. All we've done is kiss so far, which is lovely, but it sparks a deep seeded need within me. A need he awoke from a long slumber back in London and now that he's back, it wants to play again.

"This sucks," I mutter into the top of my desk. "Remind me again why I said I'd take it slow instead of just continuing on with how we left off?"

Kara pats my shoulder, causing me to twist my head toward her as she leans toward my slumped over body. She pulls a Post-It off my forehead and sighs.

"It's only been a week Tessa. You can't make a life-changing decision after a week, remember? That was your big argument with Andrew. You are so sure that someone can't fall in love after only a week so why are you shocked when you're having a hard time with the pace you've currently selected? There isn't some flashing neon sign somewhere giving you the answer. Things like this take time and unfortunately for you, my friend, this is one of them. Listen to your heart. It knows what it wants and won't steer you wrong."

With a resigned sigh, I lift my head back up, rubbing the reddening spot on my forehead where a new pain has formed. "Yeah, I know. But this whole thing of fighting my feelings for him is getting exhausting."

"So change it up a bit. Do something different. Feed your

wild side. The beast within you likes meat and Andrew's got exactly what it's looking for." She walks to the window and looks out, but not before giving me an evil smirk.

My mouth hangs open briefly. "I cannot believe you just said that. You know I've taken sex off the menu with him. It complicates things and I don't need more complications in my life."

"It only complicates them because you're in love with him and you refuse to admit it. Did you at least take my advice for the weekend?"

Kara's plan involves me spending the entire weekend with Andrew: sleepovers, meals, the whole nine yards. And I have to admit it's a great idea. If I want to really know him, the best way to do that is to spend as much time with him as possible.

"Yes, I took your advice and, of course, Andrew thought it was brilliant. He wants to cook dinner for me at my apartment so he's going to pick me up after work. Then we're going to the grocery store because you know my place isn't well stocked for dinner type meals."

Kara's nose crinkles in mock disgust as she walks over to one of the many bouquets of flowers that fill my office. Touching the petals softly, as if they may fall right off, she laughs lightly. "I swear you live like you're still in college. How can you survive off of the crap that's in your place? It's all boxed goods or soups. Live a little woman. Branch out. Do you get any meat in you, besides Andrew's?"

My mouth drops open, unable to believe she seriously just said that to me. Well, not really. I can believe it. "Seriously? Did I not just say that there will be no sex between me and Andrew?"

Turning, she walks back to my desk, getting back on her perch on the corner. "I swear you must be a nun. There is no way I'd be able to keep my clothes on with him around. How do you do it? I mean, a woman has needs you know."

"I just said no sex. I didn't say no to messing around. We just haven't come to that juncture yet."

Kara's face brightens and I'm almost afraid of what's going to come out of her mouth. "What exactly is your definition of sex then? Are you talking in the biblical sense or Bill Clinton's definition?" She wiggles her eyebrows and I roll my eyes at her.

"Oh my God, you did not just refer to the infamous cigar scandal, did you?"

Her smile grows wider and I shake my head, laughing silently. The things that come out of her mouth never cease to amaze me. She should be a stand-up comic in another life. Kara shrugs her shoulders, looking back at the flowers again. I follow her gaze and admire the bright and beautiful bouquets. Apparently Andrew has been on a mission to find my favorite flower. Every day he brings or sends me a new vase of flowers, all ranging from red roses to orchids to lilies. And with each bouquet, he asks if he's found them yet. When I say no, his reply is just a smile. He said he wants to make me happy by showering me with all my favorite things. I told him it's unnecessary but he's bound and determined to do it, so who am I to say no?

"Yeah I did. And if sex is off the market then you need to get some kind of action so I'm curious as to which flavor is off the menu. Messing around is well and good but nothing beats a good stiff …"

"Stop right there," I say, holding up my hand to her. Kara laughs, her eyes bouncing with delight at my embarrassment.

"I will not discuss my sex life with you."

"Fine. Don't let a girl live vicariously through you. But seriously, get something, anything. I don't care if it's just with a finger. It's been way too long for you. Plus it's a proven fact that it relieves stress and is an all-natural mood booster."

I shake my head, still laughing under my breath. "I'm not discussing this with you."

She groans loudly. "You are such a bore! Try it tonight with Andrew. Do something, anything. You know he's good for it."

I smack her arm. "I'm trying to have temporary amnesia when it comes to Andrew and our past. I want to learn new things about him instead of relying on what happened in the past."

Kara rubs her abused arm, scowling slightly at me. "If you keep abusing me I'm going back to my office."

That would not be a good thing because I haven't gotten the signal from Chris yet letting me know everything is ready. She starts walking toward the door and I bolt out of my chair, reaching her before she turns the knob.

"Fine, fine, I'm sorry." Placing my hands on her shoulders, I push her back to her spot on my desk. After retaking my seat, I spread the applications out again and sigh. "But seriously, I need your help. All of them are so similar I have no clue which one to choose. What do you think?"

Kara taps a finely manicured nail against her lips while she shuffles through the different applications. All the notes I took during the interview process are attached to each one, along with mountains of Post-Its, highlighting each of their strengths and weaknesses. Kara places them back on the desk, lining them up next to each other. I raise my brow, wondering what exactly she's doing and watch as she twirls her finger above the three pieces of paper, closing her eyes and then stabs one of the papers with it.

"I like this one."

I laugh, picking up the paper she selected. "Very scientific and sophisticated. Did they teach you that in business school?" I can't help rolling my eyes at her.

"Hey, you asked, I delivered. Your new assistant is picked. What more do you want?" Apparently she finds this hilarious. Then again, I said it myself that all three finalists were very close so truly it didn't matter too much. I would get along with any of them and all would excel in their assigned position.

Charlene Jacobs is my lucky winner. Twenty-two years old, recently graduated with a BA in Marketing from the University of Minnesota, working toward her MBA. On the application she states she needed real life experience for her graduate program and was impressed by the work that our company does. Definitely a plus in her category. And I know about needing real-life experience. I wouldn't be in my position if Kara didn't take me with her to every meeting she had. Strong typing skills and, according to my notes, an eagerness to learn rounds Charlene out. I can work with that.

"I'll give her a call and let her know the good news, minus the way she was selected of course. She may not be thrilled to hear about that."

Kara nods and moves to the window again. She seems forlorn and sad. Chris had better hurry up or she's going to think the wrong thing. I move to stand next to her, gently draping my arm around her shoulder.

"What's wrong?"

She sighs and looks down at her shoes. "Nothing. It's just … Chris has never acted this distant before, even when we were fighting. At least we still saw each other when we fought. He's been gone almost all week and it's sort of freaking me out."

I give her shoulder a reassuring squeeze. "I'm sure it's nothing. Maybe he's just stressed out. His work schedule has been overloaded this week, having to sit on interviews for two new assistants on top of all the regular work he's supposed to do. That's not an easy task you know."

Kara nods her head, still looking down. "Yeah, maybe you're right. But today is our five-year anniversary. You'd think he would have done something for that. It's a big deal and I know there's no way he's forgotten it. He always does something elaborate every year."

My phone vibrates in my pocket, letting me know that it's time. "I'm sure he hasn't forgotten. That man has a mind like a steel trap." I lead her to the door, my arm looped through hers. "Come on, let's grab your stuff and blow this place off early. I think we both could use a drink. My treat."

"What about your date with Andrew?"

I shrug. "I'll text him and let him know I'll be a little late due to a change in plans. You're my best friend and your happiness comes before any date. Chicks before dicks and all that."

She laughs as we walk down the hall. "I think I'm rubbing off on you. But yeah, I could definitely use a drink."

We stop in front of her door and she tilts her head to the side. "I know I left my door open. What the hell?"

Turning the knob, she walks in, but I stay behind, pulling out my phone to record what's about to happen. Kara halts in the doorway, frozen in place but lets her hands come up to cover her surprised gasps at the display before her. Dozens and dozens of beautiful orchids and potted azaleas of every color cover every available inch of her office, making my own look pitiful compared to hers. Rose petals are spread across the carpet, leading to the man standing in the middle of it all, holding a single blue orchid out to her, her favorite.

When her hands leave her face, a quiet sob fills the room. Tears are streaming down her cheeks now, tears of happiness and surprise. Somehow she manages to make her feet work, walking ever so slowly over to Chris, taking the offered flower from him.

"Chris … I just … this is amazing. I thought … I thought for sure you had forgotten our anniversary," she says between hiccupping sobs. I move further into the doorway, zooming in on their loving moment. She looks around before attaching her eyes to him. "But is it safe, you know, for everyone to know?"

A small crowd of women has gathered behind me, all sighing deeply at Chris's display. Chris moves toward her, running his fingers through her loose hair before bending down, placing his lips upon hers. I'm finding it incredibly difficult to keep quiet while recording because I don't want to ruin this moment for her when she watches it later.

And then a collective gasp is heard, the loudest being from Kara, as Chris drops to one knee before her. The smile on his face is one of complete and utter devotion and love as he looks straight into her eyes.

"Kara, you and I have been together for five years now, mostly in secret. I'm tired of hiding my love for you when I want to shout it to the rooftops that you are my everything, my reason for waking in the morning and my comfort in the dead of night. Our lives are forever intertwined, destined to be together from now until the end of eternity."

He pulls out a velvet box from his pocket, opening it to show the stunning platinum two karat princess cut diamond ring. It's the most elegant ring I've seen, a perfect match for Kara. Her hands fly to her mouth again as she blinks back tears.

"I knew the first moment I saw you that I was going to love you for the rest of my life. Your beauty, your brains, your quirky sense of humor, and even that foul mouth of yours ... everything ... the whole package that makes up you. It took us a while to get here, but I wouldn't trade our journey for anything. Every part of it brought me closer and closer to this moment. And here I am on bended knee asking if you, Kara Elizabeth Thomas, will do me the great honor in becoming my wife?"

For the first time in all the years I've known Kara, she's speechless. Tears continue to fall from her eyes as her head nods up and down quickly. Chris stands, pulling her hands away from her face and sliding the ring onto her finger, reverently kissing it when it rests in place. Kara tosses the flower she's still clutching in her right hand onto her desk, cups his cheeks and pulls his face to hers. A bright beaming smile plays across her face.

"Yes, yes I'll marry you."

They embrace each other, both showering the other with love and tears. The tears are mostly from Kara. Chris pulls her into a heated kiss and a few cat calls begin to erupt from behind me. Once they pry their faces apart, Chris pulls Kara into his side and addresses the crowd at the door. I stop recording, sliding the phone back into my pocket as Kara makes her way over, engulfing me in a giant hug.

"You knew?" she asks, tears still streaming down her face. I brush them away and squeeze her shoulders.

"He told me about it earlier this week. My job was to keep you occupied while he set everything up."

Kara turns to face her now fiancé and smiles warmly at him. Chris returns her smile and mouths "I love you" to her while being surrounded by several of the women in the office, all clucking their congratulations to him.

"Thank you, Tess, for your part in this. You know I love you wildly."

"Love you too Kara," I say before Chris makes his way to us, pulling her away from me, but only so he can stoop down and hug me himself.

"Thanks again Tess. I couldn't have pulled it off without you."

I brush away a happy tear and wave him off. "Yes you could have, but I'm glad to have been a part of it. Congratulations you two. You have no idea how excited I am for the both of you."

Kara leans her head against Chris's shoulder but is snapped upright when the same gaggle of women comes up to them, wanting to get a better look at her new ring. I stand back, watching my two friends being fawned over, letting them bask in the limelight and have their moment. Kara catches my eye as I pause at the doorway, mouthing a "thank you" to me before I head back to my own office.

A perfect scene to end my workday with. Every day should always end in love. And Chris and Kara have that in spades, as is apparent by her office. They're going to have such a happy life together.

I check my watch as I round the corner, thinking perhaps

I can sneak out early since my boss is currently preoccupied with his fiancée. And I assume they'll be skipping out early as well to … celebrate.

Laughing to myself, not really wanting to think of what those two will be doing as soon as they leave, I walk through my office door. My steps falter when I see a beautiful dark haired man sitting in my office chair behind my desk. He looks quite at home, sitting with his feet propped on the desktop, an amused smirk gracing his striking face.

Kara's off the cuff remarks pick this moment to swirl around in my head. Could I really just let go with Andrew and enjoy what we had together? It's not like I'm not used to going without sex or intimacy. I've done it before. For many, many years. Mainly because it wasn't enjoyable for me and then there was the little fact of not having a man in my life either. But Andrew opened up a whole new world for me in London, showing me the beauty of the act. How powerful the emotions can be and the intense connection that can bring two people into one whole being.

Without thinking, I close the door behind me and turn the lock to ensure our privacy. This is bold and a little frightening but exciting and natural. Everything about Andrew is natural. The way our bodies move together, the way he anticipates my needs before I know, even his little mannerisms and the gentle touches between us seem as if we've been doing it for years.

Calling upon all my seductive strength, I slowly approach my desk. Andrew's eyes follow my movements as I stand next to him, leaning my body against the edge of my desk. My fingers lightly walk up his leg, starting at his ankle and slowly make their way to his knee.

"You're sitting in my chair." My voice is hoarse and throaty yet quiet and seductive. Andrew doesn't move as my fingers travel higher, now above the knee, allowing me to feel the hard muscles of his thigh.

He reclines back slightly, putting his hands behind his head in a very relaxed position, acting like he belongs there. "This I know. You're more than welcome to sit down, though. I think I'm more comfortable than this stuffy old chair."

The rasp of his voice pushes me closer to the edge. His soft tone whispers in my ear, while still holding the hard edge that only comes out when he gets excited, making the baritone notes sing in the open space. His accent gets thicker, cradling each and every word with the sound of sex. I could listen to him talk all day in this voice and it would be enough for me.

There's a knot in my stomach as my finger plays along the seam of his jeans, slowing down as they inch higher and higher. I love how he looks in jeans. The way they hug him just right, sitting low on his hips, accentuating his lower body in all the right places. My eyes travel up to his chest as it expands on steady breaths, causing my own to become less stable, slowing and then speeding up, unable to keep in time with the emotions building inside me.

The corner of my mouth quirks up in what I hope is a seductive smile. "Is that so? Well, I guess I'll just have to be the judge of that."

Andrew is adorable when he's playful like this but adorable is not the word I want to use in this situation. Scorching, sweltering, blistering, tempting, captivating, passionate, those are words I would use to describe him at this moment. I watch with rapt attention as he removes his feet from my desk, swinging them gracefully to the ground. With his lap free and clear I swing a leg over and straddle him. Holding on to the back of the chair for balance, I slowly lower myself down, leaning forward ever so slightly to covertly inhale his primal masculine scent.

I feel reckless and carefree, something new and yet familiar with Andrew. He's the only person who has ever been able to show me that I can be something more than a timid little girl, afraid of the world because she's been slighted her entire life.

Andrew's hands grab my hips, dragging our bodies closer together, letting my heated core brush up against his erection, now standing prominently at attention below his jeans. On instinct, my hips gyrate forward, rubbing against him, sending a shock of arousal through my system. It's been too long since I've felt this feeling, too long since I've felt this good.

"Does your chair feel this good?"

Andrew is just as affected as I am right now. Need, desire, lust, all thick in the air surrounding us. Those bright blue eyes I adore dilate, making the blue almost black as I subtly grind up against him again. Andrew lets out a hissing breath before his head falls slightly backward against the chair.

"No, it definitely does not feel this good. Nothing feels as good as this."

I'm panting, unashamedly, and I don't care about anything at the moment. I don't care about the rules we've set for dating or the fact that we're still in my office and there are people milling about outside. None of it matters right now. The only thing I can focus on is the pleasure radiating through my body, being transferred from Andrew to me. My one-track mind only wants Andrew and everything he can give me. My lips crave his, wanting to taste him, feel his smooth tongue caress the inside of my mouth, owning me, making me his once again.

"Tessa, you're going to completely undo me right now. I want you too much to stop. I've missed the taste of your skin, the feel of your body beneath mine, the little noises you make when you come," Andrew whispers in my ear, pulling the lobe into his mouth. A shock runs through my system and I lightly cry out.

"Ah, Andrew."

He twirls his tongue around my ear and I can feel my body getting ready for him, aching to be touched. My hips rock forward again, causing another reaction from Andrew. I'm not sure how much longer we can resist the temptation to just let go and give in to our desires. I begin unbuttoning his shirt, placing soft kisses on the newly exposed skin.

A groan escapes Andrew's lips, furthering my own desire. He's trying to stay in control, trying to keep his emotions in check, but the look in his eyes tells me he may be losing that battle.

Wanting to embrace my new brazen self, I boldly pull his shirt out of his pants, unbuttoning it the rest of the way to fully expose his beautifully tanned chest. I inch my body back on his lap, trailing my lips down the hard muscles while my tongue darts out to taste his skin. Andrew's hips shift again, trying to seek out the friction that was once above him. I smile, scooting further back as my lips travel down to his rock hard abs, feeling the muscles contract with the soft contact.

Unable to remain sitting on him, I drop to the floor between his knees. Andrew's head shoots up, looking down at me with a mixture of confusion and lust. He wants this, but I know he's thinking about our arrangement in the back of his mind.

With a dexterity that I didn't know I possessed, I swiftly release him from his jeans, sliding them just over his hips to gain access to what I want most. His boxers follow the same path, letting his cock spring free. Andrew gently cups my face while I lean forward, placing a reverent kiss upon the tip before taking his sensitive head entirely into my warm mouth.

"Fuck, Tessa," Andrew says in a strangled moan. He brushes the hair away from my face, wanting to watch me please him, loving him the only way I can right now. Our eyes connect, making the act more intimate and personal, keeping us close together. The sounds he makes as my tongue works around the hardened flesh sends heat shooting through my veins. Yes, this is an act I'm not quite familiar with but looking at him coming undone because of me, of what I'm doing, is almost enough to send me over the edge with him.

Andrew swells with each stroke of my tongue, tracing the throbbing veins, pulling him deep and then teasing him with short, soft licks. His hands tighten in my hair and I know he's holding back.

"Tessa, I'm not going to last. It's too good. It's … fuck, your mouth … it feels too good."

His words push me further, sending my efforts into overdrive, wanting nothing more than to have him find his release. His cock jerks again as my tongue runs over the ridge of his head where I'm gifted with the first taste of his salty, sweet release as it coats my tongue. Knowing he's ready, I draw him all the way back, which causes him to fully release and pour stream after stream down the back of my throat. He groans out his orgasm and gently rocks into my mouth as I take every-thing he has to give to me. I ease my ministrations, allowing him to come back down to earth gently.

Looking into his glazed over eyes, a smile forms on my lips. I did that to him. Me. No man has ever looked at me the way Andrew does. The reverence, the worshipping smile, the sheer awe in his face at this very moment makes my heart ex-pand even more. It's a heady feeling, a power trip if you will.

I carefully tuck him back into his jeans while his breathing regulates. He's flushed, but a smile graces his face, lighting it up even more. Andrew pulls me off the floor, setting me on the edge of my desk. He moves the chair so he's between my knees and pulls my face to his, reverently kissing me. I'm a little reluctant to kiss him, knowing what we just did, but it doesn't seem to affect him.

"Mmm, I can taste myself on your tongue. Bloody fantas-tic. Let's see how you taste on mine."

"Andrew, no, you don't have to …"

But I can't get any more words out as he lifts the sweater over my head, gently pushing me down onto the desk. I hear the chair being kicked to the side with obvious impatience. The hand sliding down the column of my throat distracts me as it glides between my breasts. Fingers slip under the cup of my bra to tease a hardened nipple. Then Andrew is leaning over me, trailing his lips over the path his hand just took, pulling my cup to the side and freeing my breast. His tongue laps at the sensi-tive peak, allowing me to quietly cry out. He attempts to shush me between licks, reminding me that we're not entirely alone. But I'm too wound up, too turned on as he moves his mouth lower down my body.

"Andrew, please."

I have no idea what I'm begging for; if I'm asking him to stop, to keep going, to never stop. All I know is that I want him right here, right now. He smiles against my skin, continuing his journey down my stomach, pausing to twirl his tongue around my navel. My hips buck upward, wanting to find some sort of relief. Andrew moves his hands to pin down my hips, halting my movements then shifting them to unbutton my pants, pulling them and my panties down my legs.

My hands run through his hair, down his face and neck, caressing every inch of skin they can through his still open shirt. With a gentle nudge, he opens my legs further, exposing my slick flesh to him. The blood pounds through my veins as my chest rises rapidly, gasping for precious air while Andrew admires me, worshiping my body with his eyes.

"So fucking beautiful," he whispers.

He lowers his head, taking that first long stroke of his tongue against my flesh. My hands grab the edge of my desk, holding me down as my eyes roll into the back of my head from the sheer pleasure Andrew is bringing me. My soft cries surround us, mindful to keep them moderately quiet as he works me into an emotional frenzy; expertly playing my body like an instrument he's practiced his entire life. The sensations switch between his fingers and tongue, using both to bring me higher into the clouds. Soon, it all proves to be too much. My fingernails claw at my desk while my legs shake with the need for release.

"I want to taste you, Tessa. Let go. I want all of you. Right. Now."

Another few flicks of his tongue and I'm lost to the world,

catapulting my body high into the heavens as stars appear before my eyes. My tongue caresses his name as it falls from my lips over and over again. My inner walls spasm, clenching the fingers still thrusting inside me, making sure that every ounce of pleasure is brought to my body.

Coherent thought returns slowly as my eyes open in a flutter, barely registering Andrew hovering over me again. My body feels spent and lifeless, a feeling I've missed. He leans forward, placing a kiss upon my lips, letting his tongue dart quickly inside.

"Just as I thought. We taste good together."

Another soft kiss then Andrew pulls me up to a standing position, putting my clothes back in their respective places. His lips trail up my semi-naked torso while wrapping his arms around my waist, holding me close to him. My fingers play with the silky strands of his hair, slightly damp at the roots. The heady scent of sex fills the room and I know there's no way I'm going to be able to work Monday morning behind this desk and not think of this moment.

"Hi," he whispers once his lips find mine again. I flush, feeling slightly embarrassed, even though I have absolutely no reason to be.

"Hi," I whisper back. "I hope no one heard us. I don't think I'd be able to show my face here again if they did."

He presses his forehead against mine and laughs lightly. "You were perfect. Absolutely perfect, love." A flash of concern appears in his eyes as he stares intently into mine. "How do you feel about this?"

It's a valid question really. How do I feel about this? Amazing. Fantastic. Best office non-sex I've ever had. Okay, only office non-sex I've ever had. I know I said no sex but after this, I may change my mind.

"I feel incredible. You are amazing."

I help him button his shirt again while he straightens the sweater over my body. His fingers brush across my stomach, which growls loudly now that my euphoric high has worn off. Andrew laughs at the now familiar sound, holding my jacket out to me and helping me into it, like a perfect gentleman. Not that he was a perfect gentleman five minutes ago as he ravaged me on my desk. But I guess that all depends on what your definition of a gentleman is. After all, he did make sure I received my pleasure since he did.

Once we're put together, we head to my door. I pause after twisting the lock and turn to face him, throwing my arms around his neck. Andrew looks surprised but wraps his arms around my waist, holding me close to him.

"Thank you for surprising me at work. That was one of the best surprises yet." My lips seek out his, wanting to taste him one last time before we break out of the protective bubble of my office. "I'm so glad you're here right now."

His head dips down again and his sweetness crosses my tongue. "There's no place I'd rather be than right here with you." My stomach growls again and we laugh. "Come, let's go get some food before you waste away to nothing."

Chapter 11

THERE IS A PEACE BETWEEN us as Andrew follows my directions to the grocery store by my apartment. It's funny to see him sitting on the other side of the car since the only time I ever saw him drive was back in London, where the steering wheel is where I'm sitting. Andrew's thumb is still stroking the hand he hasn't released since we exited my building. His constant need to keep in contact with me in some way is so sweet. It's making it difficult to have that temporary amnesia with him. So much of everything that he does makes my body remember his, makes my mind remember why I fell in love with him so quickly and why we feel so perfect together.

We walk around the grocery store like any other ordinary couple. I push the cart while he wanders around, trying to navigate the aisles in search of whatever it is he's looking for. He hasn't given me any clues as to what he has planned. The only thing I know for certain is that we will not be having my usual dinner of either soup or cereal.

We pass by the floral display near the fresh fruit. The light fragrance wafts through the air as I lightly finger the petals of a Gerbera daisy while Andrew picks through the produce. With an assortment of colors before me, I look at them all, loving how the vibrant colors pop against the other flowers next to them. I notice Andrew's eyes follow my hand as I continue to brush the daisies softly, not wanting to disturb them too much. His face softens as he smiles when I finally pull myself away from the beautiful bouquets on a quiet sigh.

With our groceries in our arms, we walk through my front door, placing them on the counter in my kitchen. It didn't seem like we had purchased that many items when we were filling the cart but as we started bagging them, one bag turned into four. Apparently he wanted to make sure that we were prepared for anything this weekend.

We busy ourselves getting the kitchen back in order. I show him where the knives and cutting boards are as he rolls up his sleeves. My movements slow slightly as I stare at his newly exposed forearms. There's something about a man wearing a dress shirt with the sleeves rolled up that is insanely sexy. It's such a simple thing really, not meant to be sexual at all, but the look of it is hotter than just about anything else on the planet. Okay, that may be a stretch but let's face it, it's hot.

I pour two glasses of chardonnay from a bottle of wine that Kara left at my place the other night and slide one across the counter to Andrew, who pauses in his task. He raises his glass to mine, tapping them together as I relax against the countertop next to him. Thankfully he turned down my offer to help him cook. He probably remembers that cooking is not my strong suit and if we wanted to eat something that isn't delivered or comes from a box, it'd be best if I just observed.

"To surprises," Andrew says with a twinkle in his eye. He's apparently thinking of our little romp on my desk, and honestly, so am I. I flush slightly as I take a sip of my wine and continue to watch him work his culinary magic.

"Are you sure you don't need my help with anything? I feel bad just sitting here while you're doing all the work in my kitchen. I mean, after all, you're my guest this time."

Andrew pauses between chops, looking up at me through his lashes with a sensual smile. "No. I just want you to stand there being cute and adorable." His smile begins to smolder and there's a new gleam in his eye. "Or you can get naked. Either one works for me."

He wiggles his eyebrows and I laugh. "That's not going to happen. If I get naked, I could possibly distract you, making you accidentally chop off a finger or something like that." He just laughs, bending over to steal a quick kiss before resuming his task.

"Best stir-fry ever," I say, pushing my mostly finished plate away from me. If another bite lands in my mouth, I could very well explode at the seams. Andrew smiles and clears our plates from my small dining table.

"I'm glad you enjoyed it. It wasn't much, though."

I join Andrew in the kitchen and begin rinsing the plates before loading them in the dishwasher. "Are you kidding? That was unbelievable. It was restaurant quality good. I know I could never do that in a million years."

Andrew laughs, putting the leftovers into my nearly bare

fridge. He sighs while looking at it, closing the door with a shake of his head. I ignore it, knowing that he's disappointed in my lack of groceries and food around my place. I just don't buy food to keep around for me to snack on all day long. I get what's necessary and that's it. You don't need anything more than that. It's not like I'm constantly inviting people over to entertain.

Once the kitchen is clean, we both flop onto the couch, deciding to watch a little mindless TV. My legs are draped over his, snuggling close to his side and allowing my head to rest on his shoulder. His arm drapes over my shoulders, securing me to him in a loving embrace.

This is what I love. Just a simple night in with nothing fancy going on. Nowhere to go but the comfort of your own home, resting in the arms of a man who holds you like you are the most precious thing on this planet. Soon enough, the rhythmic beating of his heart lulls me into utter relaxation. I try desperately not to cross the border into sleep. But my eyelids feel heavy and weighted. Before I know it, a yawn escapes my lips. Andrew twists his head to look down at me, sweeping his lips across my forehead as he takes in my sleepy composure.

"You're tired, love. Come, let's go to bed."

Andrew effortlessly picks me up, cradling me to his chest and walks us down the short hallway to my bedroom. My arms hang around his neck, praying that this isn't some dream. I need to know that he's going to stay with me and keep me safe in his arms.

"Can you stand, love?" he asks.

I nod my head against his shoulder. My feet hit the floor and I sway a little when he briefly releases me from his hold.

Andrew smiles warmly at me, helping me strip out of my clothes again, only this time with no sexual context behind it. He keeps my modesty by holding my gaze while sliding a shirt over me as soon as my sweater is gone. It's endearing the way he fusses over me, thinking of all the little things I would have neglected to remember. And truly it's the little things that make the biggest impact.

My body wakes slightly as he strips out of his own clothes, leaving himself in nothing but his boxer briefs. But even with the constant hum of attraction between us, my body feels spent and tired as if the activities of the week have finally taken their toll.

Andrew pulls back the covers and then swiftly picks me up in his arms again. I laugh into his neck, thinking he really doesn't have to do this but not wanting to say anything that will stop him. The mattress is soft but the sheets are cold and I shiver slightly at the sudden change in temperature against my warmed skin.

Ever mindful, Andrew quickly crawls in beside me, allowing the heat of his body to warm me instantly. I snuggle into the firmness of his chest, my legs intertwining with his under the sheets. His lips find my hair, kissing me lightly before leaning over to turn off the lamp. My arm drapes over his body and I sigh, inhaling the sweet scent that I love.

"Goodnight, Tessa. Sweet dreams," Andrew says, kissing me once more.

"Goodnight, Andrew," I whisper back. His lips move against my hair with soft words that I'm unable to make out. My heavy lids close and the steady beating of Andrew's heart lulls me into a peaceful night's sleep.

Bright sunshine floats into the room, filling the dark space with light and warmth. And I'm warm, so warm. Almost sweltering hot. Why am I so hot? The floor is usually cold, or at least I am because the covers are never around me at that point. My eyes blink awake slowly, confusion clouding my brain. I'm warm, my face and head don't hurt and I'm still in bed. This is not my typical morning. My eyes fully open and I stare at the source of my comfort. Andrew's still asleep, allowing me the time to admire him closely without being embarrassed. Even in slumber he's impossibly handsome. The fanning of his lashes against his cheeks, the way his nostrils flare slightly as he breathes. There's even a little curl of his lip, clearly dreaming of something pleasant. Silently I hope that it's me.

My fingers twitch, wanting to touch him so badly yet I know I should let him rest. The poor man must be exhausted after what I had put him through these last few weeks. Was it really only three weeks ago that we met and found each other by some twist of fate? It seems like just yesterday yet at the same time it's as if we've known each other our entire lives. Can it be possible to know a complete stranger?

But my body has a mind of its own, letting my fingers roam over his features; a light brush of his eyebrows, watching them furrow slightly at the contact before relaxing again. I wiggle closer to him, needing the additional contact as I continue my journey, tracing the slope of his nose, rounding over his cheeks to caress the hair above his ear. My fingers maintain their loving strokes, continually threading the silky strands through my fingers. I hardly notice when his lips fully quirk into a smile.

"I will give you a million years to keep waking me like this." I can't help the giggle that escapes from being caught.

Bright blue irises greet me, the morning sun shining on them, casting a glittering spell over my own. Our heads move closer until we're nose to nose and our lips are able to reach in a slow kiss, not overly passionate but not lacking in luster. My legs move restlessly against his, my foot running up and down his calf. Andrew breaks free, nuzzling his face into the crook of my neck. Warm lips surround my lobe, dragging it slowly into his mouth and a soft moan can be heard from the back of my throat.

"Good morning, love," he says. Andrew's teeth graze against my neck making me gasp, but I hold him close so he doesn't stop. My fingers resume threading through his hair as we enjoy this peaceful moment before we fully wake.

"Good morning, handsome. Did you sleep well?" I pull back, needing to look at his face. I trace the outline of his jaw with my fingers before running them over his bottom lip. Andrew flashes me a smile and pulls me closer to him, letting me feel his morning erection at my hip. My hands travel around to his back, lightly stroking the bare skin, tracing each and every muscle I can find.

He turns his eyes to mine, making my heart flutter in my chest. Those eyes have the power to see right through me, see me for who I am and who I can be. Eyes so loving and gentle they make up the portal into this beautiful man's soul. And those eyes are firmly fixed on me.

"It was the best sleep I have had in two weeks. I love waking up next to you, seeing the dreams still floating behind your eyes. And I love how soft your lips are first thing in the morning." He leans in to verify his theory and kisses me. My lips mold to his as I lose myself in everything that is Andrew; not wanting to wake up if this is some sort of cruel dream.

But it's not. It's real. He's real. And he's here, with me, for me, wanting me. It's what I've been asking for, hasn't it?

Then why am I fighting this?

My bladder is screaming at me so I pull back to kiss the end of his nose, a gesture that he always does to me and give him a warming smile. Andrew looks confused, but I smooth the worry lines from around his mouth with my thumb.

"Don't worry I'm not going anywhere. I just need to freshen up first. I'll be back in five minutes."

When I emerge from the bathroom, I turn toward my bedroom, thinking we could resume our cuddle session. The noise coming from my kitchen has me turning that way instead, clearly indicating that cuddle time is over. The smell of coffee floats through the apartment. When I turn the corner, I'm gifted with the sight of Andrew's nearly naked body standing in front of my refrigerator, clad only in his boxer briefs. It should be a crime to be just as good looking from the back as you are in the front. Yes, washboard abs make girls drool but there's something about a well-defined back that is regularly overlooked. Every muscle is smoothed over with tanned skin, not a trace of imperfection on it. My eyes drift lower, admiring his firm ass and thighs. One can always appreciate someone who takes care of themselves. It lets you know that they can put just as much effort into other things.

I'm caught off-guard when he turns to face me as if he knew I'm admiring his perfect body. He smirks and shuts the door before slowly striding over to me as I stand there in my ratty old nightshirt. It's faded to the point of being almost see-through and has holes in places that it probably shouldn't. But it's my favorite thing to sleep in because it was the first thing I bought when I moved into my first apartment. After sleeping in my clothes for years, for lack of money or various other fearful reasons, it was nice to have something to change into at night. An overlooked luxury for some but for me, it was so much more.

I'm pulled from my past by warm hands running down my arms, pulling me close to the hard body I was admiring mere seconds ago. Soft lips connect with mine, tasting and teasing as he smiles at me. My arms find their place around his waist as I cling to him. The kiss becomes hotter, needier, and I find myself pressed against the wall behind us. Andrew's hands cradle my face as our tongues move together at a frantic pace. His hips pin my own, allowing me to feel how much he wants me, causing my own body to react in the most delicious ways. My legs tremble, my nipples harden and the pulsing throb between my legs sends a shiver up my spine as want and desire threaten to make me break my rule.

This is how a kiss is supposed to be, showing the other person how much passion there is between the two of them, how need and want are in fact the same thing. My hands travel up his back, gripping his shoulders, pulling him closer to me. I begin to pick up my leg to wrap around his waist, but he slows us down, cooling the heated air between us. It's almost as effective as dropping an ice cube into a volcano. The passion and need are still there, still crying out for him to touch me, to claim me, mark me as his. But Andrew pushes back, letting his mouth run over my jaw and down the column of my throat.

"You look so sexy standing here in that little nightshirt. I just couldn't help myself."

His words are not helping to diminish the pulse inside me as my hands travel the expanse of his back again, slightly grazing over the top of his ass before tracing along his sides.

"I could say the same thing about you."

He makes a low groan as my hands continue roaming about his body, reacquainting themselves with muscles that haven't been accessible for weeks. My lips brush against his again, causing us both to smile.

"You know this no sex agreement is killing me, right?"

Andrew's tongue traces my collarbone, making my head fall hard against the wall with a loud thud. The pain doesn't even register as he continues licking at my skin. My fingers entwine in his hair, holding him to me as my breathing speeds up, becoming more erratic and shallow.

"I know. Me too," I say breathlessly. "But we have to do it this way, even if it kills us right now."

And right now I feel as if I'm in front of a firing squad, begging to just have one last taste of pleasure before I die. And what a way to go, death by Andrew. Our lips connect one last time, slow and sweet, warm and soft before he rests his forehead against mine. Our combined breaths come in short pants, our hands moving to cup each other's face. He's my addiction, my drug, and I don't know if I'm strong enough to stop him.

We pull away from the wall, hand in hand, and walk back to the kitchen area to finish what Andrew had started before we got distracted with each other's bodies. Filling two mugs with steaming hot coffee, I give one to Andrew and I lean against the counter to watch him. His biceps flex as he brings the cup to his lips, his eyes staring intently at me over the rim.

I clear my throat and shake my head, needing to keep my

mind clear. "So what were you searching for in my fridge?"

"Well I was going to cook up some bacon and eggs, but since your refrigerator is almost bare, I can't exactly do that. What do you eat in the mornings?"

I shrug my shoulders and look down into my coffee. "I don't usually eat breakfast. It just never crosses my mind. I'm usually rushing out of here most days of the week so all I have time to grab is coffee. The caffeine keeps me going all morning."

Andrew frowns, tilting his head slightly as he looks at me. "That is not going to do, love. You need to eat more."

I look down at myself and scoff quietly. Eat more? If anything I need to eat less. Can he not see the excess lining around my stomach and thighs?

"I eat enough. I don't want to get any fatter than I already am."

I know my depreciating self-image isn't accurate and everyone always tells me the opposite of what is in my head. But the years of neglect and various other issues haven't helped in seeing me for anything other than what's in my mind's eye. Andrew must realize this because he places his mug on the counter and closes the short distance between us. He pulls me close to his body, arms protectively wrapping around my waist as he kisses the top of my head.

"You have nothing to worry about in that department. You are perfect to me, each and every piece of you."

"I just don't see what you see."

"Then I will make you see. Believe me. I have never seen a more beautiful woman in the entire world than you."

And since he's traveled the world I guess he would know. However, the nagging little voice in my head says that a man as gorgeous and perfect as Andrew also needs to have a stick figure supermodel on his arm. One that matches his beauty without working at it. I mean, he couldn't possibly be happy with just a plain Jane like me, could he?

My head slumps forward, resting on his sternum, causing him to laugh while stroking my hair lovingly. "Now that we have that cleared up, how about some breakfast?"

I pick my head up and laugh. "Well I can make toast or I can make toast, and let's see, there's also toast."

"Well with what you've told me of your culinary skills before, I'm almost afraid for you to even try making that."

My mouth drops open and he laughs even more. Picking up the dishrag, I toss it at him, narrowly missing his head, causing us both to break out in hysterics. "Just for that, you're going hungry. I am capable of making toast, thank you very much. I mean, how hard can it be? The toaster does all the work."

Andrew raises an eyebrow and I scoff. Really, how hard can it be? Then the guilt sets in, having Andrew here and not being able to give him more than toast for breakfast. I open my cupboard doors and stare at the few things inside. Perhaps he's right. Maybe I do need to keep more things in my apartment. I'm not sure why we didn't grab more things yesterday at the grocery store. Apparently all those bags didn't carry the early morning necessities.

Arms wrap around my middle, pulling me into his firm body while his chin rests on my shoulder. I can almost hear his thoughts as he stares at my selection of Honey Nut Cheerios and Cream of Wheat boxes, my only breakfast food in the apartment. Andrew lets out a sigh and I poke him with my elbow, making us both laugh a little.

Finally deciding that I *can* make Cream of Wheat with our toast, I try to get everything together for it, but with Andrew draped across my back like a clingy monkey it makes it increasingly difficult. I try to pull away, but his arms tighten around my middle, pulling me closer so I can't get away. Sighing, I give up attempting to get down my measuring cups and turn to face him instead.

"You know, this would be a lot easier if I had some wiggle room." My hands stroke his cheek, feeling that early morning stubble rough against my fingers. The smile on his face slows my heart until it matches his own rhythm.

"You can wiggle all you want against me, love. I won't complain. In fact, I encourage it."

I kiss his nose, looking into his bright shining eyes. "No more wiggling for you, Mister, until I feed you breakfast. According to some people, it's an important meal of the day. Personally I could take it or leave it."

Andrew opens his mouth as if he's going to say something but then quickly closes it. There's a flash of humor in his eyes and it makes me wonder what he was about to say. My guess would be some smartass comment, or sexual innuendo since that's the route we've steered into with this seemingly innocent conversation. Well, not too innocent I guess.

The amusement still dances in his eyes and there's an underlying fire burning brightly as well, igniting my skin right down to my core. My fingers continue to stroke his cheek, trailing lightly down to the edge of his jaw. Breakfast is briefly forgotten as his lips find mine, teasing and tasting, slowly exploring what he already knows by heart. My mouth is his as we press up against each other, each fighting the overwhelming urge to go back in the bedroom and stay there until we're sweaty and spent. It's becoming more and more impossible to fight this attraction between us; pretend that we didn't happen in London. But for the sake of our relationship, if there is one, we need to try. I pull back on a weak smile, missing his mouth against mine the minute it's gone.

"If we don't stop we'll both starve."

He nods. "You're right. We're not playing fair right now. I promise from here on out to behave in a more appropriate manner. You go sit down and relax. I'll take care of breakfast."

"You do know that I'm perfectly capable of making us breakfast, right? Besides, you're my guest and I'm fairly certain there's an unwritten rule about the guest not making the meals all the time."

Calling Andrew my guest feels strange and unnatural, especially when referring to him being here with me. Guest implies temporary visitor and as much as I fight it I know that's not what I want. He's more than that to me, not that I will admit it out loud to him.

Getting a pot out from the cabinet he smirks and points to a chair at the breakfast bar. "Yes I know you're capable of many things but I want to do this for you." He closes the small distance between us, running his hands up and down my arms. "I want to do everything for you."

Damn. How can you argue with that logic? I attempt my best pout, but it comes off as less than convincing. "Fine. But I'm making the toast." I glance between us, noting that we're still not technically wearing any clothes. "But first we should probably get dressed."

After scraping off the slightly blackened pieces of toast,

breakfast was good. Okay, so I suck at cooking. Eventually, I'll get better. Maybe with practice, or private cooking lessons. Or we'll just learn to live off of takeout, but as long as Andrew's around that will never happen. Watching him fluidly move around the kitchen is like watching an elegantly coordinated dance. Everything is seamless, flowing from one thing to the next, never a hiccup or glitch, just perfection. I swear there's nothing this man can't do.

"You make your Cream of Wheat differently than I do," I say, rinsing the dishes before putting them in the dishwasher.

Andrew gives me a puzzled look. "What do you mean?"

"Well, every time I make it, it comes out in a giant clump. That's how it's supposed to be, isn't it?"

He laughs, wiping off the stove. "I'm pretty sure it's not meant to be lumpy. That's why it's called *Cream* of Wheat."

"Well, my way is hearty. A stick-to-your-bones type of breakfast."

"However you like it, Tessa. You won't find me arguing with you about it."

We finish cleaning up, content on being domestic hermits for the day. Andrew's grand plan for us this weekend: stay inside and hang out. To me, that's paradise. No running around the city, no dealing with traffic or tourists. Just the two of us, hanging out, spending time together to really get to know the other. That is priceless and means more to me than any trip we could possibly take.

So our day consists of cribbage and Go Fish, which apparently even for a kid's game I still suck at. We watch some godawful movies and have popcorn wars like we did back at his place in London. Andrew is a lover of bad movie nights like me. There's nothing better than a horribly stupid comedy or an old Eighties movie that you thought was so awesome back in the day and watch now and can't believe that you liked it.

Once we get sick of the TV, Andrew picks up my Kindle and starts to read a book to me. I lay on the couch with my head in his lap, listening to his sexy voice that makes my panties melt. Andrew reading a romance novel out loud is my new favorite thing. If I could get a recording of him reading every single book that I own, I would never leave my house. Who needs Audible when you have Andrew?

It makes me realize that I want to have this every single day for the rest of my life. We didn't do anything fantastic, just spent time together, being with each other, making the other laugh. Andrew kept me close to his side all day, always within reach, always touching me or holding my hand. What's more is he still thought I was sexy, even though I was in nothing but sweats and a messy ponytail.

"You look beautiful," Andrew whispers in my ear.

"You're crazy," I reply back, leaning my head against his shoulder. We just stare out the window, looking at the lights in the now darkened street. Soft music floats around us from Andrew's specialized playlist that he created. Each and every song deals with second chances and finding the love of a lifetime. It takes everything in me not to read too much into it, but with those powerful songs it's hard not to.

His arms wrap around me and he shakes his head. "Only about you."

I ruin the moment by yawning loudly. As always my timing is impeccable. His soft blue eyes find mine. "Tired?"

I nod as he picks me up, carrying me just like he did last

night to the bedroom. My head is still resting on his shoulder as we walk through my apartment, turning off the lights and locking the door. I nuzzle my nose into his neck, one of my favorite places on him. Andrew puts me on the floor at the foot of my bed and runs his hands down my arms.

"I'll be right back. I just want to go get ready in the bathroom."

He smiles and nods but I can feel his gaze on my retreating form as I walk down the hall, needing to brush my teeth and gargle about a gallon of mouthwash. I lean back against the closed bathroom door and can't help but smile. Never once did I think I'd be so enthralled with a man before I met Andrew. Our day was perfect. It was everything we needed to get to know each other. Temporary amnesia be damned, there's no way that I will ever be able to stop thinking about Andrew and what we could have together.

I reenter the bedroom to find Andrew propped up against the headboard of my bed, completely naked from the waist up and only allowing the sheet to cover his lap. A million different scenarios play through my mind, none of which is rated less than NC-17. Why does a man with a body like his want someone like me? That is the great question of the universe.

Flicking the light switch off, I crawl into bed next to the Adonis, tracing his muscles with my fingers in the muted light. Andrew lowers himself onto the bed, pulling me to his side. His lips find my head, giving repeated kisses upon my crown. My arm drapes across his chest, letting my head rest on his shoulder. Our bodies mold together like two perfect puzzle pieces.

Our lips find each other in the dark, pressing lightly together, leaving us both with a contented sigh at the end.

"Thank you for today. It was perfect."

He nods his head in agreement. "It was everything I've ever wanted. I just want to be with you. You, my dearest Tessa, are everything to me. If you told me you wanted to fly around the world, I would make it happen. If you said that you wanted to just lie in bed all day and stare at the ceiling, I would crawl next to you and count the dust flying through the air with you. Wherever you are, whatever you're doing, I want to be there next to you."

My heart expands just a fraction more as I kiss him softly and snuggle back into the comfort of his chest, falling into another night of peaceful sleep.

Chapter 12

LIGHT FEATHERY KISSES RAIN UPON my face, pulling me from the peaceful slumber I was enjoying. Waking up in my warm bed is definitely preferred over the cold hard floor. Having Andrew's arms wrapped around me isn't quite so bad either. A girl could get used to waking up like this. My focus narrows to only Andrew as his lips travel across my eyes, my nose, my cheeks, finally landing upon my lips, brushing them ever so softly until a contented sigh escapes. His fingers trail a pattern across my stomach as I blink into his heavenly sapphire eyes, way too bright and shiny for this early in the morning.

"I love looking into your eyes the first thing in the morning," he whispers, placing his lips against mine again. My fingers entwine with the ones caressing my stomach, keeping him pinned to me because I don't want him to let me go. Not yet.

"Good morning. How long have you been up?"

I crane my neck to check the time on my alarm clock, but it's a futile effort. Andrew quickly brings my attention back to him. Well, sort of. His mouth blazes a trail down my extended neck, nipping and sucking as he explores the area thoroughly.

"Not long. I just wanted to be the first thing you saw when you opened your eyes this morning."

He lifts his head up, brushing back a few snarled tendrils behind my ear. The back of his hand sweeps across my cheek, causing my eyelids to flutter like a hummingbird's wings. The sensations his touch brings will never get old and I can only hope they never go away either.

Our hands travel lovingly across each other's bodies, my fingers trail up his arm, his hand runs around to press against the small of my back, pulling me flush against him. Soon my fingers are tangled in his hair, letting the dark silky strands run through them. Andrew closes his eyes and I focus on his lashes as they fan out against his cheek. He hasn't shaved since Friday, which has created some seriously sexy stubble.

His words come back to me, waking up my foggy brain which is still half asleep. He wants to be the first thing I see every morning? For a man who supposedly didn't return my affections only three weeks ago, he certainly has become well versed in saying just the right things. And would it truly be that much of a hardship to look into his face every morning? Okay, twist my arm. I'll suffer through that for the rest of my life if I have to.

Reluctantly I pull away from his touch, needing to start our day, even though staying here in bed would be ideal. However, if we stay here, I know where we'll end up and that cannot happen yet. Not until I have my mind straight and my ducks in a row, so to speak.

We both sit up in bed, the covers falling from our bodies,

revealing my nightshirt and his sculpted bare chest. Suddenly it's too warm in here as my eyes travel across the expanse of tanned skin, washing over every defined muscle until they reach where his lower half stays hidden beneath the sheet. I try to avert my eyes before Andrew notices me blatantly staring at him, but I'm too late. His quiet chuckle dances around us and my cheeks redden with embarrassment. Andrew lifts my hand to his lips, softening the mood even though his eyes are still dancing with amusement.

"Are you hungry?" I ask. His eyes spark and a slow grin appears on his face.

"Famished. What did you have in mind?" He's using his sex voice and it's killing me to have to deny him. Part of me thinks he's doing this on purpose, trying to get a rise out of me, or attempting to get me to cave. Deep down I know he wouldn't do that. Andrew knows the importance of why I'm doing this the way I am. He wants me to be sure and without a doubt that whomever I choose is the one for me.

Andrew wets his lower lip and I withhold a groan in response. Damn him. My lips quirk up in a smile and I shrug. "Well, since we had Cream of Wheat yesterday I thought we should eat Honey Nut Cheerios today."

I'm laughing as Andrew moans loudly, throwing his arm over his eyes and falling back onto the pillow in a rather overdramatic fashion, making me laugh even harder. Picking up my pillow, I playfully smack him in the stomach with it. He laughs and retaliates by pulling me down to him, my body stretching fully over his.

"What am I going to do with you?" Andrew smiles, making my heart pick up speed slightly. "Promise me you'll buy some real food soon. I'd hate to think about what you do for lunches and dinners when I'm not around." He cups my face, looking deep into my eyes, allowing me to see his concern and sincerity for my wellbeing. Having someone worry over me is too new and I really don't know how to handle it. No one has ever truly cared if I had enough clothes or ate enough food before. It's a difficult concept to grasp at times, but I'm hoping the longer I stay around those types of people, the easier it will become.

"Okay, I promise. I'll go grocery shopping soon. But until then it's Honey Nut Cheerios for breakfast." I lean down to kiss his nose, making the both of us smile before I hop off the bed so we can get ready for the day.

While Andrew is busy in the shower, I notice the laundry hamper is almost full as I pick up a few stray dirty clothes from the floor. Is it really Sunday today? Where has the weekend gone? I swear Andrew just got here and now it's time for him to leave already. A dull ache strikes my chest when I realize I don't want him to go. Everything about this weekend has been so relaxed and unrushed. It's exactly what we needed, what I needed, to prove to myself that Andrew and I can be more than a physical attraction. That we can be two people who care for each other, listen to their thoughts and dreams, encourage them to follow the path they want. And knowing we have that connection without anything physical is essential to any possible relationship.

When Andrew walks back into the room, fresh from his shower, all chaste thoughts of this weekend vanish. He's clad in only a towel, hung low on his hips while beads of water disappear into it as they run down his chest and back. My mouth feels like Niagara Falls and subconsciously I remind myself not to drool. I've seen this man naked before but not like this. Not in my bedroom. Not with my towel wrapped around his narrow waist.

Lucky towel.

Andrew raises a brow at me and smirks. "Thinking of anything good?" He adjusts the towel with one hand while reaching into his overnight bag that's sitting on the edge of my bed. I blink, repeatedly, praying for my voice to find me and not sound like some stupid horny little teenager.

"Yeah," I squeak.

Well, so much for that. If Andrew couldn't guess what I was thinking about before, he most certainly is aware of it now.

Then he drops his towel.

Oh.

My.

God.

My heart goes into arrest as he stands there in all his glory. The water droplets are still running down his chest due to his damp hair and my eyes follow their trail, no longer getting absorbed by the towel that was around his waist. No, they travel further down, down into regions that make my body scream with pleasure. I mentally record the image of his naked body in my room for use at a later date. I want this picture to be the first thing I see whenever I close my eyes or blink.

The spell is broken as he slides his boxer briefs over his hips, blocking my view of his … assets. I blink several times, willing my higher brain function to return.

Hello? Brain?

Radio silence.

It may need a few more minutes to recuperate.

Andrew slides his jeans on, leaving the top button undone, sending another round of shocks to my heart. I'm about to stride over to him and throw him down on my bed, no sex rule be damned, when my phone begins ringing on the table next to my bed. My brow furrows when I see whose name it is across the screen.

"Hello?"

"Tessa, good morning. I hope I didn't wake you," my dad says.

He sounds different. He sounds … happy. Happy to hear from me? I want to pinch myself to make sure that I'm not dreaming.

"No, you didn't wake me. I've been up for a while." There's an awkward pause between us. I wish it weren't so weird to talk to my dad. "So, what's going on?"

Andrew creates a pleasing distraction as I watch him get dressed. Only he could make putting socks on sexy. But my dad's voice on the other line brings me back to the subject at hand.

"I was wondering if you wanted to come to the house for dinner tonight."

Oh boy, another family fun night with my dad and Sharon. I must admit that things with my dad have been more pleasant lately, but after the stunt Sharon pulled at her birthday party I just don't trust that she'll hold back her opinions anymore. Apprehension shoots through my system, almost like a Botox injection, rendering me paralyzed as a million other things I'd rather do stream through my head. But he is trying and I can't discredit him for that. It's my own hang-ups I need to get over now. Well, mine and Sharon's. I can only work on my end. The other part is up to her.

I swallow harshly and nod as if he could see it. "Sure, dinner sounds good. What time would you like me there?"

The Sunday paper rustles in the background, indicating that he's at the breakfast table enjoying his morning coffee. It's a very standard, typical, mundane thing to do. It's just not how I see my dad, even though I know he is just a regular guy.

"Does six o'clock work for you?"

"Six works just fine. I guess I'll see you around then."

"See you tonight Tessa. I'm really looking forward to it. Have a good rest of the day," he says. There's a hint of a smile in his voice and for the second time I'm stunned into silence this morning.

"You too. Bye, Dad."

I hit end and toss the phone on my bed before sinking down next to Andrew. His fingers run through my hair as I lean my head against his shoulder. When his lips press against my forehead, I sigh and snuggle closer to his neck.

"Dinner with your dad tonight?"

I nod. "Yeah. Seems to be an every other weekend thing lately. I just hope to survive it."

Andrew doesn't say anything. He knows I just need a moment to sort through it. It helps that Andrew already knows the situation between my dad and me. He knows how strained it is, how distant the two of us are. But the distance seems to be closing, as evident by the recent events. He seems more open to a relationship, starting with just a simple conversation and inviting me to places without any ulterior motives. The party was my first indication that perhaps he's ready to actually be a dad to me and not out of pity or obligation. And now with this early morning invitation, we seem to be making strides in the right direction. Maybe he really does want to be in my life and vice versa.

With one last kiss on my head, Andrew stands, bringing me with him. "Come, let me make you the best bowl of Honey Nut Cheerios you've ever had."

Andrew stayed with me until the very last minute. We cleaned and danced, lounged and read, he even walked with me down the block to do my laundry. It was the best Sunday I've had in a long time, even if we didn't do anything spectacular.

But now as we drive to go get my car from the parking ramp, my nerves start to kick in. I have the sudden urge to flee, or better yet, have Andrew take me with him so I don't have to go to that house. Andrew must notice my discomfort because he places a gentle hand on my bouncing knee, instantly relaxing it.

"You'll be fine, love. I promise."

I marginally turn my head to look at him. "You think so?"

He nods. "I know so. You're stronger than you think you are Tessa. And you said so yourself, the last few weeks have been encouraging with your dad reaching out to you. I think he's really trying to make up for his lack of parenting skills from your younger years. You should let him try at least. What's the harm in that?"

My lips twist to the side as I consider it. "I guess there's no harm in letting him try to be a real dad. But honestly it's not him that scares me. It's Sharon."

Andrew cups my chin, tilting it up so I can look into his

eyes. "Don't worry about her either. Your dad will see her for who she truly is."

"You think so?"

"I know so. No one in their right mind would ever pick that shrew over you."

He leans forward, pressing his lips against mine as we stay seated in the front seats of his rental car. My body relaxes, allowing Andrew to soothe my frayed nerves. I'm not sure what it is about Andrew that gives me a calming effect so effortlessly, but I love it.

We pull away and my eyes follow Andrew as he exits the car to open the door for me. As I slide out of the front seat, I'm instantly pulled into him as he ravishes my mouth while pressing me against the side of the car. Our hands cup each other's face, binding us to the kiss, making sure that there's always contact between us. Emotions begin building inside me, begging to be released. Unspoken words float around in my head and travel down to my throat, pleading to be spoken.

But I can't and I won't. Not yet. I need just a little more time to figure out if this is really going to work between us.

As much as it pains me to do so, I pull back but he doesn't let me go far. He keeps his forehead pressed against mine, our combined breaths meeting in the space between. His eyes are squeezed tight and a look of pain goes across his face.

"I'm finding it difficult to let you go right now. I don't want this to end. This weekend was … it was …"

"It was perfect," I say, finishing his sentence. Those blazing blue eyes find mine and I watch as his lips curl into a smile.

"Perfect. Exactly. When can I see you again?" he asks, still stroking my hair with his hands.

"We still have our regular lunch dates, unless you've got meetings planned this week."

Andrew pulls back and walks us over to the driver's side door of my car. "Unfortunately I do. But I don't want to miss any time with you."

"We'll figure something out," I reassure him. And we will because if I didn't see Andrew every day it could very well break me.

Andrew nods before cradling my head in his hands. "This was the best weekend I've had so far. I can't wait to have many, many more with you, love."

I grab his waist, wrapping my arms around him. I pull him close to me, letting myself cave to my desire to be near him at all times. This is harder than I thought it would be. I don't want to let him go either but this is the way it must be for now.

"It was a great weekend," I agree, not wanting to declare that my heart agrees with the second half of his statement. All emotions along those lines must be locked away to be used in another place and time.

Andrew's lips find mine and I struggle to keep a tear at bay. This isn't goodbye. I'm still going to see him every day if our schedules work out. Maybe we can sneak in a few dinners this week if we're both not dead after our work day.

We pull back from each other, sadness gracing both our faces. Andrew opens my door for me then shuts it when I'm comfortably settled and buckled in. He raps on my window, placing his palm flat to me. I match up our hands together, noticing how much larger his hand is compared to mine. The heat from his body passes through the glass, allowing my own hand to feel it as it continues straight to my heart.

We don't say goodbye because that's not what this is. Andrew simply waves at me as I pull away from him.

This is not goodbye.

Even still, it doesn't hurt any less.

The drive to Lilydale is uneventful, which I'm thankful for. Traffic is minimal, but then again it is Sunday evening. Not many people are milling about. Most normal people are at home, eating dinners with their families, getting the necessary things ready for the work and school week ahead. They're not nervously chewing their nails as they navigate the streets of the upper class, sticking out like a sore thumb with their beat up car.

Miriam's friendly face greets me right away as I walk up to the front doors. "Tessa, so glad to see you again." She squeezes me tight, hardly allowing my arms to move to return the gesture. I laugh a little when I'm finally able to breathe again.

"Hi, Miriam, glad to see you too. How's Colin doing? Is he still working those evening shifts at the bar?"

Miriam nods and helps me remove my jacket, despite my protests. She places it on the hall tree while I remove my boots, tucking them underneath.

"Yes, he's always at that crazy pub these days. Still haven't found enough staff to cover shifts. But it's also more money for us if you want to look at it that way."

"That's true. But he must get tired of working all the time."

"Sometimes I think he's running himself ragged trying to do everything, but then he proves me wrong and I just let him do his thing. Him coming home to me in one piece every night is all that matters."

Miriam gives me a playful wink as we walk down the hall to the living room where my dad and Sharon are. My dad has his nose in a book and Sharon is reading another fashion magazine. I quietly clear my throat to announce myself and my dad looks up at me. A large smile crosses his face as he removes his glasses, placing them and the book on the table next to his oversized chair.

"Tessa, I'm so glad you made it. Please, come in and make yourself at home." He holds his arm out to the matching chair next to his and I take it without thought. My smile matches his as I sink down into the plush, soft leather. "How much longer until dinner Miriam?" he asks.

"Just another five minutes and it'll be ready."

"Thank you, Miriam."

I watch her retreat back to the kitchen then look around the room. Sharon hasn't even acknowledged my existence yet. Not that I would expect her to. It wouldn't break my heart if she didn't talk to me the entire time I was here. In fact, that would make my night.

"So Tessa, anything exciting happen lately? I apologize for not phoning you earlier in the week, but my schedule has been quite busy."

I shrug my shoulders. "It's okay. I know you're busy so don't worry about that."

"Still, I should make a more conscious effort. Tell me, how was the first week in your new position?"

I smile, thinking back upon my week. "It was good. I don't have any accounts yet, but Chris is working on transferring some to me. And I picked out my new assistant, which is an immense relief. She's a grad student at the U of M, going for her MBA. Oh! And Chris asked Kara to marry him on Friday. It was very romantic. I'm so happy for them."

"Well, you must give Kara my congratulations when you see her tomorrow."

"I will. I don't think I've ever seen the two of them this happy before. They really are perfect together."

Sharon scoffs from behind her magazine before throwing it down on the coffee table next to her, drawing my dad's attention right away. He gives her an annoyed glare, which throws me off a little. Luckily we're all saved by Miriam, who announces that dinner is ready now. The three of us follow behind Miriam, only this time my dad is not escorting Sharon by the arm like he did two weeks ago. I don't dwell on it because it's really none of my business. However, I can't help but internally gloat when my dad holds out my chair before he holds out Sharon's. That's getting chalked up to a win in my category. And the look on Sharon's perfect face is truly priceless. I'm fairly positive that her eyes would have bounced across the table if they could.

Miriam brings out our dinner, an elegant and deliciously smelling rack of lamb, complete with all the fixings. She serves my dad first, then Sharon and finally me. I smile at my plate, thankful that she's arranged it so it looks like I have more food than what is really there. She's always good at having my dad believe I'm eating more than I do. I risk a glance and note that he's smiling at me.

The silence surrounding the three of us isn't uncomfortable or deafening, which is a very pleasant surprise. The usual tension isn't quite as palpable, more than likely due to the change in attitude from my dad.

"How are things with Michael?"

I swallow hard, curious as to why he's asking about him. "Good. We have coffee every morning and see each other in passing every once in a while."

"Any plans outside of coffee with him?"

"No, he's not that type of friend. We just like to hang out together and talk. He's an excellent listener and he's hilarious. Plus it helps that he's in my building so it's easy for us to get together."

My gaze falls over to Sharon, who sneers at her plate before laughing out loud. She picks up her wineglass and holds it in front of her highly amused face.

"How is it going juggling two guys at once? Don't you get confused?" she spits at me before taking a hasty sip of her wine. I stop twirling my fork, letting it fall noisily to the plate. Holy crap, how does she know about Andrew? My leg begins to bounce beneath the table and I repeatedly tuck the same piece of hair behind my ear.

My dad frowns at her. "What are you talking about Sharon?"

The Cheshire cat-like grin crossing her face scares me as ice begins to run through my veins. "Well, I mean, she must really be getting around when she brings two guys to the same party. Kind of tacky to me, but hey, whatever gets you through the night."

Sharon slides a piece of lamb into her mouth, making a satisfied humming sound. My stomach turns and rolls around like I'm on a rollercoaster. The smug look on her face lets me know that she's not going to let this drop. Oh no, she's going to really play this up and paint me as something I'm not.

My dad looks between the two of us then turns to me with sympathetic eyes. I don't want him to think I'm a whore because I'm not. There's nothing going on with Michael and I don't know why Sharon is trying to paint a different picture than what is really there.

"It's not like that," I whisper softly. My voice is barely audible and my eyes burn with unshed tears, barely contained by my weakening will. Out of the corner of my eye, I can see my dad sitting there, waiting for some sort of explanation. I sigh, just wanting to get this over with so I can leave here quickly when all hell breaks loose. "Do you remember when I told you about the Head of Operations for the Tree of Life Foundation?"

My dad nods his head, setting his silverware down on his plate. "Yes, the gentleman who escorted you around London. What was his name again?"

"Andrew. Andrew Parker. He and I … we … well we kind of started something in London, but I didn't think it would work out because of our jobs and the distance and then we had a misunderstanding." I pause, taking a sip of liquid courage as I lay it all out for my dad. "He was supposed to be here this week but came a week early instead."

"Because of you?" he asks, tilting his head slightly.

"Yes. He found out I was going to be at the party so he showed up, letting me know he wants to pursue a real relationship with me. That he needs to be with me and only me. I was surprised and shocked to see him, but all of the old feelings came rushing back to me and I couldn't ignore them. So we've decided to take things slow. Try to date and have a real relationship."

My dad stays quiet for a moment, his fingers tented in front of his mouth. "So this Andrew, do you like him?"

I nod my head for fear of saying the words I don't want to voice yet.

Sharon just laughs. "I don't buy it. I saw the way Michael was looking at you at the party and vice versa. You two obviously have something going on besides friendship. So what did you do? Kick him to the curb when this other guy showed up? Were the sheets of your bed even cool before you brought this Andrew to bed with you?"

I shrink back as far as I can into my chair, wanting to disappear altogether. I knew coming here would be a bad idea. There was no way Sharon would leave me alone, especially now that she knows about Andrew.

A lone tear treks down my cheek as I push away my half-eaten plate, my appetite truly gone now. But I'm slightly jostled out of my self-pity by the slamming of my dad's fist against the table. I watch as he slowly stands from his chair, looming over Sharon.

"That is enough Sharon. I will not tolerate you speaking to Tessa that way. You will never insinuate that my daughter is a whore. Ever."

Sharon is stunned into silence. Hell, I'm stunned into silence. Her mouth gapes open, but then it twists into the ugliest scowl I've ever witnessed while simultaneously arching her perfect eyebrow. "Really Robert? Then what would you call it? She shows up at a party and entertains two men throughout the night. I mean pretty soon she'll be down at the corners on Lake Street along with all of the other working girls."

The look on my dad's face is borderline murderous. You

can physically see the red crawling up his face with each passing second. "I will not sit here and listen to you speak about *my daughter* that way. It is not allowed in this house!" he yells, putting emphasis on my title.

Sharon stands as well, throwing her napkin onto her plate. She stabs a pointy finger toward my dad. "You will not speak to me, *your wife*, that way Robert." She pushes away from the table. "I'm leaving for a while. Don't wait up for me." Sharon stalks out of the room with my dad still fuming silently, watching her with cold eyes before we hear the slamming of the front door followed by the loud screech of her tires.

It feels like everything just happened in slow motion. I have never witnessed an ill word spoken between Sharon and my dad. He's always appeared to worship the ground she walked on, ignorant to her feelings toward me. Although with this little display, perhaps I was wrong about that. Maybe he wasn't unaware of her actions. Perhaps he was just waiting to hit his limit.

Unable to hold it back anymore, I quietly sob to myself, my head still hanging down, letting my hair hide my shame. My shoulders shake with each sob, reliving each and every word Sharon spewed about me.

"Tessa, please don't cry. What Sharon said is not true." His hand is light on my shoulder, reassuring his statement with that small gesture. I look up and am greeted by my own eyes looking back at me. "I do not think that of you so please don't believe a word she says." I nod and he retakes his seat. His hand moves to my forearm, wanting to give some sort of comfort to me. "Now, tell me about Andrew."

How do I describe Andrew to my dad without sounding

like a lovestruck teenager? "Andrew is, well, I don't know how to explain him. He's kind and caring and always thinking of others. He treats me well and is a perfect gentleman. Obviously he's smart since he went to school at Oxford and holds the position that he does with the Foundation. Andrew is always polite and has impeccable manners. He makes me laugh constantly and I'm so happy when he's around. It's like I'm a totally different person. Well, not different I suppose. Maybe someone more like me or how I used to be, or how I could have been." My eyes fall onto my dad's, watching him wince ever so slightly at my last comment. I swallow hard and continue. "Andrew brings something out of me that I never knew I had. The way he looks at me, wanting to be around me all the time, never satisfied with any amount of space between us … I don't know, it makes me feel cherished I guess."

My dad smiles at me and I feel better. My whole body lets out a collective sigh, relaxing back into my chair, the tension of earlier now forgotten. Is it because of that smile or because I'm thinking about Andrew? Could it be a combination of both?

"I would very much like to meet this Andrew if you wouldn't mind."

I nervously chew the inside of my cheek. "You would?"

He nods. "Yes. Any man who has my daughter's attention like that is someone I need to meet."

"Okay. I could try to set something up for the three of us. I'll have to check with Andrew, see what his schedule is first."

"Good. You said he was scheduled to be here for work this week?" I nod. "How long will he be here then?"

My fingers twist in my lap and another smile ghosts my face. "Andrew said he will be here for an undetermined amount of time. He wants to prove to me that we belong together and are meant to be."

"That's good to hear. If he looks at you the way you describe him, then I know everything will work out for the best."

"I guess a part of me is scared because he's my first real relationship and I don't want to mess anything up."

My dad pauses to take a sip of wine. "How do you feel when you're with him?"

"Safe, happy, elated," I reply, not hesitating to respond.

He nods his head and smiles. "All good qualities in a man. He hasn't forced you into anything you're not ready for, has he?"

He's thinking about Shawn right now, the ex-boyfriend that ruined me. The guilt he feels over not being able to protect me must continually eat at him. It's the reason why he acts the way he does around me. My childhood and the months spent in foster care could have been prevented. I'm sure he feels guilty on some level over those years. And then the monster of the boy who I thought cared for me adds to another layer of guilt. Although he really doesn't need to feel guilty about Shawn. No one could have seen that coming, least of all him.

And the guilt needs to stay in the past because as far as I'm concerned it's over and done with. I don't want to give power to those who don't deserve it. And the figures and events of my past don't deserve another glance. There's a future for me that has the ability to erase the ugliness of what's been done. Like a magical do-over button.

I shake my head. "No, Dad, never. He's been nothing but gentle with me. And he knows about my past so he's extra cautious to make sure everything is on my terms and my pace."

He nods. "Good. I'm glad to hear that."

And that's the last we talk about the subject because it makes the both of us uncomfortable. So we spend the next half hour just talking about random topics, causing us both to laugh at the more ridiculous parts. The smile on my face has become a permanent fixture and I like it. Opening up to my dad about what's going on in my life feels good. And his genuine concern and interest in what I'm doing pleases me to no end. We could actually have a functional relationship if this keeps going.

When it's time for me to leave, he walks me to the foyer, helping me into my jacket and waits patiently while I lace my boots.

"Tessa, I want to apologize again for Sharon's behavior tonight. I assure you it won't happen again."

I sling my purse over my shoulder and shrug my shoulders. "It's all right Dad. Thank you for inviting me over. It was fun. Well, the last half was fun."

There's a smile on his face but then he surprises me when he pulls me in for an awkward side hug. I take advantage of the contact and hold him tight, pretending that we're really a family.

"Drive safe, please. I worry about you in that car of yours. Now that you have a new job, do you think you could buy something a bit safer?"

Not that I haven't had the same thoughts go through my mind before, especially when winter is fast approaching. But it still gets me from place to place and I'd rather not have a car payment right now. It may be old, but it's mine, free and clear.

"Maybe. I know I'm getting a raise and all with this promotion, but I don't know if I want to start putting myself into debt with a newer car. Money's still kind of tight for me."

He shakes his head. "You know I can help you with that."

"I know, but I want to do this on my own. You shouldn't have to carry my problems around with you. I am an adult after all. Besides that would put another rift between you and Sharon and I don't want to be the cause for you two to fight."

My dad lets out an audible sigh. "You let me worry about Sharon. Do you need anything? More clothes for work perhaps?"

I smile. "No, I'm good there. But thank you."

"If you need anything, please just let me know. There's nothing wrong with asking for help when you need it."

"I know." We walk out onto the front steps. The chill of the night air has a slight bite to it, making me wish I would have started my car about ten minutes ago. I step next to my car and wave back to him. "Goodnight, Dad."

He waves back, a large smile on his face. "Goodnight, Tessa."

The freezing cold steering wheel numbs my fingers as I make my way back to the city and my now empty apartment. It feels lifeless without Andrew here. And quiet. I don't like it. All I want to do is go to sleep and rest my head after the evening I endured.

The bed looks small now, all freshly made and lacking a large, dark-haired presence in it. Throwing the sheets back, I smile when I find a surprise waiting for me. *Sneaky bastard.* Andrew's sweatshirt, the one he wore yesterday during our lounge day, is spread across his side of the bed, the arms of it stretched out toward mine side. I know he wants me to think of him. Not that I could ever stop. There's a reason why I never washed the nightshirt I'm wearing again. It still smells of him and I don't want that smell to go away just yet. But I cling to the sweatshirt as I crawl into bed, my head on his pillow, immersing myself in everything that is Andrew before falling asleep, wishing that he was here.

Chapter 13

CHARLENE WALKS INTO MY OFFICE, bringing the large stack of files I asked her to find for me. She has been my lifesaver this week. Definitely a great pick for my new assistant, even if it was done in the most unconventional way. At least she was able to start right away after I let her know the good news.

"Here you go, Tessa. Is there anything else I can get for you?"

Her sweet smile lights up her face. I return her smile, hoping to pass it off as believable. "No, no I'm good. Thanks, Charlene. How's everything coming along with you?"

"So far so good. Everyone's been really friendly so far, helping me out with everything and answering all of my stupid questions. And, believe me, I've had a lot."

I laugh. "It's a lot to take in at first, but you seem to be getting a handle on it quickly. Pretty soon you'll be running my schedule better than me. Then I'll be back to your position and will probably end up as your assistant."

Charlene shakes her head with a nervous laugh. "I don't think so. You're an awesome boss to work for and I don't think I could ever do your job. At least not right now. Between here and school I'm kind of on overload."

"I can only imagine. If you ever need a break or if it gets to be too much for you just let me know. We'll work something out."

"Thanks. I really appreciate that," Charlene says before giving me a small wave and returning back to her cube. She reminds me of me at the beginning, ambitious yet very unsure. I guess I'm still like that, even with my best efforts to try and hide it. It's a hard habit to break, but self-assurance isn't exactly one of my strong suits.

A knock at my door has my head picking up from the newly placed files. Kara leisurely strolls into my office, throwing herself into one of the empty chairs in front of my desk. "What's up, Chickie? How's your first account going? Have you already hit it out of the park?"

"Not entirely, but so far it's looking good. I'm just happy that it's pretty straight forward. Nothing too complicated, unlike some of the stuff that you and I had previously worked on together. I have a meeting with their CEO in about an hour to go over some final details and then I should have the contract signed by early next week."

Kara claps her hands together, giving a little hoot in the process. "I knew you'd be perfect for the job." She fidgets with her nails before looking back at me. "So tell me how your love life is going so far? Anything new on that front?"

A groan escapes my lips as I begin massaging my temples. "Other than the daily headaches I'm getting, no there's nothing new."

"Still scared to admit your feelings?" she asks.

I sigh audibly, slumping back into my chair. "Yeah."

Kara gives me a sympathetic smile. "I honestly don't know why you're fighting this. You both are absolutely crazy for each other. How many dates have you been on in the last two weeks?"

"Let's see. We do lunch everyday, or most days depending on his schedule, and we had our weekend together. Does that count as one date or two?"

"Two. I think you need all the help you can get."

I roll my eyes. "Funny. We've gone out to dinner three times this week and twice the week prior, so how many is that?"

Kara taps her fingers against the armrest. "Enough for you to figure things out. You go on more dates than Chris and I do."

"But you're engaged and live together. You don't have to go on dates."

She shakes her head. "No, we need to go on dates *because* we live together. We have to work at it still, even though we're always with the other. If we don't change things up every once in a while, things will become stagnant and we'll develop a rut. And I refuse to be one of those people who take their relationship for granted." She raises an eyebrow to me and I know what she's trying to say.

"Okay, fine. So we've been on more dates than not over the past two weeks."

Kara waits expectantly for more. "And?"

I open my mouth, prepared to tell her I have no idea how to proceed further when another knock comes to my door. A delivery man stands in the doorway with a large bouquet of flowers in a crystal vase.

"Ms. Martin?" he asks, walking further into my office.

"Yes, that's me."

He hands me a clipboard to sign while placing the flowers on my desk. I hand it back to him and he nods his head after confirming I've signed in the right spot.

"Thank you. Have a nice afternoon," he says, turning quickly to leave. Kara jumps up instantly, snagging the card from the clear plastic stake before I even have a chance to look at it.

"Let's see who it's from, shall we? As if we didn't already know." She opens the envelope while my eyes glide over the flowers. Bright, multicolored Gerbera daisies, laced with peach colored roses, are perfectly arranged in the vase, which also sports a large green bow, my favorite color. He's finally figured out my favorite flowers, right down to the color of the roses. How did he manage to do this? I don't remember giving him any hints to either one of those flowers.

"Can I have the card, please? I'm fairly positive they're for me, not you."

Kara pouts, handing me the card while leaning forward to take in the sweet fragrance. "I never get flowers anymore," she pouts.

"Really? Did you completely forget what happened last week? Your office looked like a freaking flower shop."

The memory of her proposal causes her lips to quirk into a smile as her fingers gently caress the large diamond on her left finger. She laughs lightly and shakes her head. "That's not the same as getting random flowers just because he's thinking about me."

"Don't complain," I say, looking at the already open card and seeing the familiar neat handwriting scrawled across it.

> These flowers do not hold a candle to your natural beauty. I love our time together and cannot wait until I see you again. Think of us.
>
> Yours, Andrew

My fingers reach out to graze each petal, making my heart swell with each stroke as it yearns to be filled with Andrew's love and a future together with him. Kara looks up with a smile on her face as she watches my reaction. My lips twist to the side in contemplation.

"Quick question for you."

"Shoot," she says.

"Did you say anything to him about my favorite flowers?"

Kara shakes her head. "No, why?"

I sink back into my chair with a sigh. "I assume you've had a hand in it since you've been in cahoots with Andrew from the very beginning.."

"My lips have been sealed on this matter, I swear to you. I've never once uttered your favorite flowers, nor has he asked me about them. But hey, props to my man for figuring it out all on his own. Go Andrew!" she says with a fist pump to the air.

I toss a wadded up piece of paper at her and sigh. "You're

incorrigible."

Kara shrugs while ducking out of the way. "Yeah, but you love me." She stands from her chair and stretches her arms above her head. "Okay lover lady, I'm ditching you to go molest my fiancé." She gives me her customary wave over her shoulder as she exits my office.

I stare at the bouquet, amazed that Andrew has managed to figure it out. We just had lunch not more than two hours ago and he never once let on that I should be expecting a delivery today. But then again he wouldn't have wanted to ruin the surprise. I pick up my phone and begin typing out a text to him.

Andrew, thank you for the flowers. They're absolutely beautiful. How did you know they were my favorites? ~T~

Charlene comes in, looking like she's been restraining herself for as long as possible. "Wow, those are beautiful Tessa. I saw the delivery guy when I was making copies and just had to find out who they were going to. Are they from your boyfriend?"

Boyfriend? Well, there's a complicated statement. I ponder quickly on how to respond to the question.

"Yes, they're from the guy I'm seeing."

"I love Gerberas. They're so beautiful," she says, bringing her nose closer.

"They're my favorite," I reply.

Charlene smiles. "He must really like you then if he knows your favorite flower. Most guys are generic and just send red roses. I mean, they're beautiful and all, but I don't know many women who actually choose them as their favorite. My favorite flower is a lily. Brian, my ex-boyfriend, used to decorate our old apartment with them constantly."

She sighs at the memory. Another hopeless romantic like myself. I can definitely see us getting along, even becoming friends. We share way too much in common already. "I must say I agree on the whole red rose thing. I am a sucker for brightly colored Gerberas and peach colored roses. They're kind of hard to find, which is why I like them."

"Well, he certainly nailed it on the head with this arrangement." Charlene takes another moment to admire the flowers before turning her gaze back to me. "Is there anything you need before we head out for the meeting?"

Shaking my head, I start shuffling around the files in front of me. "Nope. Just be ready to leave in about forty minutes." She smiles, nodding her head, and turns to leave.

My phone alerts me to a text message and I eagerly open it.

I knew they were your favorite because I know you, Tessa. And I'm looking forward to showering you with all of your favorite things for many years to come. ~A~

Andrew's words roll through my head. How is it that he's managed to make his way into my life in such a short amount of time and know me, like really know me? He knows things about me that most people haven't a clue about. Is it because he pays attention to every little thing I say and do? Or is it just because we're fated to be together as he keeps reminding me? I mean, how can two people be so drawn to the other, know things instinctively without needing clues or urging? Andrew seems to take the crown in that category. And this little display is just one more thing to prove it may not all be in my head as I think it is.

Charlene and I return from our meeting, our heads held high and giggling like two schoolgirls while we make our way down the hall. Of course, it was a sure thing getting everything worked out with the contracts. Mr. McDannold was so impressed that he almost guaranteed the signatures by early Monday morning. For my first account, I couldn't be happier with the outcome, even if it is only a small one.

After telling Charlene to take the last half hour off, I turn the corner into my office and am surprised to see Andrew standing off to the side of my desk. My heart flutters in my chest as I admire him dressed in his suit, looking as yummy as ever.

"Andrew? This is a surprise," I say, closing my door and walking the few steps toward him. He smiles and adjusts to rest his body against the edge of my desk.

"I was just finishing up a meeting with Chris and thought I'd stop by to see how you were doing. Also, I really wanted to see that beautiful smile of yours."

His hand reaches up to tuck a strand of hair behind my ear, allowing the pads of his fingers to trail lovingly down my cheek. I bite the inside of my cheek to fight the growing feelings inside of me from leaking out.

My eyes glance downward quickly, wanting to break away from his intense gaze. "Thank you again for the flowers. They're perfect. I still don't know how you managed to figure them out, especially the color for the roses."

Andrew closes the distance even more, leaning closer to me with our noses mere inches from each other. "I told you, love. I know you. Our souls are matched together therefore I know you better than myself."

My breathing spikes at his words and his closeness. The scent that drives me wild has my blood pumping, forcing the flush across my cheeks and warmth to spread across my body. The ever-present thrum of desire swirls in the air and it's becoming harder and harder to fight against it.

Unable to withstand it any longer I sag against his chest, my legs giving out slightly underneath me. Andrew's hands instinctively grab my hips, pulling me into the safety of his body. He lightly kisses my ear before nuzzling into the crook of my neck. I sigh, allowing myself to relax into his hold. My hands find their favorite place in the silky strands of his thick dark hair. Why am I fighting this? Why is there even a question in my mind regarding us when the universe keeps placing us together?

Andrew's nose runs down the length of my neck. The act brings a round of goose bumps to the surface of my skin, making me shutter slightly in his arms. The warmth I feel flowing through my body is now gathering low in my abdomen as I tighten my grip on his hair.

My mind is telling me we need to stop, but my heart is telling me to not let go. It doesn't help my internal war any when his arms tighten around my middle and his lips trail hot kisses along the slope of my shoulder.

I release my grip on his hair and place my hands upon his shoulders. "Andrew," I say in a breathless rush, feebly attempting to push him away. Andrew's lips leave my skin as his head pulls back to look at me. Stormy eyes meet mine and I know he's fighting a war inside himself as well, although I'm sure it's different than my own.

"Tessa, I'm trying to be noble and respect your wishes but I just …"

He dips his head lower to claim my mouth in a soft kiss. A kiss that feels feather-light but also has the weight of his heart in it. My eyes roll to the back of my head as the first swipe of his tongue brushes across my lower lip, asking for entrance. And I'm fooling myself if I say that I don't want him, don't want to taste him, get my fix of him. The kiss changes from gentle to possessive as his tongue sweeps inside my mouth, moving with deep fevered strokes. A new wave of passion flows between us and I can't help the moan of sheer pleasure that escapes from me. Andrew is staking his claim, reminding me of what he has and what we are together.

"You undo me every time. I just can't get enough of you," Andrew whispers against my lips. His fingers flex against my hips and I want to submit to the temptation to just give in. His tongue sweeps the inside of my mouth again and all rational thought leaves my head. Any questions, any doubts, any ideas of not wanting him are gone. The one thing that I know is that I need him. I want him. I love him.

Then why am I putting us through this senseless drama?

Andrew's hands move from my hips and begin roaming about my body. He cups my breasts, squeezing them gently. My hands fist at the lapels of his coat, pulling him closer to me. His thumbs flick over my hardened nipples, making my head tilt up at the jolt of pleasure it brings. Andrew takes advantage of my exposed neck, licking his way down to the swell of my breasts, now peaking through the buttons he somehow managed to open.

Somehow I become aware of our surroundings, remembering that I didn't secure the door after I had shut it. Releasing his coat I attempt to push away from him but he increases his hold on me, not willing to let me go.

"Andrew, the door," I say, pointing feebly at it. Andrew spins me around, letting me slump against my desk as he takes care of the problematic door. But he doesn't move toward me right away once the lock is turned. Andrew's intense stare has me gripping the edge of my desk, my chest rising and falling with each gasping breath. Fire lights his eyes, igniting them with lust burning solely for me. He stalks me like a predator seeking its prey. My eyes roam over his body, noticing the effect that I have on him. Reaching out, he finishes unbuttoning my blouse, letting it fall open to reveal the lace bra underneath.

"Like I said Tessa, I know you. Know exactly what you want, what you need, and how to give it to you." His fingertips brush down the center of my body, between my breasts, past my stomach, then moves around to the small of my back, pulling my body to his. His leg moves between my thighs, the feel of his erection at my hip sends desire and heat rushing between my legs.

Andrew picks me up, setting me on the edge of my desk. Papers flutter off the side, along with a few other things, creating a loud thumping noise. I cup his face, pulling his mouth back to mine. This moment is the only thing occupying my thoughts. I should care about what's going on outside this office, but I don't. I should be mindful that I'm doing inappropriate things in my office. And yet I can't stop this reaction I have to Andrew. I ease my body down, offering myself to him giving it what it craves the most.

Andrew moves over me, about to unbutton my slacks when the jostling of my doorknob has both our heads swinging in that direction.

"Tess? Are you in there?"

My eyes dart from the door to Andrew and back again as Kara continues to wiggle the handle. I can feel the flush crawl up my body as I realize what I almost let happen on my desk, again. *For fuck's sake, I'm still at work.* What is it about this man that makes me completely forget everything? Andrew laughs, placing a kiss upon my shoulder before pulling me up and helps put me back together.

"She has impeccable timing," Andrew mutters beneath his breath. Once the last button is done on my shirt, he cups my cheeks and presses his lips against mine. Kara's incessant knocking is growing louder and I pray that no one is around to wonder why she's beating on my door.

"Be right there," I cry out, waiting until we both look presentable. With a final smoothing of my hair, I unlock the door and greet my troublesome friend.

The knowing grin she's throwing at the both of us says she knows we've been caught doing inappropriate things in my office. She walks in, lifting a suspicious brow to the piles of papers and various other items on the floor.

"Did I interrupt something?"

My face reddens further, feeling the heat all the way up to my ears. "No, not at all," I reply a little too quickly. Kara knows me well enough to know when I'm lying through my teeth. The smirk on her face lets me know that she's on to me.

Kara rolls her eyes at me before turning to Andrew. "Nice to see you, Andrew."

"A pleasure as always Kara," he says, giving her that mega-watt smile of his.

She occupies one of the chairs in front of my desk, patiently waiting for something, although I'm not quite sure what. Probably for me to just admit the truth. *Fat chance of that happening.*

Needing to put some distance between us, I move around my desk to sit in my own chair while Andrew takes the remaining empty seat next to Kara.

"Such dirty creatures you are. Honestly, can you not keep it together for more than five minutes? I mean really. This is a place of business you know."

Her statement causes me to laugh out loud. "Okay, pot calling the kettle black. Do I need to remind someone of the events from last week, or perhaps the last five years in the boardroom? Maybe your late night business meetings?" I say, using quotation fingers for added emphasis. Andrew and Kara both join in my laughter.

"I won't deny it. It just pleases me that I'm not the only nymphomaniac in the office. You two could definitely give Chris and me a run for our money." Kara turns her attention to Andrew and lightly smacks his arm. "And you are such a bad influence on my poor sweet and innocent Tessa."

"Bad influence, yes. Innocent Tessa? I don't think so. She has a fire in her I don't think anyone has seen and I do enjoy bringing it out, regardless of where it may be."

The heated stare he throws my way has me squirming in my chair. Damn him. He enjoys bringing out the fire in me? Well, two can play that game. Feeling brazen, and waiting until Kara's not looking, I run my tongue along the front of my teeth, using the tip to lightly graze my top lip in the process. Andrew follows the movement with his eyes and it's his turn to squirm. There. Now we're even.

"Okay, enough about me. Was there something you needed Kara?"

She grins and moves to stand. "Nope. Just saw your door closed, along with the blinds and figured I'd come see what you were up to. And now I know. Have fun you two." She gives us a wave over her shoulder as she walks out the door. She is trouble with a capital T, but God knows I love her for it.

Andrew stands and rounds my desk, placing his hands on the armrests of my chair, leaning in close to me. "Like I said, I just wanted to come here to see your smile."

I duck my head, fighting off the feeling of embarrassment and lust. Andrew pulls my chin up, placing a kiss upon my lips before pulling back and gifting me with that beautiful smile of his.

"Well, I'm glad you did."

Andrew grabs my coat and purse from the closet, holding them out like a perfect gentleman. He slides it over my arms and smooths his hands over my shoulders. When I turn to face him, he's smiling at me. Instinctively my hand cups his cheek, wanting to feel his smile.

"What are your plans for the weekend?"

He shrugs his shoulders. "I'm not sure yet. Perhaps taking a beautiful lady out on a date?"

My smile widens and I nod. "I think that could be arranged. But I do have work that I need to get done around my house, so maybe tomorrow or Sunday?"

"I think that can be arranged. Anything I can help you

with?"

"No, it's just the regular stuff. I tend to deep clean my apartment once a month and trust me, you don't want to be around for that."

"I wouldn't mind. As long as I'm with you, I don't care what we do."

I trail my fingers across his cheek. "You're too good to be true."

Andrew turns his head, kissing the center of my palm. "I can say the same about you, love."

He leans down and presses his lips to mine. We take it slow this time, careful not to ignite any embers that may still be smoldering inside us. Although, if I know us, they're always burning with a white hot passion we can't ignore.

"Let me walk you to your car," Andrew says when he pulls back. I nod and lace my fingers into his as we venture out of my office toward the elevator.

We get a surprise when we walk into the elevator and find Michael already inside. He smiles brightly at us and gives a small wave.

"Hey stranger," he says to me.

"Hey," I reply. I turn to Andrew and smile. "Andrew, this is my friend, Michael. Michael, this is Andrew."

The two men shake hands and I can't help but smile. I know what Andrew initially thought of him so I was always kind of nervous about them meeting. Even though we're just friends, it's still a little strange to see the two of them together.

"Nice to meet you," Andrew says. He shoves his hands into his pockets and rocks back onto his heels.

"Likewise. So you're the guy from London I take it?" Michael asks.

Andrew quirks an eyebrow to me and smiles. "Yes, that would be me."

Michael laughs. "I've heard a lot about you. All good, of course. Tessa and I meet for coffee every morning and your name has come up in conversation a few times."

"Has it now?" Andrew's laughing at me because my face is turning an ungodly shade of pink.

"Your name may have been mentioned once or twice," I say.

There's a brief pause and we all shuffle back and forth.

"What do you do, Michael?" Andrew finally asks.

The doors to the elevator open and I step out first, letting the guys follow behind me.

"I'm a lawyer. I work in the law firm a few floors above Tessa's office."

"My dad is friends with one of the partners at his firm. He and Michael really hit it off at the party a couple weeks ago."

"Yes, your dad has been a tremendous help to me. He's given me the names of quite a few different contacts, some of them even want me to join their firm with the promise of making partner sooner than I would here."

We stop outside of the building and I give Michael a hug. "That's amazing. I'm so glad you were able to further your career. Good thing you suggested accompanying me to that party."

He laughs and runs a hand through his hair. "Yeah, it was a good thing all right. But I was happy to help you. This is just a side benefit of the night."

Andrew tightens his grip on my hand and I smile up at

him. "It sounds like things are working out for you."

Michael nods. "In the business world, yes. Things are going well. Everywhere else in my life, not so much."

"Haven't you found someone to date yet? What happened to that girl down the block from you? The one from your gym?"

We cross the street to head to our cars. "Tammy was okay. We went out for drinks after our workouts, but it just wasn't happening."

"After one date you could tell? I mean, that's hardly enough time to judge something like that," I say.

Michael stops by his car and shakes his head. "I disagree. I don't pay much attention to the amount of time I'm with someone. There should be an instant attraction when you see someone, followed by a need to keep seeing the person. That's how you know things will work out in the long run. The more you want to spend time with them, the more you will, regardless of everything else. Time is irrelevant. Knowing when it's the right person is all that counts and Tammy wasn't it."

"Are you sure?" I chew on my bottom lip because he could have been speaking about my own life instead of his.

"I'm positive. Sure, I was attracted to Tammy, but I didn't have the desire to see her again. Not on a permanent basis. I'm getting to the point in my life where I want to settle down and come home to one person and know they'll always be there. You know what I mean?"

Andrew nods. "In fact, I do. More than you know."

He smiles down at me and I flush again. Michael unlocks his car and opens the door.

"Well, I hope you both have a great weekend. Maybe Andrew could join us for coffee some morning?"

"I'd love to join you two for coffee. I'll have Tessa give me the details and see when I can come."

Michael nods and smiles to me. "See you Monday, Tess."

"See you then," I reply.

Andrew and I continue walking to my car as Michael pulls out of his spot

"He's a very nice gentleman," Andrew finally says.

I nod. "He is. It was sheer luck that I ran into him. He's super funny and very sweet. He's like a big brother to me almost. And I can forgive him for being a lawyer. Not everyone is perfect," I laugh.

Andrew holds my gaze for a second before bringing my hand to his lips. "You're perfect."

I turn my head away slightly, trying to hide my nonstop flush. "You're biased."

He laughs and turns my chin to face him again. "Yes, I am. Only because I've found the perfect girl for me. Go out with me tomorrow?"

My smile broadens and I kiss his lips softly. "Yes."

He opens my car door and I slide into the seat. "I'll call you to let you know the time."

"Okay."

He shuts my door and waves goodbye to me as I pull out of my spot and head home, wanting to get a jump start on my chores so I can dedicate all my free time to Andrew.

Chapter 14

I'M ON MY HANDS AND knees, scrubbing a stubborn stain from my kitchen floor when a knock sounds at my door. I brush a loose tendril of hair off my face and wipe my dirty hands on my cleaning shirt. Luckily it's an older one that I don't care if it gets dirty.

I open the door and am surprised to see Andrew standing before me, dressed in jeans, hiking boots, and a sweatshirt.

"What are you doing here?" I ask, holding the door open for him to come in.

"I came to take you on our date."

I look down at myself and cringe. "I thought it would be later tonight. I'm sort of a mess right now and haven't showered yet."

He kisses me quickly and chuckles to himself. "You look beautiful."

"You need glasses then because I look horrible. Do you mind waiting until I'm done showering?"

"Not at all," he says, walking around to the barstool to sit.

"I can join you if you'd like. Help scrub your back, perhaps?" He wiggles his brows and I smile.

"Tempting, but no. It won't take me long. How should I dress?"

His eyes roam over my body and I pull on the hem of my ratty old shirt. "However you'd like, but just so you know, we'll be doing quite a bit of walking so you may want to be prepared for that."

"Where are you taking me?" My mind is curious as to what he has planned because I don't think he knows the city all that well and I'm interested to see where we'd be doing a lot of walking.

"You'll see when we get there. But we can't get there until you get cleaned up. So get moving or I'll take you in there myself."

His eyes darken with his threat and I quickly move to take the world's fastest shower.

Once I'm finally dressed in my favorite jeans and hoodie, I'm surprised to find Andrew kneeling on a towel in my kitchen, finishing up with my floor.

"You didn't have to do that," I say.

He finishes wiping up the spot before sitting upright and smiling at me. "I know, but I wanted to do it. Anything to help you out. And now your floor is nice and clean so we can go out and have our date."

"You've thought of everything, haven't you," I say, kissing his lips as he approaches me.

"Not everything, but close enough."

"So where are we going?" I ask as we drive down the road.

We pass a few familiar landmarks before I see it come into view. Minnehaha Park, one of the most beautiful parks in all the metro area. I've heard about it, but I've never taken the time to go there. And it's just down the road from my apartment.

"Andrew, how did you find out about this place?" I ask with wide eyes.

We park in one of the lots and he exits quickly to open my door. "I was looking for ideas online of things to do in the area and this was one of the suggestions. Apparently the scenery is incredibly beautiful. And it has waterfalls."

After taking a backpack out of the trunk, he takes my hand and leads me into the park with a childlike grin. He's so adorable when he's giddy about showing me something I haven't seen before. Our hands swing between us as we walk along the path with the rest of the tourists, taking in the beautiful trees and all the changing colors around us. Andrew stops every once in a while and asks to take a picture of me by some trees or a bench we pass. I oblige because I simply can't say no to him. I, in turn, grab him and take a bunch of selfies of us, some of which Andrew sneaks a kiss in. It reminds me of our tour of London and the fun we had that day.

Many people are taking advantage of the warm weather, having picnics by the river or taking family photos with nature's beautiful backdrop. It really is the perfect day for this. These unusually warm days are rare this time of the year so you must take advantage of them while you can.

The further down the path we get, the louder the sound of rushing water gets.

"We must be getting close," Andrew croons in my ear. His

closeness sends bumps across my skin. When I turn my head, he's still smiling at me, but kisses the end of my nose and pulls me close to his side.

I gasp when I see it. Right here, in the middle of the urban jungle, is this beautiful piece of nature, flowing freely over the rocks and surrounded by golden leaves and still green grass. It's almost like a grotto with the rock walls and the pool of water beneath. It's not quite flowing as hard as I would have thought, but considering winter is just around the corner, it's still very impressive. But I make a mental note to return here in the spring after the snow melts because I can only imagine what it will look like then.

"This is amazing," I whisper, gripping Andrew's waist tighter.

"Do you want to go behind it?" he asks, pointing to a dirt trail that winds around the trees and goes to the rocks supporting the fall.

"Can we?"

He laughs and kisses the top of my head. "Of course, love. Look, there are others doing it too. It'd be fun to see what it looks like from behind."

Several people are walking the trail and going behind the falls. I watch them one by one disappear behind the wall of water and I chew my bottom lip.

"Let's do it."

We walk the trail and Andrew stays behind me, making sure that I don't trip or fall over any exposed tree roots. I can hear the shutter of his camera working, but I don't know what he's taking pictures of. Hopefully, it's not of the back of my head.

We join several people who are behind the falls, all taking

pictures or excitedly talking and touching the water. The rock wall is beautiful, with its different colors and lines showing every crack and change that has happened over many, many years. We take several photos with the Falls as the backdrop before walking back to the main path.

The sheer beauty of the area is just breathtaking and it leaves me speechless. I would never have expected to find anything like this in the middle of Minneapolis.

"Shall we follow the river?"

I nod and excitedly pull him down the path. The gold and red-hued leaves form a canopy above us as we watch the water flow over the rocks. Andrew pulls me off to the side and presses me against one of the hidden trees.

He kisses me slowly, unhurriedly, lovingly, while surrounded by the sounds of chirping birds and rushing water. My hands frame his face and I take the kiss further. Our tongues meet and I melt into his body as his arms tighten around my waist.

"Words cannot describe how beautiful you look right now; your hair blowing in the breeze, the sun beating down and giving your face a natural glow. The sparkle in your eyes as you try to memorize everything we pass, all of it makes you even more impossibly beautiful."

"I could say the same about you, too. There's no one that I would rather experience this with but you."

We kiss again before pulling ourselves away from the tree and follow the path back toward the car.

"Want to stop here for a second?" Andrew points to a small open spot in the pavilion.

"Sure."

We walk over and he sets down his backpack to pull out a blanket. My eyebrow rises as he spreads it out on the ground.

"You really did think of everything, didn't you?"

He pats the spot next to where he's sitting and I comply, sinking to the ground and snuggling into his side. I close my eyes and listen to the beat of his heart. He leans back, taking me with him, and props his head on his other arm.

"This is perfect," he whispers into my hair.

"Mmm. This reminds me of our afternoon in Hyde Park. That was perfect too."

"Yes, it was, love. But every moment is perfect when you're in my arms."

"Thank you," I whisper.

"For what?"

"For bringing me here today and for being the incredible man that you always are. I have never felt as safe as I do when I'm in your arms. And you do it so effortlessly and without prompting. You know me better than I know myself." I look up to look into his eyes and smile. "Thank you for being you."

"You're welcome. I'm glad to share this with you."

We lay in quiet contentment, listening to the laughter of children nearby and the calming sounds of nature. Soon enough, my stomach growls, letting us know that we did, in fact, skip lunch. Andrew laughs while pulling me off the ground.

"Come. You know what that means."

I laugh. "That you're starving me to death by making me exercise?"

He puts the blanket back in his pack and slings it over his shoulders. "It means we get to eat. And I love watching you eat."

"You're crazy," I say, grabbing his hand as we walk back to the car.

He shakes his head. "Only you could make eating a muffin utterly erotic."

My cheeks flush. "There was nothing erotic about that. I was just shoving a pastry into my mouth."

He unlocks the car and opens my door. When I slide in, he bends down and kisses me quickly on the lips before closing my door. After the backpack is put away, he climbs in next to me and starts the car.

"It was the way you were eating it that was erotic. You would bring those little crumbly pieces up to your mouth slowly, making sure you didn't spill any of it. Your tongue would dart out before the sweet confection hit your mouth, tentatively tasting it. But it was when your eyes closed as you slowly chewed that made the whole thing come to life. Your lips would quirk up in the corners and the faintest hum could be heard. Believe me, it was very difficult to sit still next to you while you were eating it."

I flush at the memory, remembering Andrew eating the offered piece and thinking those exact same things about him. I clear my throat and look out the window, noticing we're not heading back in the direction of my apartment.

"Where are we going now?"

He gives me a wink and makes several more turns to pull up near a tiny pub. The most delicious smells float in the air as we approach the doors. We walk in and it's like your typical sports bar. A long, narrow bar occupies one entire wall. There's a chalkboard behind it, stretching as far as the bar, listing each and every beer they have on tap. And there are a lot. Three handles for each tap with ten taps total.

A waitress shows us to the back area that's less crowded than the front. He sits next to me and presses a kiss to the top of my hand.

"How did you find this place?"

I glance over the menu and see it's my kind of place. All burgers and fried foods, everything that's not good for you but tastes like heaven.

"I also found this online while looking for date ideas. It came highly recommended on Yelp."

I laugh and shut my menu after figuring out what I want to eat. "You really put a lot of thought into this."

He leans over and kisses my temple. "I just wanted to make this perfect for you."

I lean over and show him my thanks and appreciation by gently kissing his lips.

"You succeeded. It's perfect."

He laughs and points to something on the menu. "I'm glad. Now tell me, what exactly is a Juicy Lucy?"

Chapter 15

THE PHONE RINGS AT MY desk and I stifle a yawn before answering. "Tessa Martin," I say, trying my best not to sound groggy.

"Tessa? Are you all right? You don't sound well."

Hearing the concern in my dad's voice snaps me out of my funk. I sit up straighter in my chair, acting as if he were sitting in front of me rather than talking to me on the phone.

"No, no I'm fine, Dad. Just a little tired this morning. I haven't had my regular dose of caffeine yet today." That's because Michael had to cancel this week due to a new court case he's been assigned. Apparently my dad's glowing endorsement of him has increased his workload. Hopefully, it'll slow down for him soon.

"Yes coffee is a must in the business world," he chuckles. I pinch my arm just to make sure I haven't nodded off on my desk. My dad is laughing? "I have an opening in my schedule this afternoon and was wondering if you and the elusive Andrew would like to join me for lunch?"

I tap my pen on the desk while gnawing relentlessly on my bottom lip. I haven't seen Andrew since our date over the weekend, even though he's been floating around the office with Chris and Kara. We've been constantly missing each other, which only makes me crave him more.

"Well, I know Andrew and Kara are in meetings together all day so I don't think he'll be able to make it."

"Would you still be willing to accompany me to lunch then? I'd hate to pass up a chance for us to sit down and enjoy a meal where you may actually eat something," he says in a mildly scolding tone.

"I eat. It's just I tend to not eat as much as everyone else." Not to mention the fact that I don't eat around Sharon because usually after spending a few minutes with her my appetite is gone. I flip through my day planner, just to make sure that my schedule is clear for a few hours this afternoon. "Lunch today sounds perfect. What time and where?"

"Shall we say noon at Zelo?"

"Zelo sounds good to me. Thanks, Dad. Guess I'll see you in a few hours."

"Get some coffee before you fall asleep at your desk," he laughs. "I'll see you in a bit. Bye, Tess."

"Bye, Dad."

I hang up the phone but continue to stare at the receiver for just a few moments longer. Tess? My dad never calls me Tess. Somehow I get the feeling that today is going to throw me off kilter. But I shake it off and follow my dad's advice and head out to get my first cup of coffee for the day.

My morning meeting ended with just enough time for me to walk the few blocks over to Zelo, a little restaurant that's extremely popular among the businessmen and women in the area. Once again, it's another place I have yet to venture to, even though I work nearby. Living on a budget tends to make you pack your own lunch or grab side salads that are only a few dollars.

I spot my dad as soon as I walk through the front door, sitting at a table near the bay of windows. He smiles warmly at me as I place my jacket and purse on the back of my chair.

"Hi, Dad," I say, sinking down and placing the napkin on my lap.

"Hi, Tess. How has your day been so far?"

I take a quick drink of water before answering. For some reason, I feel nervous even though I have no reason to be. I mean, he's my dad.

"Good. I had a meeting with a potential client this morning and I'm about ninety-nine percent sure they're going to sign." The pride pouring out of my voice is evident. I've decided to take this newfound confidence of mine and let it show to the rest of the world. No longer will I be the weak one huddled in the corner who is afraid of her own shadow. The past three days, or even the past few weeks, have shown me that I am someone who is worth something, someone to fight for. So that's what I'm going to do. Fight for myself and my happiness.

My dad reaches out, patting the top of my folded hands while smiling at me. "I'm so proud of you Tessa. I knew you had more potential than what you were showing to the world. And I knew others would see it and recognize it someday as well."

"Well, you know what they say. You have to start at the bottom to get to the top."

He chuckles and it warms my heart just a little more to him. I haven't heard him laugh since I was a kid. And even then I don't know if that was a memory or a dream of what was or could have been. But it's moments like this with us being a typical family unit I think I missed out on the most. It makes me wonder what would have happened if he had stayed or had wanted to take me with him.

A thought hits me just then. What if things had been different? What if I had a typical childhood and was given every opportunity available? The path I followed could have been considerably different than the one I'm on now. And I don't know if it would have led me to Andrew. If our souls are indeed fated together, I imagine we would have discovered each other eventually and our feelings and attraction would have been just as intense.

We stare at our menus while I decide on how hungry I really am. He had mentioned earlier that he doesn't think I eat enough so maybe I should pick something light but will still be plenty of food to last me for the day.

When our waitress arrives, I quickly rattle off my order, glancing up at my dad for approval. He smiles, which is all I needed to know he's happy.

"How was your trip?" I ask him once the waitress leaves.

"Good. Going to those conferences aren't always my favorite thing about the job but it's still good to get my foot in the door for future prospects."

"Like you need any help in that department. Everyone says you're a shoo-in for Attorney General when McAlister's gone."

"Maybe. It'd be nice to add the title to my resume, but recent events have had me thinking lately and I'm not sure I want to go that route anymore."

I tilt my head to the side in confusion. "Oh? What's changed?"

"Some things have opened my eyes and I think I need to make a few re-evaluations."

"Sounds ominous. Care to elaborate?" I ask.

He shakes his head and laughs. "Nothing for you to be concerned with. They're positive changes, let's put it that way."

I drop it, knowing that he's not going to tell me anything more. Instead we continue with a more relaxed topic of conversation, making small talk at times in between us telling each other about our week so far. He's genuinely interested in my life, asking me questions from subjects I didn't expect him to remember from previous conversations. I avoid any topics that may stray toward my love life, changing them to safer things like his upcoming trials. But thinking of my love life makes me think of Andrew; about how happy he makes me and how truly perfect we are for one another. I just wish I would have listened to him all those weeks ago and avoided all of this nonsense.

"So what has brought on that smile of yours right now?" my dad asks me.

The waitress arrives with our food and I quickly take a bite of my Ahi spring roll to gain an extra second or two before replying.

"I didn't realize I was smiling."

He leans forward slightly. "So, whom are you smiling about?"

I wipe my mouth with my napkin. "Is it that obvious?"

He nods. "Tess, I know I haven't been the best father and I have no one to blame but myself. But over these last few years I've become more adept at reading your facial expressions and the smile lighting up your face is something new. There's joy in that smile, something I've only recently discovered myself."

There's another cryptic comment from him. I shake my head slightly. "It's nothing really. Just thinking about my meeting this morning."

He laughs again. "You could never be a lawyer. You're not very good at bending the truth. Please, enlighten me. I really want to know what you're thinking about."

I take a sip of my lemon water and clear my throat.

"Andrew," is all I say, flushing slightly at my confession to my dad of all people.

But that one word, that one name means so much more to me than the entire English language. Andrew is my everything, my whole world, my light in the darkness. He rescued me before I even knew I needed it. He saw me when everyone else passed me by.

"Ah, yes, Mr. Parker. One of these days I hope to meet the man who has captured my daughter's heart. Any man who puts that particular smile on your face is someone I want to know."

I blink back at him feeling slightly off-kilter by his heartfelt words. "I'll have to see what I can do. I haven't seen him in a few days, but I'll bring it up the next time we're together."

"There's nothing wrong between the two of you is there?" he asks, taking another sip of his water.

I shake my head. "No, nothing like that. He's just been busy this week with meeting after meeting."

"How has his project been going?"

"Good. He's received bids from several builders and secured the land needed for the build site. According to Kara, everything is going smoothly and on schedule."

"Good, I'm glad to hear that. Do you know how long he will be here then?"

I swallow hard and play with my fork. "We haven't discussed it yet. I've been avoiding any conversations which deal with his departure. I couldn't handle it last time, which is why I ran away. And we've gotten so close now that I know it'll shatter me whole if he leaves. I guess I'm afraid he'll leave me."

He pushes aside his empty risotto plate and places a hand over mine. "You have grown into such a beautiful, strong woman. Any man would be lucky to have you in their life."

"How do you know?"

"Because you are someone people want to be around. You're good, bright, intelligent, and caring. All qualities of a lovable person and someone you wish to hold on to."

That's an odd statement coming from him. He ran the first chance he got when I was little and never looked back. I must have showed my thoughts in my face because he retracts his hand and looks down slightly.

"I'm sorry about my actions when you were little and for not being around when you needed me. Maybe one day you and I can talk about everything so there won't be any more obstacles between us."

"Maybe," I whisper.

This is a bit much for a lunch conversation. I'm not prepared to dive into years and years of pain and sorrow over risotto and tuna. Not to mention I'm going to need a lot of alcohol when that conversation finally does happen.

My dad clears his throat then looks back up at me. "So Andrew makes you happy then?"

I sigh, thankful we're not going to talk about our relationship anymore. "Yes, he's the one that makes me happy and lights up my life. I honestly can't see myself living without him."

"Then I can't wait to meet the man who can make my daughter happy, even when he's not here."

I nod and return his smile. "I'd love that."

We don't even realize an hour has flown by until my dad looks at his watch and groans.

"Well, I've enjoyed our lunch, Tessa. We must try to do this again."

I push away from the table and start putting my jacket back on. "Sure, I'd like that."

He puts some bills in the book and hands it to the waitress as she passes by. It makes me happy that he's trying for some kind of relationship with me. Even more so, he sounds like he regrets the decisions he made while I was growing up. I guess time will tell if we can work things out or not.

The afternoon air has a slight chill to it as the wind has now switched and is coming from the north. I shiver slightly and stand next to him on the busy sidewalk.

"Did you walk here?" he asks, looking down the street for my car.

I nod. "It's only a few blocks so I didn't see the need to drive."

"Let me drive you back. It's cold and I don't want you getting sick."

The laugh bursts from me before I have a chance to stop it. "It's only a couple of blocks. I'll be okay. Plus the walking will do me good. Need to burn off the calories from the lunch I just had."

"That's probably the most food I've seen you eat, even if the portion was incredibly small to begin with." He narrows his eyes, but they wrinkle in the corners, letting me know he's trying to be funny.

"Well there. Now you know that I do, in fact, eat. Are you happy now?"

"Delighted," he replies. He takes another glance at his watch and frowns. "I'm sorry, but I need to get going. I have a meeting in forty minutes and it's across town. When you are able to set up a time with Andrew for lunch, please let me know."

I nod and smile. "I will. Thank you for lunch. Hope you have a good rest of your day." I move to give him a hug, but it turns into this sideways embrace. Not exactly a gesture one would give to your father but then again, we don't do that sort of thing. This is all new territory and we're still testing the waters. He pats my back but squeezes my shoulder before stepping away.

"You do the same Tessa," he says before walking down the street where his car is parked.

The afternoon has definitely given me much to think about. Our relationship is definitely heading in the right direction. And he wants to spend more time with me, which is amazing all on its own. When he's not around Sharon, he's such a different person. Then again I wonder if it's because I'm a different person now compared to who I was before. He thinks I'm strong and a few weeks ago I would have laughed at the thought. But after everything that's happened I have to agree.

I am stronger than I was. Now I just have to grab what I want with both hands and never let it go. And after work, that's exactly what I plan to do.

Chapter 16

I WALK INTO THE LOBBY of the Radisson downtown and nervously step into the elevator that will bring me to Andrew. Pressing the button for his floor, I pace the small confines of the car, resisting the urge to twist my hair or rip my fingernails off one by one. My nerves have hit me full force and suddenly I'm not entirely sure of this plan. Kara told me earlier to just do it when she texted me his room number, but she's bolder than I am.

Standing in front of room 1620, I steel my nerves and blow out a quick breath. *Okay, it's now or never.* I smooth a hand over my clothing one last time. Raising my hand, I knock on the door. Movement can be heard just beyond it and time seems to slow as I wait for Andrew to open the door. And then time stops altogether when it opens and he's standing in front of me.

Fresh from a shower, Andrew greets me in a pair of jeans and a plain white t-shirt. His hair is still damp, letting it curl slightly at the ends. I can smell his soap and cologne as they assault my senses, creating a whirlpool of sensations to run rampant throughout my body. A breathtaking smile breaks across his face when he notices me blatantly taking him in.

"Tessa," he simply says.

The sound of his voice caressing my name is all it takes for me to launch in his direction and throw my arms around his neck. He pulls me into the room, closing the door behind us before backing me into it. My purse and jacket fall to the floor as he strips them off my body. Andrew cradles my face in his hands as his tongue runs along the seam of my mouth, licking and sucking on my bottom lip. I grant him the access he seeks, letting our tongues collide with a heated passion.

He pulls me away from the door and walks us backward into his room. I stumble slightly while removing my heels, never once dragging my mouth from his. My fingers twist into his damp hair before running down his neck and chest, worshiping every line they come in contact with. Hastily I pull his shirt over his head, needing to feel his skin against my fingertips.

Andrew's hands roam over my body, kneading the soft and willing flesh, molding it to do as he pleases. He starts to unbutton my shirt, letting it fall from my shoulders when the last one is released. He makes quick work of unzipping my skirt, letting it pool around my feet.

He breaks our kiss to step back and look at me from head to toe. The intensity of his gaze makes my nipples harden and moisture to gather between my legs. My breaths are short and quick and I lick my lips when his eyes finally fall back on mine. Lust and raw, unadulterated need fill his eyes. His deep, sexy groan echoes through my ears as he stalks closer to me, undressing me with his stare.

"Tell me this means you're mine, you being here right

now."

I nod slowly, letting a seductive grin appear on my face. "Yes, I'm yours."

"Finally," he says, attacking my mouth again with renewed passion. He guides us to the bed, pressing his body into me so I can feel every hard inch of him. His need, his desire for me excites me more as my hands trail up and down his back.

I work at the waistband of his jeans and slide them down his legs, using my feet when I can no longer reach. Then he pins me to the mattress, his tongue caressing every available inch of skin from my neck to my breasts. His dexterous fingers unsnap my bra and he slides the lace from my body, tossing it over his shoulder to join the rest of our clothes.

"So beautiful," he says before leaning down to take a hardened nipple into his mouth. The warmth of his tongue has my hips bucking up to find his as he gently pulls the desire to the surface of my body. His thumbs loop into the top of my panties, pulling them down quickly, leaving me naked and writhing beneath him. He caresses the rounded curve of my behind, pulling me into his straining erection again, leaving only his boxer briefs as a barrier between what we both want.

His heated kiss returns to my lips. My hands quickly remove the barrier between us and send it to the floor with everything else. Andrew moves to the side and leans over me. Passion burns brightly behind his blue irises as he licks his lips while worshiping my naked body with his eyes.

"Tell me you want me," he says, running his hands through my fanned out hair.

"I want you," I breathe.

My fingers trace the contours of his face, gliding across

his cheekbones, his nose, his chin. Then they slide down the column of his throat and past the planes of his pectoral muscles before rounding his sides to the muscles of his back. I pull him back to me, needing to feel the press of his body on top of mine.

"Tell me you need me." His eyes lock with mine again.

"I need you. Andrew, please, I need you so much."

Widening my legs, he settles between them, letting his erection press against my slick entrance that is craving to be filled with him. It feels so good and yet it's almost a sweet torture because he's close but not close enough. I need to feel more of him, need to feel his desire and passion as it covers every inch of me, inside and out. I just need him to show me how much he wants me.

His fingers trail down my body again before sliding between us. A single digit enters me and it is absolute bliss feeling him stroke the spot deep inside me that only he knows how to find. My head presses into the mattress, letting a loud moan escape my lips as his finger continues to dip in and out of my body.

"You're so wet, love."

I clutch the comforter when he adds another finger, stretching me, preparing me while bringing me closer to the edge. My mind goes blank, only concentrating on what Andrew is doing to my body, focusing on each and every touch and caress, inside and out. His lips and tongue move to the same rhythm as his fingers, leaving me gasping for air in his mouth. It's too much, too good. I'm not sure how much longer I can stand it, feeling every muscle in my body tense, ready to find their release.

"Please," I beg, needing him to be inside me.

He moves his thumb to press against my swollen clit and it's enough to send me spiraling into oblivion, gasping out his name as everything constricts then relaxes when the orgasm rolls through my body. He swallows my screams, kissing me with a renewed passion.

My lids feel heavy but open again when I feel him press gently at my entrance. Our eyes connect and I nod my head, giving him permission. He props himself on his forearms and runs his fingers through my hair. The nature of our kiss changes to one of reverence as he presses each glorious inch of his cock into me, stretching me, reminding my body of what it feels like to have him inside me.

Cupping his face, I hold him to me, waiting until he's fully inside before running my hands over his body. My ankles wrap around his waist, pulling him even deeper.

"I've missed you so much," Andrew says, beginning a slow rhythm. I raise my hips to meet his, keeping our eyes locked together. So much expression in his face as he brings both our bodies to the heights they crave. "You were made to fit me. Absolutely perfect in every way."

I grab his face, kissing him hard and pour all the love I can into this one simple act. The love I feel for him grows with each thrust, knowing it's me he came here for, me whose body drives him wild and makes him crazy with need. He takes care of me, making sure all my needs are met as the familiar tightening of my muscles let me know that my whole world is about to shift again.

With a few more thrusts the world falls away as I claw at his back, my orgasm rocking me to the core, leaving me gasping for air.

"Yes, Tessa, yes."

A few more strokes and I feel him still above me, tense and then release as he pours himself into me, filling me completely. He brings his head to the crook of my neck, still chanting my name while licking away the beads of sweat that have formed on my skin. I cling to him as if my life depends on it, feeling his own sweat slicked skin as my fingers trace circles on his back.

My whole body feels spent and deliciously sore, a feeling I haven't felt in weeks. Not since the first time Andrew made love to me back in his apartment. He leans up on his elbows, trailing his lips across my jaw line before covering my mouth with his.

"I've missed you so much." Andrew nuzzles into my hair as my fingers thread through his. He fully relaxes and moves to lie next to me, pulling me into his side while stroking my hair.

"I've missed you too. And I'm so sorry about everything, about how I left and how I've been acting since you've been back. I've wasted so much time …" I trail off, my voice breaking at the end. A lone tear falls down my cheek, but Andrew brushes it away with his thumb.

"You have nothing to be sorry for, love. All that matters now is we found our way back to each other. I won't let you slip through my fingers again. I don't think I could survive it."

I pull his face to mine, kissing away the pain I have caused the both of us through a series of misunderstandings and insecurities.

"I won't either," I whisper.

My hands trail down his body, gliding over the muscles of his arms before playing with his fingers. He brings our hands up, pressing the palms together before interlocking our fingers. We stare at the connection, two hands joined together, making us one being.

"We belong together, you and me. This is it for the both of us. What we have is special and uniquely ours. We are all each other needs and I will spend the rest of my life showing you how happy you make me."

I kiss him softly and smile. "I like the sound of that."

"And do you know why?"

I shake my head and stare at him. "No, why?"

Our hands press against his heart. It's beating so fast it makes me nervous about what he's about to say. He smiles then kisses me deeply, stealing my breath again.

"Because I love you, Tessa."

My body stills at his words. I want to pinch myself to make sure I'm truly awake and this isn't some dream or imagined post-orgasmic high. Our eyes lock together and whatever doubts I had are erased because the answer is staring back at me, plain as day.

"You love me?"

"Yes, my sweet girl. I've loved you since the first time I laid eyes on you at the airport. I don't know how long I stood there and watched you gazing at those around you before I decided to make my move and sit next to you. Your beauty captivated me from the beginning, drawing me in until I couldn't think about anything else but you."

My brows furrow together in confusion. "But if that's true, why didn't you say it to me after our night in your apartment?"

Now it was his turn to look confused. "I did. I repeated it over and over again as I held you in my arms, never wanting to let you go. And then I said it again during the video conference we had the following week."

A tear slips down my cheek as I recall him mouthing something to me but not being able to make out what he said. Now, holding that image still in my mind's eye, I can see it clear as day. His beautiful lips forming the words 'I love you', just like they do now. Andrew brushes the tear away and kisses the corner of my mouth.

"I have never loved anyone before you and will never love anyone else but you. You are my forever; the other half of my heart, my soul, my existence. Fate brought us together and I believe it now more than ever." His fingers trail over my lips, tracing the curves. "I love you, Tessa."

I cup his face and feverishly bring my lips to his. "You have no idea how long I've waited to hear you say that, although apparently I just need to listen better."

He smiles and it warms my heart even more. "I will continue to say it until the last breath leaves my body. This I promise you."

We kiss again and I feel complete. "I love you too, Andrew. So much it hurts."

He pulls back and threads our fingers together again. "You will never hurt again. I'm not planning on going anywhere without you ever again."

Our hands fall to his chest, resting comfortably over his heart. My lids grow heavy and struggle to stay open. Andrew adjusts us so I'm able to lie comfortably on his shoulder.

"Sleep now, love. We'll start fresh when we wake."

I nod my head and fall into a contented sleep, clinging to his body and thanking fate for bringing us back together.

Chapter 17

SOFT LIPS FEATHER KISSES ALONG my neck as I slowly come back into consciousness. I have no idea how long I've been asleep, but I'm really enjoying Andrew's version of a wake-up call.

"Wake up sleepy," he says, peppering kisses across my jaw. I wiggle and squirm under his touch. He lets out a quiet laugh and runs his hands along my sides, causing me to squirm even more.

"Andrew, stop. I'm ticklish," I laugh.

But he doesn't relent. Instead it fuels him on further, digging his fingers into me and creating a torrent of laughter to escape. My sides begin to ache with the assault as I twist my body from side to side.

He stills his fingers and moves them up my sides, brushing against my bare breasts before cupping my cheek, tilting my head toward him.

"I could listen to you laugh all day. It's my most favorite sound in the world. And the way your face lights up is nothing short of spectacular."

He leans in close, pressing our lips together to savor and taste each other. I still can't believe that I wasted so much time running from him, running from my feelings. Love is about trust and I know this man will do anything for me. He's told me a thousand times before but now I will actually start to listen.

Andrew's lips begin to drift from mine, creating a burning trail down my chin and over the column of my throat before settling at the hollow dip above my collarbone. My fingers run through his sex-mussed hair, gently pulling at the silky strands. His hand moves over my breast, plumping and caressing it, making the nipple pucker into a tight little bud.

"I have half a mind to keep you captive in this room for all eternity so I can ravage you day and night." His mouth covers my aching nipple, lightly sucking and licking it.

"I like the sound of that," I say, letting my hands drift across his shoulders and follow the lines I find in my exploration.

I can feel a smile against my skin as his lips travel lower across my body. Desire heats my blood again, making me squirm for an entirely different reason now. But as his lips dip into my belly button, my stomach announces its displeasure, growling loudly once again in his presence. I groan and cover my face with my hands, rolling over to the side in an attempt to hide.

"The thought is very tempting however I do believe I need to feed you." He gets up and stretches his arms above his head as I peek through my fingers, getting a glimpse of the naked Adonis I'm sharing a bed with. "And you're staying here tonight. I won't sleep another night without you next to me."

I move to prop myself against the pillows to sit up against

the headboard, bringing the sheet with me to cover my exposed chest. "That was my plan anyway. I'm not sure I could be at home by myself when I could be lying next to you instead." I lick my lips quickly before looking back up at him, my voice soft and fragile. "You keep me safe at night, warding off all my nightmares and protect me from myself or whatever it is that's trying to tell me something through my dreams. It's something I've never actually felt before in my life and I'm going to hold on to it with everything I have."

Andrew sits next to me, running his hand across my cheek before cupping it behind my neck. "Felt what?"

"Safe."

He leans over, brushing his lips against my own. "I will always keep you safe Tessa. You don't have to be afraid of anything ever again. I'll do everything within my power to guard you at all times."

A tear slips down my cheek and I kiss him with unrushed passion, a sweet and lazy movement while trying to convey all my feelings into this one simple act. He pulls away, kissing the tip of my nose and smiles.

"As much as I would love to stay here all night to make up for lost time and forget everything else, we do need to eat." He leans closer to me, pressing our foreheads together. "We need to keep up our strength." With a wink, he stands and leaves me feeling like a puddle of mush on the bed. I watch him walk over to the dresser and pull out a pair of sweatpants which hang low on his gloriously naked body. That impeccable V peeks out over the top, drawing my eyes to it and I can't help but stare unabashedly at him. His body is perfect in my opinion. Tall, lean, not overly defined but still so strong.

He catches my stare and smirks, giving me that sexy grin of his. But the smile quickly falls off his face as I stretch my arms above my head, letting the sheet fall from my body to expose my naked breasts. He runs a hand over his face and adjusts his pants when I attempt to roll off the bed. His reaction makes me smile.

"Do you want to go out and eat?"

"Actually, can we order in? I'd really just like to stay here wrapped in your arms," I say, picking up his discarded white shirt and slipping it over my head.

I walk over to him and wrap my arms around his middle, clinging to him tightly. Andrew holds me to him, rubbing his hands up and down my back, soothing me while quieting any and all worries inside my head. "If that's what you want then that's what we'll do. Besides, I like the idea of just the two of us staying in. We can feed each other naked," he teases, wiggling his eyebrows. I laugh and sit back on the bed, curling my legs underneath me.

Andrew grabs a menu from the restaurant downstairs and sits next to me as we go through it. My head falls against his shoulder as he wraps his arm around my waist, pulling me closer to him. This is what I've missed the most, the closeness between the two of us, him knowing my needs before I do.

After calling to place an order for a selection of appetizers, Andrew stalks over to where I'm still seated on the bed. His eyes look feral, hungry with need and desire as he takes in my current state of undress.

"You look so sexy sitting there in just my shirt. It's driving me crazy to know you're not wearing anything underneath it." The bed dips when his knee presses down on it, making me crawl backward on the bed as he climbs above me.

"I love wearing things that smell like you. If I could wear this all day long, I would."

Andrew runs his nose along mine, sending a shiver down my spine. "If people saw you like this I may not be held responsible for my actions. You're mine, love. No one gets to see you this way but me." He grabs the hem of the shirt, slowly dragging it over my body before tossing it back to the floor. "Perfect."

Instinctively my arms move to cover my now bared breasts but he shakes his head, pulling my arms away and holding them down. "No hiding from me, ever. I want to see every inch of your beautiful body."

A blush creeps across my skin, heating it even more than what Andrew is doing simply with his words. His finger trails over my cheek before tucking my hair behind my ear.

"Okay, no more hiding. But if I get cold you're going to have to warm me up," I exclaim.

Andrew moves over me, settling between my thighs as he presses his forehead to mine. Fingers trail across my ribs, making me sigh.

"I have many ways to warm you up. Do you happen to know the best way to do that?" I shake my head and he smiles. "By getting completely naked." He rolls his hips into me. "Skin to skin contact." Another roll. "With lots of friction." I gasp loudly as his growing erection hits me in just the right spot.

My eyes lock with his and I trail a finger across his sensual lips. "Then I guess we'll have to put that hypothesis to test." His bare chest is pressed against mine and I can feel his warmth permeating my skin.

"I would love to." He dips low, capturing my lips in his. A knock sounds at the door and he smiles against my lips. "But first we need to eat."

He jumps off the bed and walks to the door, still naked from the waist up. I really hope it's a male delivering the food and not a female. I sit up and prop myself against the pillows again, contemplating on getting his shirt once more. But Andrew comes over with a tray of goodies and sits next to me.

The air quickly fills with delicious smelling food, making my stomach rumble once more. Popping a piece of strawberry into my mouth, I narrow my eyes at him as they travel up and down his body.

"What?" he asks while taking a bite of food.

"How come I have to be naked and you get to have clothes on?" I pout.

A spark appears in his eye as he stands from the bed and slowly drags the pants down his hips, over his thighs, then letting them drop completely to the floor. My brain misfires as I gawk and stare at him, still unable to believe that this gorgeous, perfect man is mine.

"Better?" he asks, pulling me into his side as he reclaims his spot.

"Much. Thank you."

He smirks and grabs a berry, tracing it around my lips. "If you want me to take my clothes off, all you have to do is ask."

He pushes the sweet fruit between my lips. The juice runs out of the corner of my mouth, but Andrew quickly licks it away. *Holy hell,* I think to myself as my nipples tighten. It feels as if all of the air has been sucked out of the room, replaced by the feelings of desire and passion. I want to say forget the food and let me feast on his body, but I remind myself that we have all night together. He's not going anywhere and neither am I.

We continue to eat, feeding each other pieces here and there while talking about everything except the last few weeks. Andrew tells me more about his family, asking me if I want to go visit them this summer. The thought of meeting his family is enough to give me hives but at the same time it delights me beyond belief because he's making plans for us in the future.

Once the food is gone, we turn on the TV, flipping through the channels before stopping on my favorite Thursday night program.

"I can't believe I forgot it was Scandal night," I say, snuggling in close to his side.

He chuckles and kisses the top of my head. "Well then let's watch your program."

As we watch the show, he asks me a few questions since he's never seen it and I happily catch him up during the commercial breaks. When the show is over we channel surf some more before just letting it fall onto whatever program we find. Not that we are watching the TV anymore. Andrew turns and pounces like a ferocious predator, sending everything flying off the bed as we roll around and lose ourselves in each other. Our lovemaking is heated and incendiary but filled with so much passion that I could feel it right down to my bones. After several hours we fall asleep, tangled together in each other's arms, right where we're supposed to be.

The morning sun pierces the darkness of the room, begrudgingly waking me up. Andrew's arms are still tightly wrapped around me as I cling to his chest. With my head tucked safely under his chin, I bring my lips to the hollow dip at the base of his throat. A groan sounds from the back of his throat and I smile against his skin.

"Good morning, my love," I whisper. Strong arms flex around me before soft lips meet my forehead.

"Mmm, I'm pretty sure that's my line."

"I know it's your pet name for me, but I thought I'd try it out on you."

Andrew stares at me, gazing deep into my eyes. Something passes over them but then is quickly gone. I furrow my brow.

"What is it?"

He shakes his head and sighs. "It's nothing."

Rolling over, we look at the time flashing on the digital clock and groan.

"It's already seven o'clock. We better get up and get moving for work. I'm going to be late as it is and I didn't bring any extra clothes with me."

I start to move away from Andrew, but he holds on tightly, not letting me move an inch. "Stay home with me today. I don't want to share you with the world just yet."

"Why does that sound way too tempting? Don't you have meetings with Kara and Chris today?"

A slow smile lights up his face as he shakes his head. "Not today. There isn't another meeting scheduled until Monday so I have given myself a three-day weekend."

Three days solely dedicated to Andrew? Could I handle that? I've never skipped a day of work in my life, but this beautiful man has me wishing we were on a deserted island with no responsibilities ever again.

I press my lips together and dart off the bed, walking to where my purse had been placed on the dresser after being hastily discarded the night before. Pulling out my phone, I type a quick text to Kara.

Hey, not going to make it to work today. I'm going to entertain the COO of the big account we have to make sure that he's completely satisfied.

I hit send and bite my lip as I look over at Andrew, who is now sitting up against the headboard with the sheet just covering all the necessary parts of his body. Wearing a smug smile, like a cat that ate the canary, he motions me toward him with his finger. Lascivious thoughts begin running through my mind as my eyes run up and down his body.

The phone beeps in my hand and I glance down at Kara's response.

LOL! I bet you are! Make sure he's completely satisfied and you better not come back to work until he is!

My face turns bright red as I laugh at my audacious best friend. Andrew quirks an eyebrow to me and I walk over to show him the message.

"So I believe I have permission to stay home today."

He laughs and grabs my waist, making me squeal as he plants me on his lap, my legs on either side of his thighs. Taking the phone from my hand, he places it on the nightstand and turns back to me, running his fingers through my tangled hair.

"And what is home?" he inquires.

I lean down, pressing my chest to his and kiss him with every feeling that's pent up inside of me, aching to be released.

"Home is where you are."

Andrew's hands run up and down my naked back, tracing small circles as they make their way into my hair. Our foreheads touch and I close my eyes as his warm breath whispers across my lips.

"Yes, it is. You are my home, Tessa. You are everything that I never thought I would have."

"I love you," I say as I pull back the sheet and slowly sink onto him.

"I love you, too," he replies, grabbing my hips to guide me until he's fully sheathed inside.

My heart melts as our bodies mold into each other, slowly combining into one again and again all morning long.

Chapter 18

SUNDAY AFTERNOON WE FINALLY PULL ourselves out of Andrew's hotel room, mainly because we haven't seen the outside world since Thursday, and I didn't have any clean clothes. Don't get me wrong, being naked was fun and highly pleasurable but it was time to return to reality and the outside world.

We decide to work on my Sunday chores together, which means it's laundry day, my most hated chore of all. Andrew brings his bag of dirty laundry, saying that he wants to help me around the house today. He's too good to be true because I don't know many men who actively want to do chores and mundane everyday tasks.

We walk hand in hand down the street to the laundromat, stopping every once in a while to kiss against a random building or tree we pass. When we arrive at the laundromat, there are a few people also standing around, waiting for their clothes to get clean. That doesn't stop Andrew from finding a chair for us, pulling me into his lap while he reads to me from my Kindle. Several strange glances come our way, but we ignore them as I curl into his lap and listen to the sound of his voice. I link my arms around his neck while pressing my lips to his lifeline, which is steadily beating just beneath the surface of his skin. It's a simple gesture, but to the both of us it's the most precious moment ever. Every moment together means more than the last, even if we're not doing anything special.

After several hours, we're back in my apartment with clean clothes in hand. Andrew is in the kitchen making us lunch while I straighten up the living room, getting it ready for our afternoon of lounging around. We play cards and eat our food while sitting on the couch, pausing briefly to get things to drink or make out like a couple of teenagers whose hormones have gone wild.

"So what are your plans for tomorrow?" I ask, sitting down on his lap after bringing our empty dinner plates to the kitchen.

He holds me tight against his chest and nuzzles his nose into my hair. "Well, I have meetings scheduled with Kara and Christopher for most of the morning. I figure we can leave here together since we're both going to the same place. Seems logical, don't you think?"

"I agree, as long as you don't mind having coffee in the morning with Michael. We always meet before work. Are you okay with that?"

He smiles and tucks some hair behind my ear. "Of course. He did invite me after all."

"Good. I'd love it if you two became friends. He's really sweet and funny with a personality to match my own." I pause and think about that statement. "Okay, maybe a personality that compliments my own. He's more of the outgoing type where I'm the wallflower."

Andrew laughs. "So you're saying you're attracted to people who are opposite of you?"

"Isn't that obvious? Look at who all is in my life. You, Kara, Chris, Michael, my dad. All of you are the polar opposite of me. All of you are strong and confident, which in turn makes me want to be the same. And I think it's finally starting to work."

He nods and kisses my forehead. "Yes, I do believe it is."

Andrew stands and wraps my legs around his waist. "Let's go to bed. Then in the morning we'll meet up with your friend and we can start transferring my things over here."

I raise an eyebrow to him as he carries me down the hall. "You sound like you're moving in with me."

He chuckles and kicks the bedroom door shut behind us. My feet hit the floor next to the bed and he gives me a heated look as I stare up at him.

"I am. I told you that I'm not spending another night apart from you." He grabs the hem of my shirt and starts to pull it upward. "And that's final."

My shirt falls from my shoulders and he guides me to lie on the bed. I lean up on my elbows to watch him remove my flannel pants. He teases me by trailing his lips across each inch of skin that becomes available. Then he removes his clothes piece by piece before pulling my body to the edge of the bed and kneeling between my legs.

"I'm so glad you're here." I trail my fingers along his jaw and he twists his head to kiss my palm.

"I'm not going anywhere. You will be the first thing I see in the mornings and the last thing I see before we sleep. I will hold you in my arms to protect you and keep you safe. Then I

252

will worship every inch of your body to show you how much you mean to me."

The world falls away as his lips trail up my inner thighs and then slowly cover the sensitive flesh between my legs. If this is what it's going to be like all the time when he lives here, then I can't wait.

We walk into the Caribou Coffee shop and I immediately see Michael sitting at our usual table. He smiles brightly and waves us over. Andrew follows behind me and shakes Michael's hand as we join him at the table.

"Good morning," Michael says, sliding my coffee over to me. He then faces Andrew and shrugs apologetically. "Sorry, I would have gotten one for you as well, but I didn't know you were coming."

Andrew waves him off. "Quite all right. I'll just head up to the counter to get one. Do either of you need anything?"

I shake my head and smile. "No, I'm good for now."

"No, thank you," Michael responds.

Andrew stands and kisses the top of my head before going to brave the long order line. I turn back to Michael, who has a rather large grin on his face.

"What?" I ask.

He shakes his head. "Nothing. It's just, you look happy."

I take a sip of my coffee after blowing on it. "I am happy."

"So everything worked out between you two?"

I nod. "It did. All misunderstandings have been cleared up and we're moving on."

"Good. I'm happy for you. You deserve something to go right for once."

"I almost feel like I should hold my breath or something. It's like I'm waiting for the other shoe to drop because it seems a little too good to be true. Nothing ever goes this right in my life."

Michael twists his lips to the side. "That's not true and you know it. What about your promotion? Or the fact that your dad has come around and is including you more and more in his life?"

"Yeah, I guess."

"Can you say that things have gotten better since you returned from London?"

I pause to think about it. "Yes, they are substantially better than before I left, that's for sure."

"So how does Andrew fit into things now?" he asks.

I look over my shoulder at the man in question and smile. He's talking to some random stranger behind him, laughing at whatever the man has said. If I know him like I think I do, he'll more than likely buy his cup of coffee as well because that's what he does. He gives without needing anything in return and always thinks of others before himself.

"We haven't talked about the future too much, but he did tell me over the weekend that he loved me, so I have to think that everything will fall into place."

Michael leans forward and places a hand on mine. "Congratulations. I know you were worried about him not returning your feelings before. It's good to hear that it wasn't true."

I shake my head. "No. As a matter of fact, if I had been listening I would have realized it a lot sooner."

"The important thing is you're listening now. Things will work out. I have a feeling about you two. I just hope he doesn't take you back to London because I would miss our almost daily coffee dates."

We laugh as Andrew approaches the table again. "What did I miss?"

I smile at him and shake my head. "Nothing much. Just Michael's addiction to caffeine."

"Hey, I'm a lawyer. It's pretty much what my body runs off of most days of the week, along with most nights."

Andrew holds up his cup in salute. "I'll drink to that."

Michael begins telling us the story of his latest case, flailing his arms around while talking animatedly. It makes the three of us laugh and I take a moment to appreciate this scene. Andrew is engaged in conversation with Michael, asking him questions about the American legal system and how it differs from the British one. It makes me happy that the two of them seem to get along. I was nervous at first because of the whole party incident, but Andrew knew deep down that there was nothing more between Michael and me other than friendship.

"So, Michael, is there someone special in your life yet?" Andrew asks.

Michael shakes his head. "No, unfortunately, I'm still playing the role of the lonely bachelor. I just haven't found that special someone yet. When I do, I hope to have half the chemistry as you two seem to have with each other."

I tilt my head to the side. "What are you talking about?"

Michael's cheeks pink up slightly as he looks down at the table briefly. "I wasn't going to say anything, but since you two have made it official, I guess there's no harm in mentioning it.

I saw you two dancing together at the party a few weeks ago. Even though I could tell there was some tension between you two, the looks you gave each other told me that it was all just a show. Your true feelings ran deeper than what was on the surface. I saw it again one other time while I was waiting for the elevator in the lobby. You both must have come back from lunch together and were laughing at something. But the furtive little glances you exchanged showed the amount of adoration and love you both hold for each other. I knew you would find your way eventually. Tess just needed to get out of her head and listen to her heart."

"You saw all that?" I can't believe he witnessed all that and never once said anything about it.

Michael nods. "I did. And it makes me want to find someone who will look at me the way you look at him. So if you happen to know anyone, by all means, send them my way."

He laughs, but I can tell there's a hint of sadness in it. I guess I never realized he was lonely.

"I don't know many people so I won't be much help. But if I see someone I will definitely send them your way."

"Thanks, Tess. I'm just kidding about that. You don't have to play matchmaker for me. I'll find someone eventually. Just need to keep my eyes open."

"It's all about being in the right place at the right time," Andrew adds, grabbing my hand.

"Yes, it is."

We spend the next half hour talking sports and catching Andrew up on the latest football games. He says he hasn't watched much American football before, but he's going to have to learn to love it if he wants to stay in a relationship with me.

Michael glances down at his watch and starts to stand from his chair. "I suppose it's about that time. Time to hit the grind again."

We dispose of our coffee cups and exit the shop to head down the block to our building. Andrew keeps a hand to the small of my back as we walk down the street.

"It is positively freezing out here. Aren't you two cold?" Andrew asks when a large gust of wind kicks up. The warm weather from the weekend has disappeared and brought back the usual temperature for the season.

"This is nothing. Have you ever experienced a Minnesota winter?" Michael asks.

"Afraid not."

"Oh, you're in for a treat then. A word of advice, though. Just because the sun is shining doesn't mean it's warm outside. Always dress as if there's going to be a blizzard because it can pretty much happen at any given moment."

"Really?"

Michael and I both nod our heads. "Really."

"Remember the blizzard of '91?" I ask Michael.

He laughs and holds the door open for us. "I remember my mom talking about it. It was Halloween and you guys up north got around three feet of snow dumped on you overnight, right?"

I nod. "I was little so I don't remember much of it. According to my mom and dad, the snow was so high it covered half of our living room windows to the point we couldn't see out of them."

Andrew shudders as we step into the elevator. "You are not making a good case for this state right now."

I look up at him and smile. "Don't worry. That was a fluke blizzard. We haven't had another one like that yet."

"Some have come close, though," Michael adds. I send him a glare and he just laughs.

"Not helping." I turn back to Andrew and smile. "You'll love winter here. It's so beautiful when it snows."

"I can't wait to experience it and see the difference between a London winter and a Minnesota winter."

"Be prepared to be shell-shocked," Michael says. The elevator stops on our floor and we move forward to exit.

"Enjoy your day in court," I say, waving goodbye to Michael.

"I will. You enjoy your corporate life down here. Coffee again tomorrow?"

Andrew nods and quickly shakes his hand. "We will be there."

"Great. See you then," Michael says as the elevator doors close.

Andrew turns to me and smiles. "You were right. He's a good gent and funny to boot. I can see why you're friends with him."

I kiss his cheek and link my arm through his. "I knew you two would get along."

We walk down the hall and stop outside the conference room.

"Lunch again?" I ask.

He shakes his head. "Not today. Chris and I will be tied up during lunch so I won't see you until after work. But that also means that I get to pick you up and take you home."

I smile at the thought. "Home. I love the sound of that

coming from your lips."

He leans down and gently brushes his lips across mine. "Good. I love you."

"I love you, too."

Andrew kisses me one last time before entering the conference room. I turn and walk toward my office, thankful that Michael seems to be right. Everything is working out as it should for once in my life.

Chapter 19

IT'S THE WEEKEND BEFORE THANKSGIVING and everyone is getting ready for the big holiday, making travel plans or arrangements for family to visit them. And since Andrew moved into my apartment a few weeks ago we don't have to worry about travel plans anymore. Surprisingly it's been a seamless transition incorporating both our lives into one. And his arguments for moving in turned out to be entirely valid, like taking one car to work instead of two. It's good for the environment and saves on gas. Brilliant. It also has saved me from physical pain since I have stopped falling out of bed altogether.

Luckily he didn't have many things to move over from his hotel room. And I'm afraid to bring up the dilemma of what is going to happen once his project is done here and he has to go back to London. I try not to think about it because it makes me sad. We'll deal with it when the time comes and so far it's still several months away.

Andrew is at the grocery store, picking up some essentials for dinner tonight. He still hasn't warmed up to my version of dinner. Apparently breakfast food is meant for breakfast and not for any other time of the day. But since he does the majority of the cooking, I'm not going to complain. It's like having my own personal chef sometimes.

Wanting to keep myself busy, I plug my phone into the stereo dock and start swaying to the music as Madonna's "Like a Prayer" blares through the speakers. Picking up my duster, I alternate between dusting and singing into it, bouncing to and fro as I drown out everything around me except the music.

"I love the way you sing."

Andrew's voice in my ear startles me, making me scream and damn near jump out of my skin. I twirl around to face him, clutching my chest and willing my heart to resume its normal rhythm.

"You scared me half to death!"

He laughs as the last few notes of the song fade and transitions to "Your Song" by Elton John. Andrew pulls me close, tossing the duster to the side and wrapping his arms around my waist. Looping my arms around his neck, I press my body into his as we sway in the middle of the living room. Unlike the last time we danced together, we're not in fancy clothes or shoes. Jeans and sweatshirts can be just as sexy sometimes. Andrew presses his lips to my ear, whispering the chorus to me softly.

I take the words to heart, loving that he's communicating to me through music. My body melts into his, becoming putty in his hands as he holds me upright and guides me across the room. The love song swirls around us, reminding me of how important he is to my life.

The music dies and is replaced by the shrill ringtone of my phone, breaking our spell and impromptu dance. I reach up on my tiptoes and gently kiss Andrew before grabbing my phone from the dock to answer it.

"Hello?"

"Hi, Tess."

"Hi, Dad." He sounds funny and the tiny hairs on the back of my neck stand up. "You seem different. Is there something wrong?"

He clears his throat and lets out a breath. "Tessa, I just got a call from the institution. Your mom apparently became ill a few weeks ago. The doctors have been giving her all sorts of treatments and medications, but her body was resisting them. Some complications arose and … " he pauses before going on again, "they ultimately claimed her life. I'm so sorry honey, but she's gone."

I stare at Andrew for a moment, but I don't really see him anymore. It's as if I'm having an out of body experience. Nothing is registering in my mind. No sounds, no movement. Everything is blurry, blending together into one giant black hole. The phone slips from my hands, landing at my feet with a soft thud. I hear someone quietly crying, not sure where it's coming from. My body goes limp and falls to the floor. Somehow Andrew's arms wrap around me and guide me into the safety of his body. Bringing my knees to my chest, I curl up into a tight ball and begin to cry gut wrenching sobs that wrack my whole body with pain.

Andrew's voice tries to break through the ringing in my ears. He must be talking to my dad because he's not asking me any questions.

My mom is dead.

My mom is dead.

My mom is dead.

This is all my mind can focus on, the only thing it knows for certain. She was fine and then she wasn't. She was alive and now she's dead. And worse, she died alone, thinking that no one cared about her. No one was by her side when she left this world. But someone had to have been there with her. She was placed in the hospital so a nurse must have been there, right?

But the one person that should have been there wasn't. I wasn't there in her final hours when she needed me most. I did the best I could to take care of her when I was growing up after my dad left. Even though she was sick and hated me for his departure, I still loved her. And now she's gone. And I didn't even get the chance to say goodbye.

Time ... space ... everything falls away with that thought. My body moves, but I'm not in control of it, as I'm lifted into the air. Tears fall from my eyes, pooling onto Andrew's shirt as I continue to cry. Andrew's voice breaks through again, pulling me back into the present. The words are still jumbled in my head, but the worried tone of his voice can be heard. I can feel the press of his hand as he strokes my hair lovingly.

Somehow I gather enough strength to pull away to look into his worried face. He's pale and scared and I can only imagine what I look like if I'm the reason he appears this way.

"I'm so sorry, love. Don't worry, I've got you. I'm here," he soothes, trying to relax me. His thumbs brush away some of the tears that continue to fall and I take deep, gasping breaths, attempting to get air back into my lungs.

"My mom," is all I can say before another round of tears breaks through again. Cradling my body, he holds me close while continually pressing his lips to my forehead.

"I know. Your dad told me. It's going to be okay, I promise." I stare blankly at him, wanting to believe in what he's saying. "She wasn't in pain, love. She passed in her sleep."

I nod against his chest, half paying attention, half processing everything that's happened since my world crumbled within the last ten minutes.

"Tessa, look at me." Andrew pushes me gently from his body, framing my face with his hands. I blink twice in partial recognition, but everything blurs with another round of tears. His voice is fading again and I feel weak as if all the energy has been zapped from my body. Soft lips kiss mine, coaxing me back from the edge of consciousness, but the tears continue to fall on their own.

"Your dad needs us to leave right away. We're heading to his house. Can you stand?" His voice sounds pained, scared. Why is he scared? I don't understand.

He sets me down on the couch, making sure a pillow is under my head before he moves around the apartment, darting in and out of rooms and stuffing things into a bag. He then grabs his keys and my purse before putting my tennis shoes on my feet. I'm lifted back into his arms, where I nuzzle my nose into his neck, pulling in deep breaths to calm me down. His strength amazes me as he covers me with a jacket and locks the door behind us, never once putting me down.

Cold leather meets my back as he places me in the front seat of the car. He guides my face to meet his, bringing us nose to nose. "Love, you're frightening me. I need you to stay with me. Can you do that?"

I blink several times as I try to focus on his face. Blue eyes stare at me.

My mom's eyes were blue.

Were blue.

My mom is dead.

Mommy.

I start crying again as Andrew buckles the seatbelt for me. My head falls back against the headrest, suddenly feeling very tired. The scenery around me moves fast beyond the window I'm staring out of. Blurs of barren trees and tall buildings fly by without fully coming into recognition.

Andrew's hand squeezes mine, but I can't squeeze it back. It hurts too much. Everything hurts. My eyes hurt, my head hurts, my heart hurts.

I never even got to say goodbye. She never heard me say that I loved her one last time. Yes, she was neglectful for most of my life, showing me more emotional pain than love, but she was my mom and I needed her. And now she's gone, forever.

The car slows to a stop outside my dad's house. I stare out the window, blinking repeatedly but not crying anymore. Somewhere along the way I stopped crying, as I listened to Andrew's voice constantly telling me that everything will be all right while never letting go of my hand. But it's his face that pops into view as my car door opens. He's crouching down next to me, releasing me from the confines of the car.

I look over his shoulder and see the house. *Daddy. I need my daddy. Daddy will help me.* The overwhelming urge to see my dad has tears flowing again, but not out of sadness. Warm lips brush against mine, contrasting against the cold wind beating against my face. I turn my head slightly and finally see him, my Andrew, kneeling in front of me, helping me deal with everything I'm going through.

"Andrew?"

My voice sounds hoarse, almost distant, and my throat feels like sandpaper due to all the tears I have cried already.

"I'm here, love. I'm going to take care of you, I promise. And so is your dad. We're both here for you."

He helps me out of the car and I wobble on my feet as they hit the ground. With his arm wrapped around me as support, we climb the stairs to the front of the house. A gust of wind wakes me up further and I focus on the person standing in the doorway with outstretched arms, looking at me with sad eyes.

Daddy.

"Tessa, honey." He pulls me into his arms, swallowing me into a loving embrace. He kisses the top of my head and releases one hand to shake Andrew's, who is standing behind me now. "How long has she been like this?"

"Since your call. She comes in and out of it, but she hasn't said much. I think she's still in shock."

My dad nods and walks us into the house. He stops us near his study and releases me, allowing Andrew to pull me back into the safety of his body.

"I just need to grab a few more things and then we can head up north. Feel free to have a seat in the living room. I'll only be a few minutes."

"Thank you, Robert."

Andrew leads me down the hall while my dad disappears behind his study door. We walk to the small loveseat, where Andrew pulls me into his lap. I can feel his lips press against my head and I finally snap out of my trance, noticing everything around me.

Andrew, my Andrew, is here, holding me, comforting me,

loving me. And my dad is here. He's coming with us. Both of them are here with me so I'm not alone.

I turn my head and half smile at the most beautiful face I've ever seen. "Andrew?"

His hand continues to smooth over my hair, gently threading his fingers through the strands. "Yes, love, I'm here. I've got you, don't worry."

"We're at my dad's house?"

He nods and kisses the tip of my nose. "Yes, your dad is coming to help us out."

Realization finally sinks in as the haze clears from my brain. We need to go up north, to the institution, to finalize things and see my mom. And it gives me great relief that Andrew and my dad are coming with me, so I don't have to do this alone.

I'll never be alone again.

"Thank you. For everything. For sticking it out with me, for helping me, and for being here so I'm not alone."

"You will never be alone. I promised that you would never be alone again and I meant it. I'm here and so is your father."

His beautiful blue eyes are still filled with pain as they move back and forth over my face. I trace his lips with the tip of my finger, running it along the curves before trailing it down his chin, letting my hand fall limply into my lap.

"My mom is dead."

He nods, holding me tighter in his arms. "Yes."

A tear slips down my cheek though it doesn't hurt this time. "Okay."

Andrew holds me, knowing that I don't need anything more than to feel his arms around me.

The fog has lifted and I'm finally coming back into myself, putting together bits and pieces of the last hour of my life. "And Daddy? Where did he go?"

Just then he enters the room, placing his suitcase on the floor before walking toward me. "I'm here, honey."

Remembering that he held me at the entrance to the house, I stand upright and close the distance to him, wrapping my arms around his waist. I bury my head in his chest while he holds me.

"It's okay, Tessa. Daddy's here."

I step away and look into his sad eyes, the same eyes as mine. Andrew approaches behind me and presses a kiss to my temple.

"I think the shock has worn off," he says, wrapping his arm around my shoulders. I cling to his waist and press my head against his body, thankful to have his support.

My dad looks at me and gives a genuine smile. "You haven't called me Daddy since you were little. I just realized now how much I've missed that."

I release Andrew to give my dad another hug, noticing that he is hurting from this as well. He was married to my mom after all. He had to have cared about her at some point.

Out of the corner of my eye, I see someone else enter the room. "What in the hell is going on here?" Sharon sharply states. I jerk back, startled by her outburst and Andrew wraps his arms protectively around my waist, pulling me back into him.

"Sharon, stop your yelling. Tessa's mom has passed away and understandably she's upset."

She walks over to the three of us, putting her hands on her

hips and scowls. "So what does that have to do with you? You divorced the woman years ago. Why do you care about what happened to her?" she asks, tapping her foot impatiently. Andrew's grip tightens around my waist as she glares at me, her mouth firmly locked into a sneer.

"The hospital called me because they were unable to reach Tessa due to a mix-up in updated contact information. And since I was the next person on the list they called me. So I'm taking Tessa and Andrew up north to help them take care of everything."

"Like hell you are!" she bellows. "She's your EX wife! You don't owe her shit anymore." Her voice echoes throughout the house, swirling around me and creating those feelings of inadequacy again.

My dad straightens up to his full height and turns an angry eye to Sharon. "Yes, I am Sharon. Tessa needs me right now and I'm going to help her. She won't have to do this alone."

Sharon swings her icy gaze to me and I shrink back. "She has her current fuck buddy to help her out. She doesn't need her dad running to help her with every little problem that life throws at her. You've helped her with too much as it is. She's an *adult*. Let her fucking figure it out on her own."

Andrew moves me to the side protectively, trying to stand as a shield between me and my cruel stepmother.

"I would advise you to change your tone, Sharon. You are out of line. Tessa needs the both of us right now," Andrew says. My eyes bounce between the three of them, watching each expression morph into something else. Sharon's morphs to disgust, Andrew's changes from disdain to anger, and my dad stays eerily calm, except for the red slowly creeping up his neck.

"Sharon, this is not up for discussion. And I sure as hell do not need your permission to do anything. I'm leaving tonight with Andrew and Tessa to help them with her mother's estate. It's the least I could do after what happened all those years ago. Show some respect for God's sake. She lost her mother and you're acting like it doesn't matter."

Sharon scoffs and stabs her pointed finger into the middle of his chest. "The least you could do? If you owe anyone anything, it's me. I'm the one who saved your life from that little brat over there. I'm the one you should be thanking and showing gratitude to."

Confusion takes over the anger in my dad as he tilts his head to the side. "What are you talking about? What did you save me from?"

"If I hadn't intercepted that fucking phone call from Child Protective Services, you would have been held back in your career, putting all your focus into poor little Tessa instead of the law firm. I *saved* you when I told them you were not interested in taking her in when her mom was committed. Don't you see? She would have held you back. She would have dragged you down like the little leech she is. You wouldn't be in the position you're in today without my intervention. So I'm the one who needs you. You're my husband, not her fucking dead mommy's!" Sharon explodes, releasing years of resentment and anger all at once.

I move to Andrew's side, still clinging to him but now I'm morbidly curious what Sharon's involvement in my adolescence was. But my curiosity is nothing compared to the fire that shines in my dad's eyes as he stalks slowly toward his wife.

Sharon straightens her posture, but there's a slight tremble in her arms, letting us know that she's not quite as put together as she appears.

He leans in close, leaving only a foot of space between them. "Am I to understand this correctly? Child Protective Services called me and *you* decided to send her to live in foster care, with some strangers instead of her own family? You sent her to live in filth, made to believe that I didn't want her and let those people treat her the exact same way? She's my daughter, my flesh and blood. You turned her away when she needed me most and you think I should be grateful for that?"

Anger radiates from his body towards Sharon, who has taken a defensive pose, but is not backing down. She actually believes she didn't do anything wrong, that she saved him from a life of burden to a teenage daughter who would do nothing but bring him down.

Sharon straightens her shoulders again, matching his glare. "Yes, I did. And I paid a lot of money to make sure the case moved along quickly and quietly. You didn't need some bratty seventeen-year-old girl hanging around, especially one who opened her legs to whoever came knocking and then didn't even know how to properly satisfy him."

Shane. Holy shit, she's bringing up Shane. My lungs feel deflated as I try to breathe, except it feels like I'm suffocating. How could she be so cruel?

Andrew takes a step toward Sharon. "If I were you I would watch your mouth. You are talking about my girlfriend who has had countless assaults and other indecencies done to her that should never be wished upon anyone. Abuse takes on many forms and so far both of her maternal role models have done the opposite of what she's needed. It would be in your best interest to not speak ill of her again."

Sharon swings her icy gaze to Andrew, letting a slow, creepy smile play upon her lips. "She has you snowballed, just like everyone else. Let's face it. She's not some innocent little girl who needs rescuing. She's a manipulator, a whore, and a spoiled brat who doesn't want to deal with anything. And why should she when daddy dearest will come clean up the mess for her."

My dad moves to stand between Sharon and Andrew, looking down upon his wife with unrepressed hatred. "I don't owe you anything, you gold digging snake. You didn't do me a favor by keeping her from me. You destroyed my life." He reaches down, grabs her left hand and takes off her wedding rings. "Get the fuck out of my house right now. I will send your things to you. You are nothing to me and no longer welcome here. And, believe me, I will destroy your life if you step foot in this house again. Leave, now!" he bellows, letting his voice echo around the completely still room.

Sharon's face pales. "You're throwing me out? How dare you! You're choosing her over me? She's a nobody!"

"No, I'm choosing my daughter. You, Sharon, are the nobody. And if you want any sort of decent settlement in the divorce, I suggest you leave right now and never look back. My lawyer will contact yours," he says, effectively dismissing her with an eerie calm.

Sharon's shoulders scrunch up as she clenches her fists at her sides. "Fuck you!" she screams and turns on her heels, stomping out of the room. Moments later we hear the front door slam and her car tires squealing out of the driveway.

I can feel Andrew's whole body relax in my arms before he pulls me around to the front of him, framing my face in his hands.

"Are you okay?"

"Yes," I whisper. I turn to look at my dad, who appears absolutely heartbroken. Shame and regret play across his face as he takes a cautious step toward me.

"Tessa, I'm so sorry. I never knew. I swear to you that I never knew what Sharon did. If I had received that call all those years ago, I would have come for you. You must believe me."

He opens his arms and I instantly gravitate to him, wrapping my arms around his middle. He holds me close, kissing the top of my head and I feel the first tear slip down my cheek. It's not a sad tear, but one filled with relief. *He does love me.*

"I know now you would have. It's not your fault. I don't blame you for Sharon's actions. They're hers to take responsibility for, and hers alone."

When I step back, I see his eyes are watery and watch as a tear slowly rolls down his handsome face. He brushes it away and doesn't speak any more on the subject. I think enough has been said already.

"I'm sorry you had to witness that Andrew. I'm sorry any of us did. But you will never have to deal with her again, either of you."

I nod my head and link my hand with Andrew's, watching him bring it up to his lips and gently press them against the back.

"Let's just focus on what we need to do over the next few days," Andrew says, leading us toward the front door, grabbing our coats on the way out.

"I could only get a couple days off from work, unfortunately, which means I need to be back here by Wednesday," my dad says.

"It's okay. I called Christopher and Kara to let them know what's happening, clearing both our schedules for the week so we can take our time getting everything done."

We walk into the garage and watch as my dad places his suitcase in the trunk of his car before turning to us. "You'll follow me up there?" he asks Andrew, who nods in response. "I've already made hotel reservations for us so we will be all set when we arrive."

"Excellent. Thank you, Robert."

We exit the garage and head back to our car. Andrew holds open my door and waits for me to buckle my seatbelt before shutting it and getting in on the driver's side. He gives me a smile and begins following my dad for our journey north.

Andrew keeps a hand on my knee as we make the two and a half hour drive to where my mother is, or was I guess. The pain isn't quite as bad anymore when I think about her. Having Andrew nearby helps quite a bit, as well as knowing that my dad is there to help me too.

We don't say much as the world passes us by. Once we're out of the metro area, the scenery changes as we leave behind the urban jungle for long stretches of trees and the open road. Towns are sprinkled here and there and are barely visible from the highway. The one thing I'm grateful for is that it hasn't snowed yet so the roads are dry and not as hazardous as they could be this time of the year.

I turn to look at Andrew's profile as he concentrates on the road. Just his presence is enough to calm me down from any stressful situation. He grounds me and brings me back to the world I now have a place in.

I switch the radio on, looking for a little white noise to drown out any remaining thoughts in my head. We listen to song after song, sometimes humming along with the melody, sometimes just letting the words wash over us in silence. Then an older song comes on, one I haven't heard in years. Allison Krauss's soulful voice fills the car and it's like she's reaching into my brain and saying the words I'm thinking as I look at the beautiful man sitting next to me. Without thinking, I start softly singing the words out loud to him.

Andrew turns his head and smiles. He grabs my hand, kissing the palm lightly as his eyes twinkle in our brief contact.

"Thank you for saving me from myself today. I don't know what I would have done if you hadn't been there for me." I reach up and place the same hand on his cheek before he threads our hands together, resting them over his heart.

"Love, I will do anything for you. I told you, you are mine and I am yours. We will take care of each other for the rest of time and then beyond that. As long as we're together, nothing can harm us."

If I thought it wasn't possible to fall further in love with this man, I was mistaken. Time after time he shows me how much he cares for me, wanting nothing more than my happiness. He makes me feel as if I'm the most important thing in the world. And I honestly believe that he will save me from everything and everyone, including myself.

When we arrive at the hotel, Andrew parks our car next to my dad's and gathers our luggage together. After checking in and getting our room keys, we say goodnight to my dad, agreeing to meet up in the morning so we can get things started. As we ride the elevator to our room, I slump against the wall, feeling the weight of the day's events finally dragging me down. I begin to move but am swept up in Andrew's arms instead as he carries me down the hall. I want to protest, but my body is so tired that all I can do is lay my head against his shoulder and cling to him.

Andrew drops our bags on the floor at the foot of the bed and slowly sets me down.

"You're tired. Come, let's get you ready."

He strips me out of my clothes, tapping the body parts he wants me to move. Before long I'm in one of his shirts that hang limply on my body. He strips down to his boxer briefs, scoops me up and settles us both under the covers. Holding me against his chest, he nuzzles his face into my hair, whispering sweet endearing words to me.

"I love you."

"Everything will be all right."

"You are so beautiful."

"My brave, strong girl."

I twist around, needing to see him before I succumb to the sleep my body is so desperately craving. "Andrew?"

"Yes, love?"

I press my lips against his softly, slowly moving them with love and appreciation. "You are my hero, you know that? I feel so much stronger around you. You make me brave and give me hope when I think it's lost. Nothing is quite as scary as it seems as long as we're together. You are my everything and I just want you to know that."

He smiles and kisses me again, reassuring me without words that he feels the same as I do.

Chapter 20

"WAKE UP, LOVE."

I stir and rub my face into the pillow, wanting to stay in the warm cocoon the blankets have created for me. Pulling the covers over my head, I sink further into the mattress, hoping it's enough to make the world go away.

"Don't want to," I grumble through my protective fortress.

Andrew laughs and drags the covers down my body, leaving me shivering with the sudden assault of cooler air. I liked my big warm blanket wrapped around me, although it's nothing compared to being wrapped up in Andrew's arms. I sigh wistfully as I open my eyes, not instantly recognizing my surroundings. Then I remember the reason why I'm sitting in this hotel room.

Mom.

I brush away the tangled mess that I call my hair from my face as I sit up, turning to see the bright smiling eyes of the man I love. He's dressed in black pants and a gray button-down shirt. His hair is still wet from a recent shower and he smells like his body wash and cologne, my two favorite scents.

I let my body slump forward, landing on his shoulder while I deeply inhale his calming scent. He laughs and kisses the top of my head, seemingly amused at my lack of energy this morning.

"Are you trying to tell me you like how I smell?"

I nod my head against his shoulder and my whole body melts into him, wanting nothing more than to wake up to this smell every day for the rest of my life.

"Mmhmm," I say in a muffled voice.

Andrew picks me up and places me on his lap. Wrapping my arms and legs around him, I lean forward and press my lips to his in a quick morning greeting.

"How are you feeling this morning?" He runs his fingers through the hair loosely hanging near my face and I lean into his touch when his palm meets my cheek.

"Better," I say, taking a mental inventory of my emotional and physical state. My head has stopped pounding and my stomach no longer aches for no apparent reason. My eyes aren't nearly as dry and painful as before but not having cried within the last twelve hours has helped. "I know the next few days are going to be tough, but I'll be okay, as long as you don't go anywhere without me."

He smiles and presses his lips against mine again. "Never. I'll be stuck to you like glue."

"Good." I stand from his lap to stretch. "What time are we meeting my dad?"

Andrew looks at his watch and twists his lips to the side. "Half hour? Can you be ready by then?"

I nod. "Half hour it is," I say, disappearing into the bathroom so I can attempt to feel human again.

It's your standard hotel bathroom, complete with giant vanity countertop and bathtub/shower combination. It makes me miss the hotel bathroom in London with its extraordinary opulence and high-end fixtures. Obviously not everything in life is going to be like that.

Standing under the hot spray of the water, I can feel each and every muscle relax as the knots slowly wash away. Rolling my shoulders, I hunch forward, allowing the water stream to hit my most tender spots where I carry all of my stress. With each passing moment, I relax further and let my mind prepare itself for what's to come.

Yes, it will be hard. It may be downright excruciating, but as long as my dad and Andrew are with me I know it'll be okay. It still amazes me the transition in my dad, going from seemingly indifferent and judgmental to loving and concerned. But I could have also been projecting some of my own insecurities onto him, only seeing what I wanted to see. Ever since I came to Minneapolis, he has been attentive, offering to pay for my schooling, my apartment, clothes, anything I could ever want. And because my past dictated so much of my life I was too stubborn to accept help due to the idea that obligation was making him do it. Knowing what I know now, I can see that wasn't the case. Yes, guilt may have played a little bit, considering my situation after I was placed into foster care, but I believe he just wanted to get to know me.

Once I'm dressed and feeling better about my appearance, I walk back into the main room and find my dad sitting with Andrew at the table near the windows. Both men look up and smile brightly at me when I join them. Andrew pulls out a chair for me, making sure it's the one next to him, of course.

"I ordered some breakfast for you," he says. I clasp his hand as he uncovers a dish in front of me, displaying a plate loaded with scrambled eggs, bacon, toast, and hash browns. The smell alone has my stomach rumbling in eager anticipation of food.

"Thank you. I didn't even realize I was hungry until just now."

My dad folds up his paper, placing it off to the side as he watches me eat my breakfast.

"Good morning, Tess," he says, taking a sip of his coffee.

"Morning, Daddy," I mutter through a bite of my toast.

He laughs, making his eyes crinkle in the corners. I take a bite of everything on my plate, humming my pleasure and only pause to take a sip of the orange juice that Andrew just put in my glass.

"What?" I ask, letting my fork hover over my plate as I look between the two of them.

"Nothing. It's just, I've never seen you eat so much before," my dad says, still laughing at me.

I roll my eyes and wipe my mouth with the napkin. "I told you. I do eat. I just don't eat when I come over to your house, mainly because of Sharon. She makes me lose my appetite with her condescending comments and opinions about me."

He reaches over and pats my hand. "Well, you won't have to worry about that again. How did you sleep last night?"

A blush creeps across my cheeks. What dad wants to hear about his daughter sharing a bed with another man? Not that we did anything last night. It's the mere fact that we are sharing a bed together which causes my brief embarrassment. Most fathers tend to threaten or clean their guns in front of their daughter's boyfriends. But this is different. He really has taken a liking to Andrew, even though they've only met once or twice before this.

"She was a little fitful but otherwise got some decent sleep," Andrew answers after I fail to speak up. I turn my head and smile in appreciation while continuing to eat my breakfast, letting my dad and Andrew talk sports and business.

Once my food is mostly gone, I shove it away and place my hands on my full stomach. "I think I'm good for a while." Both men laugh and shake their heads. Andrew looks out the window and I follow his gaze, noticing that we're staying right on the water. We must be in Canal Park, the ever popular tourist section of Duluth. That's where most of the higher end hotels and shops are, along with some of the best views of Lake Superior.

"The lake is so beautiful, very calm and surprisingly large. It's almost like looking out at the ocean," Andrew observes.

"This part of the state is really magnificent. The lake, the trees, the hills, all of it placed together in absolute perfection. If you both decide to spend a few extra days up here, you should go on a tour of the area. I'm sure Tessa remembers a few places to go so you can grab the full experience," my dad says.

I look over at him and nod. "I think I remember and if not I'm sure we can figure it out. Sightseeing isn't exactly high on the list of things to do right now and I don't know how much extra time we'll have."

"I'm sure we'll have a better timeframe after we speak with the people at the institution and the cremation society" Dad gently clears his throat and leans forward, folding his hands on the table. "Are you sure this is what you want Tess?"

I nod. "Yes, I'm sure. There's no point in having a burial. She didn't have any family, except for me, or us, rather. Cremation just seems like the logical thing to do. Plus we can spread her ashes over the lake." I look out the window and my heart constricts slightly at the memory. "She always loved the lake." A lone tear rolls down my cheek, but Andrew brushes it away quickly.

"Then that's what we'll do. Whatever you want, honey."

"Thank you, Dad, for being here." I reach out and grab hold of his hand, squeezing it lightly. With the other, I take Andrew's hand and squeeze it as well, drawing strength from both the men in my life.

"No need to thank me, Tessa. You're my daughter. I'm always here to help when you need me. I'm just sorry it took this long for it to happen." The sadness in his eyes almost makes me start to cry again.

"It's okay. You didn't know. It's in the past now and I don't want to dwell on the past anymore. I think we both need a clean slate, starting now."

"I'd like that."

Once everything is cleaned up, we head out to the vehicles, ready to make our way downtown.

"Why don't we take mine? No sense in bringing two cars down there," my dad says.

"Sounds like an excellent idea," Andrew agrees.

Andrew lets me sit up front while he folds his body into the backseat of my dad's car. It's a short drive so he says he doesn't mind. We make our way downtown and my chest begins to tighten slightly as we pass the familiar sights from a time I don't want to remember. Andrew squeezes my shoulder, somehow knowing that this place has mixed memories for me.

We park in the lot for the institution and walk into the building, greeted by a blast of warm air. It feels good in contrast to the icy cold wind outside. Somehow I've forgotten how much the wind hurts when it blows directly off the lake. The lady behind the registration desk greets us warmly and points us in the direction of the administrator's office.

"You can just have a seat in the chairs over there. Mr. Peterson will be with you shortly," she says, smiling brightly at Andrew. I laugh because no one can resist his charms, not even sixty-year-old receptionists.

We find three available seats in the waiting area. Andrew sits to my left while my dad sits to my right. Andrew places his hand on mine and I tug them both into my lap, feeling surprisingly calm. The pain doesn't hurt quite as much today now that I'm here and ready to face everything though I don't think I could handle another breakdown.

"How are you holding up?" Andrew asks me.

I try to give him a reassuring smile. "I'm okay for now, although if I lose it again at least I'm in the right place." Both Andrew and my dad stare blankly at me, apparently not amused. "Sorry, bad joke."

Well, I thought it was funny. Andrew rolls his eyes in the same way I do to him and it makes me laugh. Wow, tough crowd. *Mental note, don't crack jokes about going crazy while sitting in a mental hospital. Got it.*

A door opens to the right and an older, portly gentleman steps out.

"Ms. Martin?" he says, extending a hand to me.

I stand and greet him, shaking his hand in return. "Please, call me Tessa."

"Hello, Tessa. I'm George Peterson, the administrator here at the hospital. I first want to give you my deepest sympathy for the loss of your mother."

Tucking a lock of hair behind my ear, I swallow hard and nod. "Thank you."

Mr. Peterson then turns to my dad and shakes his hand. "Are you her father?"

"Yes. Robert Martin."

"Very nice to formally meet you." Mr. Peterson turns to Andrew next.

"Andrew Parker. I'm Tessa's boyfriend."

"Very pleased to meet you as well," he says, shaking Andrew's hand. "Let's go into my office and we can discuss things further."

The three of us follow Mr. Peterson into his office, taking seats in front of the desk that occupies the middle of the room. His office is exactly what I had imagined it would look like. Plaques and certificates adorn the walls, proudly proclaiming his many accomplishments and accolades. A large shelf filled with books takes up the whole wall directly behind his solid wood desk. A small leather couch and round end table sit on one side of the room and more shelves on the opposite side, along with several windows that overlook the lake.

Mr. Peterson opens a folder on top of a pile and folds his hands over the papers inside. "Tessa, again, I'm very sorry for your loss. I know this is a difficult time for you and that you haven't had much time to process everything. We will understand if you have any questions regarding how you'd like your mother's body to be prepared."

I nod, reaching for Andrew's hand in support. "Thank you but I have made a decision in regards to my mother. After discussing it with my dad, we've decided that cremation would be the best option."

Mr. Peterson nods his head, writing notes on the paper in front of him. "I assumed as much but wanted to make sure. Have you been in contact with the cremation society yet?"

I look to my dad and he nods. "Yes, I contacted them this morning so they are anticipating her arrival this afternoon."

Mr. Peterson scribbles some more notes and then looks at us over the rims of his glasses. "Of course. I will contact them as well and make all the necessary arrangements for you." He turns his attention back to me and slides several sheets of paper before me. "Tessa, as her next of kin, I just need your signature on a few documents and then I can let you folks be on your way."

I nod and start signing my name on the designated lines, reading each paragraph carefully to make sure I understand what I'm signing. Once they are all complete, I hand them back and he places them in the folder.

"Since Mrs. Martin was a ward of the state, all of her expenses here have been covered."

I nod again and blow out a quick breath. "Thank you, Mr. Peterson, for all of your help. Is there anything else we need to do here?"

He smiles and stands, shaking each of our hands again. "All forms have been signed so there is nothing left to do. Thank you for coming in and I hope you're able to enjoy the rest of your day."

"Same to you," I say, flashing him a half smile before exiting his office.

Once we get back to the car, Andrew pauses and wraps me in his arms. "Still okay, love?"

With a smile, I press my lips to his and nod. "Yes, I'm okay."

We decide to take Andrew on a quick tour of the city so my dad drives us around, pointing out different attractions and giving a brief history behind them. We drive up to the Skyline Parkway and follow the winding road as it twists along the rocky hillside, showing the most breathtaking views of the city and lake below.

After stopping at a little café to eat a late lunch, we drive back to the hotel. My dad retires to his room, saying he needs to contact his friend who is one of the best divorce lawyers in the state. I definitely do not want to be around for that conversation.

Andrew and I settle onto the bed and decide to watch some TV to pass the time. I curl into his side, resting my head on his shoulder as we channel surf and laugh at some of the dumb commercials we find. After an hour, we get bored and decide to play cards instead. Andrew shuffles the deck and then proceeds to beat me four times at cribbage, a game I had taught him just weeks ago. It makes me laugh and also appreciate these moments because they're so easy and laid back. I've never been this comfortable with anyone before, being able to do absolutely nothing and have it mean so much at the same time.

Later, we meet my dad for dinner at one of the restaurants down the street. It's still strange, this newfound relationship with my dad, but the more we spend time together, the more I'm surprised at how quickly we're falling into our roles of father and daughter. If you saw us together, you'd never know that we didn't see each other for ten years at some point in my life.

We leave my dad at his room once again after dinner and Andrew and I decide to walk on the boardwalk along the lakeshore. It's a rare clear November night, with only a slight chill in the air from the wind blowing off the lake. The moon is high in the evening sky, dancing across the water as it ebbs to the shore, casting a silver glow onto the world below. Stars twinkle and dance above us as we walk hand in hand along the lake. Andrew pulls me close as a gust of wind kicks up and blows my hair every which way, making me laugh as I attempt to tame it down again.

"Did you really grow up around here?"

I stick my hand into the back pocket of his jeans and lean closer into his body. "Yeah. We passed by my old apartment on the way to the institution this morning, but the house I grew up in is thirty minutes north of here."

"Were you still near the lake?"

"Sort of. The town was right next to the lake, but I couldn't see it from our house since we lived on the outskirts of town." I pause, looking at the water as a memory flashes into my head.

"When I was little, my mom and I would drive to one of the beaches in town to collect rocks on the warmer summer days. We would spend hours combing every inch of sand and rock, finding those little agates nestled among everything else. I'd wade into the lake but not too far because the water was so cold. I could only stand to be in there for a few minutes before my lips would turn blue and my feet went numb. Then we'd come back to the house and wait for my dad to get home and have dinner together. It wasn't very often, but it was nice when it happened."

Andrew stops and pulls me in front of him, my back to his chest. We watch the waves lap against the sand, listening to the wind and water. There's a calming effect it's having on me, especially with Andrew holding me in his arms. "It really is beautiful. I can only imagine what it looks like in the summertime, full of lush green trees and boats on the water."

I nod and smile. "It's beautiful in the summer, but it's also pretty in the winter when ice forms on some of the bigger rocks by the shore and the trees are covered in a thick blanket of snow. Everything always looks better after the snowfall, when it's freshly white again. Almost like getting a brand new start."

We turn and start walking back to the hotel. Andrew doesn't say much but just listens to me go on and on about living in this area. I tell him some more happy memories I have of my childhood and skim over the less than pleasant ones. We pause beneath a streetlamp and face each other. Andrew's hands reach up to brush some hair from my face and I get mesmerized once again by the light reflecting in his eyes, making my heart beat in double time.

"I can't wait to build memories like those with you," he says, pulling me close to his body. The way he looks at me has my blood igniting, sending sparks shooting through the veins just below my skin.

Unable to resist any longer, we close the distance between us and kiss beneath the light. It starts out soft and slow, as one would expect a kiss in public. But then it shifts and changes, turning heated and passionate as our hands wrap around each other's bodies, tangling in hair and wandering beneath our coats. The cold wind is gone, along with the outside world, as Andrew becomes the sole focus of mine. The minute our tongues touch and dance together, intense desire settles low in my body. Andrew feels it too because his breathing changes and his fingers dig deep into my hips, pulling me tight against his body.

"Let's go back and make a new memory right now," he says, trailing his lips along my jaw line.

Somehow I'm able to respond as my eyes flutter between that happy place of open and closed when his lips press against my skin. "Hurry," I whisper and feel his smile against the pulsing vein in my neck.

With a tug of my hand, we practically run back to the hotel, pausing only to put the Do Not Disturb tag on our door before falling into bed and creating our memory.

Chapter 21

MY DAD RECEIVES THE CALL from the cremation society about mid-afternoon the next day, letting us know that my mother is ready for us. To me, it seems so sudden, but I suppose after having arrangements made, and possibly my dad's name thrown around, there wasn't a whole lot to do. It's not as if we were planning a burial or memorial. We just needed the cremation services.

"Where would you like to spread her ashes?" my dad asks me.

Holding the urn in my hands, my mind blanks for a moment as it tries to grasp the reality of the situation. I'm holding my mother in my arms for the last time and now have to decide where she's going to rest. We had already agreed the lake was the best place but now that the moment has arrived, it seems surreal. Almost like it's not really happening.

"Tessa?" Andrew asks, rubbing my back gently.

"Home. We need to go back home, back to Burlington Bay. That was her favorite place to go look at the lake in town."

They both nod and Andrew helps me into the front seat of my dad's car. The drive will only take about a half hour, but it could be the longest half hour of my life. So many emotions swirl through my body, making it difficult to pinpoint one that wants to take dominance. But over everything else, there's a peace about the whole thing because I know this is the final journey with my mom, where I can let go of everything that's happened between us.

We drive in silence for most of the way. Andrew asks a few questions, but I stay quiet, staring out the window as the scenery passes us by. It's been eight years since I've stepped foot in this town and it appears nothing has changed. The same small shops greet you as you drive through town, along with some familiar faces. Even with the November winds blowing, the town is still busy, getting ready for the snow to hit and the tourists to come back for their winter activities.

Burlington Bay is on the other side of town, tucked into a secluded little spot where rocks jut out and dip into the lake. It's quiet and peaceful, a perfect place to lay my mom to rest.

I exit the car first, walking slowly through the sand as my shoes sink with each step I take toward the water's edge. Andrew joins me about halfway down the beach, wrapping his arm around my shoulders as I cling to the urn in my hands. My dad appears on the other side and we pause, taking a good look at our surroundings. Birds fly overhead and the waves lap against the sand, ebbing and flowing with ease. The wind blows my hair around my face as I amble to the water's edge. Whitecaps tip the waves further out and I stop and watch them roll to greet us.

"Do you need any help?" my dad asks.

I shake my head and give a sad smile. "No, I've got this. I took care of her for so long ..." I start, breaking off as tears threaten to fall.

Andrew's hand rests on my shoulder, comforting me. I lean my head against him quickly and smile. "If you need me, I'm right here," he says, leaning down to whisper in my ear.

"I know."

"I love you," he whispers before joining my dad back up at the top of the beach.

There's something comforting about hearing those words pass from another person's lips. They fill up every crack and crevice of your body until you're whole again. Even though they're just words, they're powerful words. Words that can destroy but also rebuild and heal. And that's what he does to me every time he says them. He's healing me.

But for now, there's another piece of me that needs to rebuild and heal. I need to let my mother go, to forgive her for the wrongdoings of my childhood because she wasn't herself. She wasn't the mother of my earlier years. Just a broken shell of a woman who was lost in her own world where nothing mattered and no one could reach her, not even me.

I clutch the urn tighter against my chest as I approach the water. The wind dies down to a dull breeze, almost as if it knows there's something more powerful happening at this moment. I can barely feel the chill in the air as I stare into the vast expanse of water before me. Waves lap against my boots, dragging sand from the shore to the lake as it swirls into the darkness of the water.

I grip the top of the smooth blue urn, lifting it gently to reveal what's left of my mom.

"I love you, Mommy," I whisper. I press my lips lightly against the smooth surface on the side, giving her one final kiss.

Lifting my face to the heavens in a silent prayer, I spread her ashes before me. The waves pull the ashes underneath, washing her away and setting her free. I place the lid back on the urn and blow a kiss to the air. "Goodbye, Mom."

I turn back to where Andrew and my dad are standing, each giving me a sad smile. But the weight of my emotions comes crashing down upon my shoulders and I'm unable to keep the pain inside me any longer. I drop to my knees, hitting the cold sand and sob uncontrollably.

Andrew is instantly by my side and I instinctively turn to him, crying into his shoulders as his arms wrap around me, enveloping me with his love. I cling to his neck, grieving for the loss of my mother and also the release of my childhood. I let everything go to finally be free from the weight it's always put on me. When my sobs subside, Andrew cradles my face, letting his thumbs brush away the remaining tears that trickle down my cheeks. Our lips meet as we hold each other, both of us kneeling in the cold sand. He helps me to my feet and we walk back to my dad, who also has tears streaming down his face, looking just as broken as I do.

I hand Andrew the empty urn and walk to my dad, throwing my arms around him. We comfort each other and close the rift between us until it's no more.

"I'm so sorry I left you alone to care for your mother. I honestly didn't know she was that bad. If I had I known I would have helped the both of you. But when she called me after receiving the first check when the divorce was final and told me to not bother with her or you anymore, I knew something was wrong. Then she closed the bank account, leaving me with no indication that she had another. I was at a loss. But my pride was too big to admit my wrongdoing and I ignored her. I ignored you. And I will forever regret that decision because you were an innocent child and deserved her parent's love."

I hold him tighter, wanting to let him know that I've forgiven him. "It's okay, Dad. You didn't know, and I'm okay now. My childhood formed me into the adult I am today and I wouldn't change anything about me." I glance over at Andrew with a smile. "Everything happens for a reason. Some call it luck. I call it fate. And I wouldn't change it for the world."

He lets me go and hands me back to Andrew with a smile as he looks at us. "Yes, honey, I believe that things happen for a reason. At the time, you don't fully understand it but eventually you're shown the way."

I brush off the remaining sand from my clothes and take the urn back from Andrew. We walk back to my dad's car with my arm looped through Andrew's. As we pull away from the lake, heading back towards Duluth, peace falls over me. One I have been searching for over the last few years of my life. In death comes new life and with new life comes hope. Hope of something better, doing things differently, and learning from your mistakes. Today I healed my soul by letting my mom go and finding comfort in my dad. But that soul is no longer mine. No, I have given that soul to someone else when I was in London, along with my heart.

I reach my hand back over my seat, seeking out Andrew's. He wraps his hand around mine and I squeeze, just needing the connection.

We make small talk on the short drive back to the hotel. My dad tells us his divorce attorney has the papers ready for him to sign as soon as he gets back to Minneapolis. Apparently he drew up a rough draft on his computer a few weeks ago and was just waiting for the right time to send them to his friend. I talk about some of the newer contracts I've acquired and my strategy for helping them grow their business and get in contact with several builders. Dad gives me a few names of people who could also help, which is huge because I never had a contact on the inside with a few of them since they're so exclusive.

"Anything to help you out, honey," he says, smiling at me. His eyes flicker to the backseat and connect with Andrew. "How is your project going, Andrew?"

"It's going well. Everything is progressing smoothly on this end and it sounds like it will be completed by May or June."

"So all of your contracts have been signed and things are ready to go?" he asks.

Andrew nods. "They are."

"What are your plans now that this project is virtually complete for you?"

My stomach drops because I didn't realize that Andrew's job over here is basically complete. He's signed all his contracts and made sure everything is set up. There's no reason why he can't foresee the project from London. But his hand reaches up and squeezes my arm as if he knew what my riotous mind was thinking.

"I have a couple of things lined up actually. I just started the process on a new venture that should keep me here for a long time," he says.

I turn in my seat, needing to look at his face. He just smiles, not giving anything away.

"What new venture?" I ask, puzzled.

Andrew leans forward and brushes his lips softly across mine. "It appears that Charles and Priscilla have agreed that an office will be needed here to manage all the centers we're planning to open in the U.S." He pauses and looks to my dad, who silently nods his approval. "And they agree that I am just the person to lead the way."

I stare at him, dumbstruck because I can't believe what he's saying. Is this real?

"So you're staying here?"

He nods and runs a finger gently down my cheek. "Yes, love, I'm staying here. No more traveling around the world, only within the States, and not for extended periods of time since my role will be different now."

"What about your position in London?"

"They've already promoted another promising intern, the same way they promoted me."

I blink a few more times, still trying to wrap my mind around this.

"What about your home? Your family?"

His thumb gently brushes across my bottom lip. "They are just a plane ride away. Besides, my home is with you. Is it all right if I stay here with you forever?"

I laugh and grab his hand, kissing his knuckles the same way he does my own, not caring that my dad is witnessing this whole event.

"It's more than all right. It's perfect."

Chapter 22

ANDREW IS CLINGING ONTO ME for what appears to be dear life with his legs and arms banded tightly around me. I'm so hot that I feel almost faint. I attempt to disengage his body from mine, peeling an arm off my stomach only to have it return with force, pulling me closer into the hardness of his chest. A grumble erupts low in his throat as his lips kiss the back of my head.

"No, stay here. I'm comfortable," he says. I laugh and lightly elbow him in the side.

"Well, I'm glad you're comfortable. Could you at least turn down your internal furnace a little? I'm dying over here."

He laughs, rolling me onto my back as he presses his body against mine. Vibrant blue eyes meet mine as a slow, lazy smile brightens his face.

"Good morning, love." Andrew leans down, kissing the tip of my nose. But that's not enough for me so I grab his neck and pull him down closer, peppering kisses along his jaw, following an invisible line to his ear before curling around and finding his mouth.

"Good morning," I say, watching his eyes dilate with desire at my sudden morning assault. "What time is checkout? I'm assuming we're leaving around the same time as my dad?"

He shakes his head and runs his fingers through the hair fanned out beneath me. "We are not. I've arranged for us to stay another night. I want to take your mind off things and to relax a bit. Create new memories up here, happier ones," he says, brushing his nose against mine. "So we're taking a mini holiday."

I blink at him a few times, twisting my lips in confusion. "A holiday?"

"Yes, love. A holiday. After the intensity of the past few days, you need a break to relax and center yourself again. What better way to do that than by showing me the beauty in this area."

I wrap my arms around his shoulders and tilt my head back as his lips trail down my neck. "Mmm, that sounds like fun. But do we have to leave the room? Can't we just find the beauty in here?"

"Oh, I plan on exploring the beauty in here as well."

His mouth moves further south down my body. I throw my head back on a gasp as he connects with a rather sensitive spot, creating a familiar pull low in my stomach. Exploring outside of this room is forgotten as stars appear before my eyes and we explore each other instead.

Once we clean ourselves up, we meet my dad downstairs in the lobby around noon. Throwing my arms around him, I hug him tight and place a kiss upon his cheek.

"Thank you so much for being here. I don't think I could have done it without your help."

He kisses the top of my head and releases his hold on me. "I'm glad I was here too. How about the three of us start instituting family dinner night on Sundays?"

"Three?" I ask.

He laughs at my puzzled look. "Yes, three. As in you, me, and Andrew."

"I would love that. What do you think, Andrew?" I turn to glance at his smiling face. He pulls me into his side with a laugh.

"Sounds wonderful. It would be my honor to be invited to your family dinners."

The two men shake hands and smile at each other, passing a silent communication between them again. I told myself I wasn't going to dwell on it and just let fate work her magic, so I roll my eyes and thank the heavens they get along so well instead.

My dad picks up his suitcase and, with a final wave, walks out of the hotel toward his car. I turn to Andrew and pull the knit cap lower on his head, making sure his ears stay covered. He performs a similar check on me, making sure my fleece headband is securely over my ears.

"Ready to explore?" I ask.

He nods, kissing me quickly before grabbing my gloved hand and dragging me outside into the bitter cold wind. We walk around Canal Park, exploring the different shops and taking in the various smells coming from each restaurant we pass.

A ship comes into the harbor and we run as fast as we can to watch it pass beneath the lift bridge. It's a huge tanker, more than likely ready to carry a load of iron ore through the channels and out to sea. Salties are not uncommon ships around here though a lot of the business just goes from one great lake to another. Once the bridge is lowered, we walk the length of the harbor and stand at the lighthouse on the end while admiring the open water before us. Andrew holds me from behind, wrapping his arms around my stomach and kissing any open area of skin he can find around my neck.

Once our bodies seem almost frozen solid, we head back to the hotel to grab the car, wanting to move this little exploration elsewhere. Plus, the car has heat. It's much nicer to explore when you're not a popsicle.

We make several stops around town, some places to eat, some to stretch our legs and walk a bit. We go back up to the Skyline Parkway and climb Enger Tower, allowing us a bird's eye view of the entire city below. Afterward, we stop at one of the observation sites along the road and just stare at the twinkling lights of the city, dotting along the water.

"It's beautiful here, Tessa. I've honestly never seen anything like it before. Just the vastness of the lake once it gets away from the city and the shoreline is amazing."

I nod and smile. "When you think of a lake, you think of this small body of water, something you could putter around in a boat and see every side of it. But here, there's just nothing but water as far as you can see. Except Wisconsin over there," I say, pointing to the bridges that connect the two states and the hills on the other side of the water. "Looking back on it now, I do feel lucky that I grew up in this area. Of course being the age that I was, I didn't appreciate it properly but now that I'm an adult, I can sit back and look at what's around me. Maybe this summer we can come back up here and hike in some of the state parks. There are a couple of them that even have waterfalls we can explore."

"I'd like that. But for now, I think I need to explore something else," Andrew says, unhooking my seatbelt and dragging my body over to straddle his lap. In an instant, our jackets are off and our hands are on each other, slipping beneath our clothing as our mouths connect and explore. I love the way he feels as my hands roam underneath his sweater, feeling each and every muscle tense and relax from my feather light touch. Grinding my hips into his, I feel his arousal press into my core, causing me to gasp into his mouth. There's no light or sound except for our breaths and beating hearts. We devour each other like a couple of lust hungry teenagers who snuck out of the house to make out without being caught.

As if someone was reading my thoughts, bright red and blue lights flash behind us, flooding the car with color. We pull away from each other when a rapping noise is heard from the driver's side window. Andrew sits up as I scramble off his lap, trying gracefully to get into my seat and failing miserably.

"Good evening you two," the officer says. He bends down low, showing us his uniform and graying hair, stocky build, and slightly amused smile.

"Oh, good evening officer. Um, is there something we can help you with?" I ask, feeling the flush of embarrassment taking over my face.

"I saw your car parked here and was wondering if you were having any car troubles."

Andrew shakes his head. "No, no troubles, officer. We were just … observing the scenery." Andrew barely gets the sentence out with a smirk. I bite my lip to stifle my own laugh while Andrew does a very awkward cough to hide his.

The officer shakes his head and lets out a small chuckle himself. "Might I suggest a different spot to observe the scenery? Perhaps one not quite so public?"

I have to turn my head away so I don't bust out laughing because this whole entire scenario is too funny. Here I am, a straight-laced girl who has never done anything wrong in her life, never broken a rule or done anything even remotely lewd in public, meets a handsome man and suddenly I'm doing public displays of affection and getting busted by the cops.

"Yes, sir. We will leave right now and take our observations elsewhere," Andrew says.

I snort because I can't contain it any longer. I keep my face turned away from the officer, but I can hear him laugh as he walks back to his patrol vehicle and drives away, plunging us back into darkness once more.

Andrew and I look at each other and start laughing uncontrollably.

"I can't believe we just got busted for making out," I say once words come back to me.

He frames my face in his hands, pulling me close and kisses my lips again. "Let's get back to the hotel before we really get ourselves in trouble."

We back out of the spot and start heading back down the hill toward the hotel.

"And what else could we get in trouble for?" I ask.

Andrew glances at me quickly with a wicked grin. "Indecent exposure."

We both laugh again and dream of different ways we could have been busted by the officer until we park the car in the hotel lot.

Once in the safety of our room, where we can't get into trouble, Andrew pulls me into him and takes off my jacket, leaving it in a pile on the floor.

"What would you like to do now, Tess?"

I shrug my shoulders and wrap my arms around him. "I'm not sure. What did you have in mind?"

He nuzzles my neck and slowly kisses along the delicate skin beneath my ear.

"How about a nice hot bath? I'm sure you'd like the chance to relieve some of your tension from the past few days."

"You've already helped me with that. Whatever stress I had has left my body completely."

Andrew picks his head back up and brushes the hair away from my face. "Well then, how about you let me pamper you by doing this for me. It would give me great pleasure for you to relax in a warm bath."

I raise a suspicious brow to him. "What have you got planned?"

He shakes his head and leads me to the bathroom. Sitting me on the closed toilet seat, he begins running some bath water for me and pours in some liquid to mix with the water. The scent of vanilla fills the air, instantly letting my shoulders drop. Andrew begins undressing me, taking each piece of clothing off in a slow, sweet torture and kissing every exposed area of skin as my clothes fall one by one to the floor. When I'm fully naked, he picks me up and holds me against him while kissing me slowly; distracting my mind from any other thoughts except him.

I walk into the water and slowly sink down until only my head is sticking out. Bubbles float around me, tickling my chin as Andrew bends down one last time to brush his lips against mine.

"This is your time to relax. I want you to enjoy this."

"Where are you going to be? Don't you want to join me and help me relax further?" I ask, swishing the bubbles around with my hands.

He shakes his head and stands. "I have something else planned. I'll be right outside if you need me." He closes the door behind him, leaving me to soak in a vanilla filled heaven. I take his advice and let the soothing heat relax my muscles and clear my mind, enjoying this moment of tranquility.

When the water turns tepid, I pull myself out and grab the robe Andrew left on the counter for me, tying it loosely around my waist. When I enter the bedroom, I stop and blink several times, trying to take in my surroundings. Dozens of lighted candles are scattered around the room, giving off the most romantic glow I've ever seen. Several vases filled with colorful flowers are placed on the tables and nightstand, filling the room with their soft fragrance. I walk further into the room and bring a hand to cover my trembling lips, doing my best not to cry. I'm completely overcome with emotions as I slowly turn in circles, getting the full view of what Andrew has done for me.

My eyes search for him, but he's not here. Perhaps he left to go get something else? Although judging by what we have in the room I'm not sure what else it could be. I walk over to the window and look out at the lake. The moon is high again, casting its silvery glow upon the water, making it shimmer and sparkle as the light dances across the water.

My eyes close as I feel him approach, even though he hasn't touched me yet. Strong arms wrap around my middle, pulling me into the comfort of his chest. Feather soft kisses trail along my neck and I tilt my head to grant him better access.

"Come to bed, Tessa. I need you."

A chill runs down my spine at the familiarity of those words. But it's lost again as he gently bites down on my shoulder, walking us back toward the bed.

"Yes," I breathe.

Andrew lays me down, placing me in the middle of the giant king sized bed. He trails his fingers down my cheek, along the column of my throat before dipping inside the opening of my robe. His lips follow the same path, nipping and sucking on the supple skin before taking a hardened nipple into his mouth.

My hands smooth over the contours of his back, feeling his muscles undulate with each movement as his body continues to move over mine. He looks up when his lips reach the belt of my robe, slowly threading it through his fingers and pushing the plush material aside.

"You are so beautiful," he says, locking his eyes with mine. Moving my hands to his hair, I thread the thick locks through my fingers, giving a slight pull when his tongue dips into my belly button. Goose bumps coat my skin and I can feel the wetness build between my legs.

I pull him back up to my mouth, needing to taste him and dive into his warm mouth until everything else fades away. Our tongues meet in a well-rehearsed dance, knowing the exact movement the other will make. He's the air I breathe as passion overrules everything else. Before long, his pajama pants and boxers join my discarded robe as his hips settle between my thighs.

"Tell me you want me" His mouth drags across my collarbone, making me claw at his back in a mixture of sweet torture and delight. Words are lost to me as his mouth continues to move down my body. The instant his tongue connects with my aching nipple, my hips fly up and I cry out my want for him.

"Tell me you need me," he grunts, spreading my legs wider with his knees. The hard press of his erection hits me as he rubs himself against my wet center, making me bite down hard on my lip. He replaces his cock with two fingers, slowly opening me, making me climb higher and higher off the ground.

"I need you. Please, Andrew, I need you so much," I pant out, unable to hide the desperation in my voice.

Andrew must feel it too because he quickly positions himself at my entrance and slowly slides into me with skilled control, making me feel each and every hard inch of him as our bodies join as one. My eyes flutter closed as sensation after sensation wraps around me. When Andrew fully rests on top of me, I'm aware of our joined heartbeats, pulsing as one. I'm wrapped around him like a second skin and he lets out a guttural moan, bringing me closer to the edge with that sound.

I open my eyes as he begins to move slowly inside me. He brings himself up on his forearms, hovering over me as we move together in perfect harmony. Every move my body makes is because he's guiding it, knowing it better than I do. He knows how to bring it the most pleasure, how to satisfy each and every craving without ever needing to feel hunger for it. I wrap my legs around his waist and pull him closer, urging him deeper inside me. The first spasm has my inner walls clenching and the orgasm hovering just on the edge of explosion.

"Tell me you love me," he whispers against my mouth. The sight of him rocking back and forth, hitting the deepest parts of me causes me to cry out, wanting to release each emotion that he invokes so naturally. Loving him was never an issue. Trying to keep my emotions at bay was the hardest thing I have ever done and I realize now what a waste of time it was.

Andrew grabs my hips and rolls onto his back, forcing me to be on top. I brace my hands against his chest as I begin to move again, chasing after the orgasm that was there moments ago. Only this time I'm in control. I'm the one regulating the speed, playing his body while bringing him extreme pleasure and getting my own from watching him. He reaches up and cups each of my breasts, squeezing lightly and making my head roll back with a loud moan.

"Tell me, Tessa," he growls. He bucks his hips up hard to hit my clit in just the right spot, making me see stars. The rolling waves outside pale in comparison to the waves crashing upon the shore inside me. Nothing can be heard over the roar of blood in my ears. Then, all the tension in my body releases at once, sending me soaring high into the clear night sky.

"Andrew … I love you," I cry out, unable to hold it back any longer. My body is still shaking as he grabs my hips, guiding me faster until I feel him pulsing inside me, crying out my name with sheer reverence. My limp body falls on top of his, taking in shallow breaths as the waves calm inside me. Andrew's fingers slowly trail over my back in the same way I trail them over his after an intense love making session. It really does relax your body and it feels oh so nice.

"I love you, too," he whispers, kissing my sweat-slicked skin.

He rolls us to the side and brushes the damp hair away from my face. Shadows from the candlelight dance across his face, highlighting his gorgeous blue eyes and light scruff across his jaw. My fingers trace the curve of his lips, his cheekbones, and his jaw. A realization dawns on me as I quickly survey the room, transporting myself into a scene that I've played out in my head on an almost daily basis. This room, the candles, the lake, his eyes. It's him, the man from my dreams, only he's been right here the entire time. It's always been Andrew.

A tear rolls down my cheek but is quickly brushed away. "What's wrong?"

I shake my head and kiss him softly. "Nothing's wrong. Everything is perfect." I swallow hard, trying to find my voice. "You know that dream I always have?" He nods, brushing back some hair from my face. "The scene never changes. It's always me standing in a candlelit room, looking at the water and the same man is always there, but he's always nestled in the shadows so I can't fully see him. All I could see was his eyes, these beautiful sapphire blue eyes. Not knowing that I've actually been staring at them for the past few months, losing myself in them over and over again. My body recognized you instantly from the very first moment we met. I'm just sorry it's taken my brain this long to catch up. But it's you, Andrew. It's always been you. You are the love that I've been waiting my whole life for."

He traces my jaw with his fingertips, eyes bright and shiny with emotion. "Believe it or not, I saw you in my dreams too, just before I met you. That's what made me stop and look at you in New York. Your hair, your eyes, your nose, and that sweet smile. It was like my world stopped and started anew. It's why I couldn't stop looking at you or stop touching you. I had to make sure that you were real and not a figment of my imagination." His lips brush across mine with the sweetest smile I've ever seen. "It was always you."

Fate truly did a number on us, sending us both signals to make sure we didn't miss what was in front of us. Had I not paid attention and taken a chance when all the signals were right in front of me, I would have missed out on loving this beautiful man beside me.

Our arms wrap around each other, keeping each other close in a loving embrace. And as I listen to the steady beat of his heart, I feel complete for the first time in my life. His fingers run gently through my hair and I fall asleep, listening to his confessions of love and thanking fate for bringing us together.

Acknowledgements

Did you know this book used to not exist? When I originally wrote this, both books were combined together, making it one, very long manuscript. Because I was tossing around the idea of publishing, I reached out to a few of my favorite indie authors and asked for some advice. When I told them the word count, they suggested breaking it into two, which I agreed with after looking at it again. This also gave me room to expand the story and give Tessa and Andrew their much-needed room to grow. So after writing the first draft, taking it apart, breaking it down and rebuilding it, it has come to this. An amazing journey to a destination I never thought I would see when I started this whole thing.

So many people helped me along the way and words can never express what your help has meant to me. From the bottom of my heart, thank you!

To my husband, my source of support and best friend. He's done so much for me during this whole journey that I don't know what I'd do without him. Taking care of our four beautiful girls has been the biggest help by far. With just the simple words "whatever you need", I knew he was ready to support me throughout everything.

Billie, what can I say that hasn't already been said. You were the first to fall in love with this story and have been through everything with me during this whole process. You've questioned my moves, suggested and praised my changes and have diligently read this book chapter by chapter. You've picked me up and yelled my name to the rooftops because you believe in this series and think the world will too. Your support has helped bring me to where I am and I love you for it!

Patricia, Tara, and Stacy ... I love you all so, so much! Your constant support has been nothing less than amazing. Your messages, your emails, and overall ways to make me smile have been a lifesaver throughout this process. Thank you for listening to me babble on during my low days and for cheering with me when I felt like I was on top of the world. You have no idea how lucky I am to have found you and am thankful to call you some of my best friends!

Amanda, Andi, Gloria, Heather, Jenn, Melissa, Samantha, Stephanie, and Stephanie: YOU ARE AWESOME!! The videos, the messages, the pictures ... all of it has meant the world to me. I know that I can rely on you for whatever help I need. Whether it's to laugh or cry with me, I know that you'll always be there. I love and value our friendship and am thankful that we were brought together! Thank you for being my never ending rocks of support!

To the Vixens and all my friends, your support and positivity, your words of encouragement and excitement for this series have been amazing. I love you all and am proud to be a Vixen! #VixenLove

Murphy, again, what can I say. I had zero ideas regarding my cover and you've turned it into something amazing. As soon as you showed it to me, I knew it was perfect. Somehow you knew what I wanted with only that little summary of the book. And you nailed it!

And to you, the readers, words cannot express what your support means to me. I am so delighted that you took a chance on Tessa and Andrew and have given them a place to live in your heart. Without you, I wouldn't be doing this. And don't worry, this won't be the end of this series. It's been highly suggested to me that someone else needs their story told and I may start putting something in the works for that.

Truly, from the bottom of my heart, I love you all! Thank you so much for reading!

About the Author

Jodie Larson is a wife and mother to four beautiful girls, making their home in northern Minnesota along the shore of Lake Superior. When she isn't running around to various activities or working her regular job, you can find her sitting in her favorite spot reading her new favorite book or camped out somewhere quiet trying to write her next manuscript. She's addicted to reading (just ask her kids or husband) and loves talking books even more with her friends. She's also a lover of all things romance and happily ever afters, whether in movies or in books, as shown in her extensive collection of both.

You can find Jodie at:

Facebook: www.facebook.com/jodielarsonauthor
Twitter: www.twitter.com/jlarsonauthor

Made in the USA
Columbia, SC
11 February 2023

11535538R00174